Praise for T...
Hearts

"The War in Our Hearts, for the most part, deals less with plot than with the internal thoughts and feelings of its characters. Insecurities, fears, hatreds, and joys are exposed in a way that rivets the reader's attention, connection, and support.

No matter how tough circumstances seem, Jamie, Aveline, Estelle, and George learn to celebrate their bond of love that, without being contrived, enables more than survival. Hope is a very real entity that each seeks and learns to value.

One may wonder how such cruel and evil people exist, but Seyler focuses her message more on the birth of compassion, fairness, and strength through turmoil and tragedy.

Remarkable, highly recommended historical fiction."

Viviane Crystal, Historical Novel Society

"I felt like every piece of the story was strong and essential to bring it to the place it did.

A beautiful and evocative read."

R. S. Hogan, author of *Shrouded Loyalties*

"Set primarily in the trenches of WWI, The War in Our Hearts tells a story of courage and redemption, of innocence destroyed and the healing power of love."

Marian L Thorpe, author of the *Empire's Legacy* series

THE WAR IN OUR HEARTS

Eva Seyler

Edited by Meggan Padvorac

Library of Congress Control Number:
2021902615

Typeset in Georgia and Josefin Sans

E-Book ISBN: 978-1-7360297-1-8
Paperback ISBN: 978-1-7360297-0-1
Audiobook ISBN: 978-1-7360297-2-5

For Elizabeth,
who said WRITE YOUR BOOK
at me so many times
that finally
I did.

PART ONE

9 November 1916

France

— Eva Seyler

CALAIS

Estelle Graham hesitated on the dock, scanning the sea of faces as humanity flowed around her on either side of the gangway. Even standing on her toes did not afford her the height required to find her husband's face in this crush of people. Lips pressed together and eyes narrowed at the crowds which threatened her stability, she stood her ground and kept watch for twenty minutes. The crowds thinned, and still there appeared no sign of her husband, nor of anyone else whom he might have sent in his place to deliver the girl whom Estelle was supposed to take home with her in the morning.

At last left alone, Estelle sighed impatiently, unable to squash her disappointment at not immediately being reunited with her beloved husband and introduced to her new daughter.

She stood for a moment, contemplating her options. It was not yet noon; she had time before it grew dark to find a way to Montreuil-sur-Mer, where the British Army had its general headquarters. If she could get there, she could perhaps be enlightened as to her husband's whereabouts. She set off at a brisk pace towards the center of Calais, her mind spinning in circles as she considered the situation. Why had *nobody* come to meet her?

She spotted a man driving a cart and hailed him in French. "Are there any trains to Montreuil-sur-Mer?" she asked. When he said yes, she climbed onto the cart and held out a handful of coins he could not resist. He drove her to the station, where she paced restlessly, waiting for the next train out.

It arrived at last, so full of soldiers that she was obliged to share a compartment with several young men on their way to the front, but she hardly noticed their presence in her preoccupation.

When she alighted in Montreuil-sur-Mer, she asked directions to the general headquarters, housed in the city's military academy. On arrival, she went inside and spoke to the first officer she saw.

"I am looking for my husband. He was supposed to meet me in Calais today, and he did not come. How can I find him?"

He blinked at her as if it were an alien concept for a woman to actively seek out a missing husband. But he only asked, "Who is he with? What is his name?"

"Captain Augustus Graham," she answered, also giving his division and the address she used to write to him. "Lord Inverlochy. Just Graham to his friends." Mentally she added, *And Jamie to me.*

"Come along with me," said the officer, beckoning her to follow him upstairs.

She waited outside his office for what seemed an interminable amount of time. Anxiety welled in her throat, as it so often did since her husband had gone to France over a year before. She could not let herself entertain the cruel idea that her husband might have been killed in the few days since she'd received his telegram, asking her to meet him in Calais today. Surely he had simply been delayed, or there had been unexpected fighting, and he couldn't get away after all.

But Jamie was the essence of dependability; surely he'd have at least sent word if something had happened to prevent him coming.

Jamie's brother George was here in France, fighting alongside him. *He might have come,* she thought reproachfully, curious whether life on the battlefield had done anything to help her happy-go-lucky solicitor brother-in-law grow up a little.

At last, the officer came out to her. Estelle shot to her feet, expectant. Hopeful. Dreading.

"I have found him," he said, "but I am afraid my news is not good."

Estelle swayed; through her numbness, she felt the officer take her arm, guide her gently back to the chair, and sit beside her. "Lady Inverlochy, your husband is in the casualty clearing station in Allonville."

"Not dead, then?"

"For now, yes, he is still alive."

"Oh, thank God," Estelle said fervently. "I must go to him."

"My dear lady, it is not a safe place for women."

"You will arrange transport for me. I don't care how, but get me there. Tell them anything you like. Tell them I'm a nurse, because I will be his." Something in her eyes did not allow for any further remonstrance on the officer's part. He shrugged as if to say, *Well, don't say I didn't warn you*, and went to do as she ordered.

Someone brought her a pot of tea, which she drank slowly. Another two hours had trickled by before anybody could be found to take her out of Montreuil. As she was about to leave, the officer again tried to convince her to let a man go in her place, but she shook her head and leapt to the seat of the wagon.

"Intrepid old thing," the officer murmured. He saluted her as the wagon lumbered away down the road. She sat, straight and regal, conversing cheerfully with the driver, as though the wagon seat were a throne and she hadn't a care in the world.

It was really only a way to distract herself from the harsh fact that her husband might already be dead by the time she arrived. She had no details about his exact condition or injuries; she wanted nothing except to get to Jamie, assess his situation, and simply be there beside him.

The wagon crept along for hours, navigating the water-filled ruts and nearly tipping twice. It arrived at last at 13th Stationary General Hospital, where Estelle was given into the care of a van driver transporting medical supplies to Allonville. The nearer they came, the more the countryside looked like a dead and eerie moonscape, trees blasted and splintered and dark against the colorless sky, the cold and frosty earth pitted from artillery shell explosions. The light of the full moon intensified the weirdness of the scene. Jamie had told her it was bleak here, but even her vivid imagination had fallen short of this ugly reality. She shuddered, thinking of her husband living amidst such desolation for as long as he had, and wondered how anyone survived it.

ALLONVILLE

A T THE CASUALTY clearing station, Estelle had to wait yet again for someone to have time to escort her to her husband's side. An agonizing quarter of an hour went by before a familiar energetic presence burst through the door behind her. She didn't even need to look to know who it was.

"George!" she cried, turning and running into the arms of her brother-in-law. He held her close and kissed the top of her head.

"Estelle, darling, I'm beastly sorry about all this," he said at last. "I wanted to come meet you myself this morning, but I wasn't allowed to leave. Everything's been in confusion around here since—"

"Tell me what happened to him."

But before George could answer her, a nurse came to show Estelle to the cot where Jamie lay.

"Don't get too close to him, lady, unless you want nits," the nurse instructed blandly and shuffled away.

Estelle took one look at the deathly pallor of her unconscious husband's face and dropped to her knees by his cot, clasping the beloved hand unnaturally hot with fever, surrounded by the groans and curses of dying and injured men. It seemed to her that her husband was the eye of this hurricane of pain, the sole silent sufferer. *Lice be damned*, she thought, and she rested her head beside his on the pillow and softly sang to him one of the songs he used to sing to her.

Come, my beloved!
Through the sylvan gloom

I wander day and night;

Oft I call thee;

Come, my joy and my delight—

Her throat choked with tears, and she could not go on. She stroked his unshaven cheek and tried not to cry, but the tears dampened the pillow anyway.

She felt a hand on her shoulder and raised her head to see George standing nearby. He gave her his hand and she rose to her feet.

"It's time to go," he said softly.

"I'm not leaving," she protested. "He needs me!"

"I know you'd rather watch over him, as would I, but you can't tonight," George said, consolingly, guiding her back toward the door. "But I've only been given permission to leave long enough to come collect you, and my time's up. I'll take you back to the house where we're billeted. Won't be a glamorous ride, I'm afraid—" Out in the cold night air once more, he motioned to a motorbike with a lopsided, apologetic grin. "And I wouldn't offer it to any lady but you. Better tie down your hat, though."

Estelle hiked up her skirt, climbed on behind George, and hung on for dear life as he tore away along the rough road. She didn't mind the speed—at home, she was infamous for her not-quite-reckless driving—and would have enjoyed her first motor-bike ride very much indeed, had she not been so preoccupied with thoughts of her husband. It was impossible to converse without shouting; she'd have to sit tight and wait for George's explanation of what had happened until they reached their des-tination.

CHÂTEAU BLANCHARD

ORTY-FIVE MINUTES later, George escorted Estelle through the door of the country house where the officers lived. A kind-faced, elderly gentleman welcomed them.

"You must be Monsieur Blanchard," Estelle said, extending her hand. "I'm Captain Graham's wife."

"Oh, Madame Graham," M. Blanchard said, guiding her inside. "I am terribly sorry about your husband. Is he improving, do you know?"

"I've seen him. About any improvement, I cannot say."

"I'm going to take her to his room," George said. "She wants to fetch his things, and she'll be staying here for the night."

"Of course," M. Blanchard said with a little bow, and let them pass.

George and Estelle stepped into the noisy room where the officers of the company gathered in the evenings. The laughter and singing faded into silence when they saw her standing there. She stood, small but imposing in her well-tailored suit with its fur collar and smart hat, queenly despite the windblown hair and liberal splatterings of mud. As one body, the men rose to their feet as they might have done for the king. They all recognized her at once. Their captain's photograph of his stunning wife had been passed around frequently, in a running prank among the men to put it in odd and sometimes irreverent places, without ever getting caught in the act of moving it.

One young man, not one of the merrymakers, sat morosely on a window seat with a black cat in his arms, absent-mindedly stroking its fur, but the sudden silence made him look up. He straightened at the sight of her. "Oh, Lady Inverlochy!" he exclaimed, interpreting the presence of his captain's wife as a sign that Captain Graham was gone. He looked positively haunted as he stepped forward and, she thought, not old enough to be here at all. "It's fair vexed I am—we did all we could to save him—"

"He's not dead yet," Estelle said, almost curtly. "And he won't die if I can prevent it. George, do please show me to his room."

The young man, cat still tucked into one arm, stared after her and George as they went upstairs. George opened a door and waved Estelle in.

"Here it is." He lit the lamp and disappeared, returning a moment later with a pitcher of water for the washstand. "If you want to wash up at all, this will be here. Come down when you've finished, and we'll talk," George said.

Estelle nodded and closed the door after him, and another sob escaped her throat. Her husband might be dying, and these men didn't appear to care. Making merry like that! She knew, she *knew*—her husband had told her death was such an everyday occurrence here, they'd become immune to it in general—but none of those other men who had died were hers. She tossed her muff to the bed and moved toward the little table, pulled out the chair, and sat in it. She had many questions for George, and she would get her answers, but she craved a few minutes alone first.

The flickering lamplight cast weird shadows, and Estelle rested her cheek flat against the worn wood of the table, closed her eyes, and imagined how he had sat here writing to her nearly every evening for the last five months, and at other desks in other billets for the months before that. Here in this room he had slept and dressed and been lonely, as the head of an unusual family: Captain Jamie Graham, his orderly Oliver MacFie, and little orphan waif Aveline Perrault. After a moment, Estelle opened her eyes again and took in the room: the two narrow beds, the walls covered in drawings—cramped but cozy too. On one cot, two kit bags rested. One she recognized as her husband's; she had embroidered a rose on one strap of it. The other one must be Aveline's.

Where *was* Aveline? Nobody had said a thing about her in all these hours, and Estelle's conscience pricked her with shame. In her preoccupation with her husband's welfare, she had forgotten all about the girl. Surely she would soon be going to bed. Estelle wanted to have some time to speak with her before going to sleep, and she didn't even know where the girl slept in this big house.

She went downstairs and beckoned for George to come, and they whispered together for a moment. Estelle drooped, and she hid her eyes behind her hands a moment before turning and slowly walking back up the stairs, moving as if in physical pain. She locked the door behind her. Leaning back against it, she looked through a stinging blur of tears at the kit bags.

They were waiting for their owners to carry them out, to take them along to Calais to meet her today. But the bags were *here*, not with their owners, and they would not go to Calais today, or any day soon. She fell to her knees and held Jamie's bag in a tight hug, sobbing until she had tired herself out.

She rested her head on one arm and opened her beloved's bag with the other hand. A small notebook rested on top of the neatly folded clothes inside. She knew it; it was the journal she had sent him last Christmas. She gave him one every year, and every year, he filled it from the first endpaper to the last. She smiled at its familiarity as she paged through, not really reading, eyes scanning the sight of his familiar backhanded script. It made her—well, not *happy*, exactly, considering the circumstances—but comforted, to see it.

At first, it contained the ordinary logs of daily activities, dull as a Scottish winter sky, and as precisely detailed as if he had expected cross-examination on every fact later. Then, abruptly, the pages came to life. It turned into an *illustrated* log, and his handwriting was interspersed with that of a younger person, a wee lassie who had recorded much of the last several months of Jamie's life in his journal as seen through her eyes. Her heart warmed inside her when she read all the handwritten conversations between her husband and the girl. She imagined them sitting here together in this room, chatting without ever saying a word, a bright spot in Jamie's long and weary days.

Aveline Perrault, not quite fourteen and about to become her own adopted daughter, was not going to come home with her. Not now. Not ever. This day had been a hoped-for, longed-for day for all three of them, and now it was as thoroughly blasted as the landscape through which Estelle had traveled that day. The tears started again.

Nobody saw her climb into her husband's bed, curling up under his blanket. Nobody heard her sobbing into his pillow, clutching his diary to her breast. The day had been long and exhausting, and at last, emotionally as well as physically drained, Estelle fell asleep.

WILLIAM DUNCAN

IN THE MORNING, her eyes shadowed and heavy-lidded, Estelle dragged herself out of bed, tidied herself as best she could, and went downstairs. Gone was the spunkiness which usually defined her; today she looked pale and beaten and sad. With the calm air of someone accustomed to giving commands and being obeyed, she requested the two kit bags be brought down for her and that she be taken back to the hospital.

While they waited for a car to be arranged, George helped her take all Aveline's drawings off the walls of his brother's room. He seemed to sense she was not in a mood for conversation and remained uncharacteristically silent.

Afterward, as she got into the automobile, the young man from the night before, the one with the cat, ran to her and handed her a harmonica. "Captain Graham left this on the piano the last time he was here, ma'am," he said.

She took it and stared at him. "Who are you?" she asked at last.

"William Duncan, Lady Inverlochy."

"My orderly," George elaborated.

Jamie's harmonica lying on her open palm was a voiceless, useless thing without his breath to bring it to life, but Estelle nodded thanks to him. She lay it on top of the clothes in her husband's bag. The notebook, however, she carried in her own hands. She would not let it out of her sight. It was hers. No matter what the future held, it could speak his words to her as long as she lived.

"I'll come call on you and Jamie as soon as I can," George promised Estelle. He closed the car door for her and waved as she was driven away.

Back at the hospital, Estelle spoke to the nurse in charge. "No change in his lordship's condition, I'm afraid, Lady Inver- lochy," she said. "Come with me. I'll find you a chair, and you can sit with him."

PART TWO

29-30 August 1916

Somme, France:
Two Miles Southeast of Albert

THE FARMHOUSE

THE FARMYARD WAS a desolate wasteland of dead grass and mud in the wet late afternoon light. No sign of life greeted the eye: not the comforting, homey clucking of scratching hens or lowing of cows, nor the welcoming glow of light in the windows of the shabby old farmhouse. Even the garden lay unplowed and unplanted, overrun with weeds.

Captain Graham and his orderly, Oliver MacFie, sat in their vehicle. They had run a load of supplies to the trenches in the morning without incident, but with a relentless drizzle having fallen all day, the vehicle had stalled and stuck in the muddy road on the way back, twenty yards past the gate of this farmhouse. They could not get it running again.

Not as if getting the motor to run would help much in getting out of the mud. The men peered through the pouring rain to the house, bleak and hopeless as the shell-scarred landscape still within sight.

"I *knew* we'd never make it back unless we took the horses," Graham muttered darkly. It was a constant point of contention between him and his superior officer, who was not even here and had to be contacted by telephone, that the motorized vehicles were a hindrance, not a help, in this terrain and weather. "You're a genius, Oliver, can you do anything for this engine?"

MacFie rested his arms on the driving wheel and said nothing for a few minutes. "I could fix it," he said, "only I havenae anything to fix it *with*. And she's still stuck in the mud. We've shovels, aye, but nae engine parts."

"Let's see if anyone is in at the house," Graham said at last, staunchly.

He turned up his collar, and together they ran the fifty yards or so down the lane to the farmhouse, vaulting over a low stone wall on the way. Graham knocked at the door.

No answer.

He opened it and called out to find whether anyone still

lived here—privately, he was of the opinion that if anyone *was* still here, they were insane to have stayed this close to the fighting—but no human voice responded. Instead, the heavy silence answering him had an eerie quality in it. It did not sound like emptiness to him; it sounded like something lying in wait, ready to spring. There ran a prickle down his back that he did not like.

As if he'd read his companion's mind, MacFie gave a low whistle and shuddered. "There's evil here. I feel it in my bones," he said in a whisper. He and Graham walked further into the farmhouse and looked about. "Think we should stay here 'til the rain stops?"

"We'll have to," Graham answered, glancing over his shoulder out the open door. The drizzle had turned to sheets of rain. "Not a chance of getting the truck out of *that* muck, let alone get it running, in this downpour. At least it's not cold—" His quick, dark eyes took in everything around them. "Is anyone here?" he called out again, in French. Still silence.

He lifted a dingy muslin curtain and looked toward the north. "I wonder if there are horses in the barn," he said, straining at any thin thread of hope, even though he doubted anyone within thirty miles had horses left that hadn't been requisitioned by the army. "If there is one, we might borrow it and ride back for a hand with the truck."

"Let's go look," MacFie said.

They dove into the deluge again. The entry to the barn was no door, only a gaping hole. Graham's spirits sank, knowing nobody would leave valuable horses thus unguarded, but he stepped into the gloom of the barn anyway. His back was prickling again something fierce, but he tried to ignore it and switched on his torch to search. He moved its beam up and down around the perimeter. Deserted stalls, moldy hay, old sacks, horse blankets, and rubbish. Not a horse, not a mule, but—

But there *was* a girl there, sitting halfway upright against the back wall, arms slack at her sides, feet straight out in front of her, eyes unblinking, lips parted, motionless. For a moment, he feared she was dead, shot perhaps, but he saw no wound, and

she flinched and squinted when her eyes came under the beam
of the torch.

THE GIRL

"**M**ADEMOISELLE?" GRAHAM SAID, his voice soft. She didn't answer. He approached her, moving slowly as though she were a wild animal that might dart away from him when he got too close, but she did not stir. Only her eyes moved, unfocused but watching, tracking along with his movements, rolling slightly as he came nearer.

He crouched beside her to get a better look at her face. He glanced down the body of the tiny, elfin figure and noticed her skirt was rucked about her waist, and her exposed thighs were a mess of blood and slime—

"Lord have mercy," he gasped, and understanding dawned on him and his orderly at the same moment. They exchanged a look of horror. The pricking along Graham's spine intensified. The notion of finding a horse was forgotten.

Graham bit his lip, steeling himself, and spoke to the girl in French. "May I take you to the house?"

She stared a moment before responding with a slow nod, as if in a trance. He stood and offered a hand to help her up, but the girl shook her head. She mimed with trembling, hesitant hands, splitting something in two, and pointed to the space between her thighs. Graham flinched this time. He understood what she meant. She must be in terrible pain. He lifted her as carefully as he could. She made a voiceless gasp of agony that chilled him through more than if she had screamed aloud, and she tensed and reached frantically toward a corner where his torch beam revealed a black kitten crouching.

"Get the cat," Graham said. MacFie placed the bundle of fur into the girl's arms, and she relaxed as she hugged it.

She was not heavy, and he had no trouble carrying her back to the house. She hid her face in his shoulder, eyes closed, oblivious to the rain. Graham took her inside and laid her on her bed and stepped back. "I wish we had the doctor with us." Pressing his lips together, he went on resolutely. "Well, get me some water. I'll clean her up." Someone had to do it.

He brought a chair close beside the bed and sat while he waited for MacFie to return. The girl stared at him with dull and hungry eyes, perfectly still except for reaching out to hold his hand. She seemed to be begging for something. His protection, perhaps, or simply his company? He wished she would speak and break the eerie aura of silence hanging about her like winter morning mists over Loch Ness.

When MacFie returned with the water, a couple of towels, and an oil lamp he had found and lit, Graham leaned toward the girl, who still clung to his hand, and explained in French what he intended to do. Was it all right with her? She nodded, and Graham again steeled himself to the task.

This was awkward. He was not a doctor and didn't want to look at some little girl's privates, but their billets were too far to walk to in the rain and dark while carrying a small girl who had just been so fearfully abused. MacFie stood watch at the door, arms crossed, back leaning against the doorframe, while Graham examined the girl's injuries. Nothing broken as far as he could tell, but there was plenty of bad bruising that would take time to heal, and her wincing made it obvious that it was very painful. He washed away the mess with a light, careful touch, all the while cursing under his breath the perversion of the fiend who would do this to someone who still had the body of a child. When he had finished, he covered her with her blankets and turned to his orderly.

"Bring me some laudanum from the truck, Oliver."

MacFie came back with the stuff a few minutes later, and Graham offered it to the girl, who took it without resistance. He suspected she was in shock. He'd let her sleep for now and question her further in the morning.

But he didn't leave the room right away. He sat beside her, watching the deepening twilight out the window without really seeing it, until long after the drug had done its work and she fell sound asleep. It was near nine o'clock. He noticed with dismay, as the minutes ticked by, that the girl's face and wrists and even her throat were coming out in nasty bruises. The person who had done this looked to have had a grip of iron and didn't care how much damage he caused, as long as he got what he wanted. What would have happened to the child had they not found her? Died of exposure and shock? It made him sick to contemplate.

THE FARMHOUSE CELLAR

AT LAST, GRAHAM roused from his meditations and noticed the room for the first time. There was a cheery patchwork quilt on the bed, which had been tidily made before he had turned it down to put the girl to sleep, and a tatty old doll sat propped against the pillow.

Someone had covered the walls with drawings—quite good drawings, which appeared to depict the girl's daily life on the farm, although he found it hard to imagine any adult permitting such defacement of walls. Was this girl completely on her own? That idea made him uneasy indeed, especially since he had passed this place going and coming at least a dozen times in the last month. The delivery end of the nearest communication trench was only four hundred yards away, and he never even dreamed there might be trouble here. He supposed he'd blithely assumed its occupants had evacuated, which is what he'd have done had *he* lived this close to the fighting. It had never occurred to him that perhaps its inhabitants were unable to leave.

He set about discovering any clues as to the girl's identity. Her bureau drawers didn't have much in them. A few pinafores, one other frock, some woolen stockings and underthings, all neatly folded, and one tattered, grubby book of art plates by Michelangelo, and similarly battered copies of *Les Trois Mousquetaires* and *Les Misérables*. He sighed. He had only wanted to find a way to get back to his billets, and now he had this girl to consider.

Even so, he wouldn't dream of leaving her alone here. Not after what had just happened. He would treat her the way he would want any of his own three sons treated in the same situation.

He took the lamp and stepped from the girl's room into the bare and shadowy kitchen. MacFie had found a few candles and lit them. There were some tinned goods on the shelves, stale crusts of bread on a cutting board, and a few unwashed dishes sat out. The place was clean otherwise.

"Check what's in the tins and get us something to eat," Graham said. "We can't go until daylight, now we have the girl to think of." He stepped into one of the other rooms to have a look. It was another bedroom, and it looked as neglected as the kitchen, with a droopy bed, bare board floor, and a locked desk. Graham picked the lock with his knife, hoping to find some relevant information.

He saw a stack of notebooks and composition books, dating back to 1910, full of stories told in the same kinds of pictures all over the walls in the girl's room, and copies of faces from the Michelangelo book. The composition books all had AVELINE PERRAULT scrolling in fanciful lettering across the fronts. Locked up for safekeeping, he supposed. He poked into the pigeonholes of the desk. There were record books here, with the name Armand Perrault inside, full of financial accounts of the farm. Graham's detail-oriented mind was pleased with how carefully and painstakingly the records had been kept. He couldn't have done better himself. He read in them a tale of comfortable poverty dwindling to bare subsistence. It appeared the farm had gone defunct last year about this time. Armand had noted when the horses had been taken by the army, when the cow had gone dry and they'd had to butcher her, when they began dismantling the barn for firewood, and details about working in town to make ends meet. There was also a record of schoolwork completed. Armand must have been Aveline's teacher. The records stopped on the 18th of August.

Eleven days ago.

Graham looked perplexed and rubbed the back of his head distractedly. Who was Armand? Father? Brother? Where was he now? It was hard to imagine such a consistent and meticulous record-keeper neglecting his task for eleven entire days.

MacFie startled him with a cry from the kitchen. "Come quick, my lord!"

Graham rushed out. MacFie hunched over the opening of the cellar under the kitchen floor, retching, and the stench of decaying flesh greeted Graham's nose. It was so terrible, it took several minutes before he could work up the courage to look in, switching on his torch and shining it into the gloom.

The rats feasting below them scuttled away from the light. It was a very dead corpse, bayoneted five times and lying in a heap at the bottom of the stairs. His head, at an unnatural angle to the rest of his body, had cracked open on impact. "Cellar floor's all blood around him. I dinnae think he'd quite died yet when he was put there," MacFie observed grimly.

"Looks like his neck broke too." They exchanged glances. The man below them had obviously been young, though his eyes were gone and his skin discolored with death. Why was he here and not in the army?

"Shut it." Graham backed away. "When the rain stops, we'll dig him a grave and bury him, but for now, there's nothing else to do."

MacFie gladly shut the cellar. Graham, ill at ease, went back to the desk and poked about some more, hoping he could deduce what had led to the vicious murder of this man. But nothing obvious revealed itself. He gathered together an armload of the records, journals, and important-looking papers into his bag anyway, for later examination. While he was doing this, MacFie called that he had some food ready.

After they'd eaten, although the rain showed no sign of ever letting up, MacFie found a shovel, and they stripped off most of their clothing and went outside and dug a grave for the dead man. The earth, heavy but soft from the rain, yielded easily to their digging, and it did not take long. When they deemed it deep enough, they tied their shirts over their mouths and noses and went back into the cellar with a mothy horse blanket they had found in the barn. They laid the man on it, wrapped him, and together, carried him out to the grave and covered him over. Muddy and exhausted, they washed themselves as best they could, put their shirts back on, rolled out beds on the floor of the girl's room, and took it in turns to sleep and keep watch.

AVELINE

THE RAIN STILL poured relentlessly in the morning. Before daybreak, MacFie set off on foot back toward their billets to get reinforcements, and Graham stayed behind with Aveline. She did not wake until mid-morning. He came in to check on her and found her sitting up while her kitten played with her bedraggled hair ribbon. He stood in the door with his hands behind his back, wishing he had his wife's knack for effortless conversation, putting anyone, friend or stranger, instantly at their ease. He always felt lost if he had to make conversation, especially with children, and the only way he knew to put people at ease was if he was drilling them. It was not exactly the same thing.

"Are you Aveline Perrault?" he asked her at last, in French. She nodded distractedly, absorbed in playing with her kitten. "How do you feel this morning?"

She shrugged.

"Can I get you some breakfast?"

Again a nod.

Graham retreated to the kitchen to fetch what remained of MacFie's morning concoction, optimistically referred to as "porridge" by its creator, and a moment later, he returned and sat beside her bed.

"How old are you?" he asked, holding out the dish and a spoon to her.

She held up ten fingers, then three. Thirteen. And she tucked into the "porridge" as if starving. Only a starving person would not discriminate against whatever was in that stuff.

She looked rather undeveloped for a thirteen-year-old. He'd have guessed she was nine at the most. Malnourished, perhaps? Why was she here in this farmhouse all alone? Did she know about the body in the cellar? There were so many questions he needed to ask her, and she had yet to speak to him. How could they communicate?

"Thirteen," he mused. "Can you speak? I need to know how I can help you."

She shook her head but mimed writing, and he rummaged in his nearby kit bag and pulled out his journal and a pencil and handed them to her.

She opened with a question of her own. *How did you know my name?*

"It was a guess. I looked in the desk in the other room to find out why you were here all alone, and I saw it on your notebooks."

She blinked at him, her expression unreadable, and bent over the paper again. She set to scribbling in a fury, as if desperate to lay out for him what had happened to her. She began by drawing a picture, all evocative shadows, ominous: a man's silhouette looming in the doorway of the barn, rimmed with the murky summer light. *I could not see his face,* she wrote underneath. *But the way he stood there, it made me cold all over, and I backed away from him. He kept coming until I was trapped against the barn wall.* Aveline shuddered involuntarily, and her pretty handwriting squiggled. *He smelled awful and he had an ugly moustache. He shoved me to the dirt floor of the barn. I could not move. It was all I could do to breathe—* Another lightning-fast sketch of herself, the muddy boot of the man on her chest, holding her in place while he undid his trousers and exposed himself to her. She stabbed at her sketch with her finger, her eyes wide. *The thing between his legs. What was that?*

Graham cleared his throat a bit awkwardly, but he told her. She looked at him hard, eyes perplexed, lips parted, and she scribbled another sentence. *Do you have one of those?*

"All men do," he said, blushing, fixing his eyes on some invisible point on the ceiling. After a moment, he heard the pencil against the paper again, and he turned back and watched the words pouring across the page.

I didn't know what he was going to do, and I wanted to run, but I couldn't. He was so big, and I was so scared. She hunched over the paper as if trying to become invisible, and her hand holding the pencil pressed hard into the pages, leaving grooves. *He muttered at me. I don't know what he said. I don't know German. I was trapped under his weight.* She wrote slowly as if she hardly dared to give any reality to what had happened. He pried my legs apart, and he shoved something between my le*gs, inside me, so far inside me. It burned and tore and split me into halves, and I gasped out silent sobs because it hurt so much, and I wanted to die.*

She stopped, the pencil hovering over the page, doodling shaky, hesitant squiggles around the words she had written. She glanced at him, but he only waited quietly.

Her dusky eyes dropped their gaze again, and she twirled the pencil between her fingers in agitation for a few minutes before she could continue. *I couldn't make myself move. If I could have called for help...but I couldn't make any sound. Not even a tiny squeak. Whatever he did went all the way to my throat, choking away my voice. I would have screamed for help otherwise. I can talk. I mean, I could until then. But I guess nobody was around to hear even if I had.* A lone tear splashed onto the paper, distorting the words under it. *A leaf thrown into a flame, shriveling into instant nothingness. That's how I feel. I was me, yesterday. I don't know who I am now.* A burning leaf emerged under her pencil, the lines of the flame hard and dark, the leaf faint and fragile in comparison.

Her distress was intense, and Graham had to battle the sickening anxiety that always welled up inside him when he remembered a similarly unspeakable thing he had witnessed when he was seven years old. It took a few minutes before he could ask his next question with any semblance of disinterested calm. "When did he do all this?"

She slumped back against her pillow, propping the book against her raised knees. *Soon before you came. Maybe fifteen minutes before you came, he left me.*

Fifteen minutes. That beastly man might still be lurking around—though more likely the sound of the truck engine, and his and MacFie's voices outside, had spooked him and he'd left.

What sort of man was this German, and why was he wandering around behind their lines without getting caught?

His thoughts drifted away for a moment while another sketch emerged onto the blank page beneath the girl's pencil, this one less frenzied in its execution. The barn door, the treetops visible through it, and sparkling diamonds of rain dripping from it like elegant strings of beads. It was what she had seen from where she sat, having dragged herself upright, chest heaving from the terror of the man's cruelty: tranquillity and beauty. Something to focus on besides evil. She could discern beauty and drink in its peace even when her body had been savagely violated mere moments before. It took her a quarter of an hour to finish it, and Graham watched a softer look come over her face, as if the act of drawing were medicine for her, as if she could evict her sadness through her pencil.

It was what he did too, only instead of drawings, he made music when he was tense or frightened to calm himself. Perhaps this wee lassie was a kindred spirit. She looked at it with satisfaction, the fear and anxiety gone from her. Instead of being tense and skittish, she was relaxed and at peace. Then she wrote, *What is your name?*

He had watched her intently, and now she wanted to engage him in this strange conversation. He opened his mouth to answer her but stopped himself. He held out his hand for the pencil, and she handed it to him. He wrote under her picture: *Capitaine Augustus Edmund James Graham, Earl of Inverlochy.*

She grinned. *Are you making that up? Nobody has that many names.*

I do. All my family has that many names. Sometimes more.

Does everyone call you Capitaine Augustus Edmund James Graham, Earl of Inverlochy all the time?

No. My friends call me Graham. My wife and my brother call me Jamie.

She fixed her twilight-blue scrutiny on him. *Your French is good. But you are English.*

I am not English. I am Scottish. They are not the same.

She looked at him with a blend of awe and perplexity which bewildered him. Had he upset her by his brusqueness, corrected her too harshly?

"What is it?" he asked her.

A slow smile crept over her face. *You are left-handed. Like me.*

WHAT TO DO WITH A STRAY ORPHAN LASS

WHEN MACFIE RETURNED on horseback with another man, Graham helped them get the truck running and out of the mud, but Aveline was constantly on his mind. What to do with her? There was a war on, and he couldn't be there for her indefinitely. He would have to find out who her people were and get her to them as quickly as possible. This was no place for a wee lassie. He had work to do, and there wasn't room for her in any of it.

But he was reluctant, all the same, to turn her over to strangers, knowing what had happened. She had shared her story with him, which could not have been easy for her. It made him more personally bound to her, heightened his sense of responsibility to be sure she was safe.

It was mid-afternoon before the truck was hauled out of the mud and the engine repaired. The mechanic drove the truck, with Graham, Aveline, and the cat beside him, while MacFie took the horses.

CHÂTEAU BLANCHARD

SINCE HIS DIVISION had moved south for the offensive at the Somme, Graham and his men, when not in the trenches, lived roughly halfway between the front and Amiens, where his superiors, referred to by Graham and his men as the Dread Staff Officers, were stationed.

The house Graham had commandeered for his company's use belonged to a couple named Blanchard, simple but well-bred folk in their early sixties. They had been so charmed by Graham's courteousness, his fluent French, and his insistence on perfect order, that they were entirely willing to have the men stay there. Graham and several others, mostly officers, lived in the house, and the rest of the men camped out on the grounds.

The Blanchards gave Graham M. Blanchard's study for any of his work requiring a desk and telephone, and a bedroom for MacFie and himself; his other men were divided among the rest of the spare bedrooms, and he was adamant that the men behave themselves and not cause distress for the owners of the house.

There was no small stir when Graham carried Aveline inside. Graham and Mme Blanchard arranged hot water and soap in a tub in the kitchen so Aveline could have a proper bath and wash her hair. He brought her a warm blanket to wrap herself in and a cup of hot tea to drink in front of the kitchen fire while he combed her hair for her, while Mme Blanchard found a safe corner for Aveline to sleep, near her own bedroom and the kitchen.

After the doctor had given her a proper medical examination (she agreed to this only if Graham stayed in the room and held her hand), Graham tucked Aveline and the cat into her little bed. She mimed writing, and he handed her the notebook and pencil, and she wrote, *Promise me you won't send me away. I'll do anything. I'm strong, and I can do lots of things.*

He sighed. "I can't promise that, little one. But I will do all I can for you."

She smiled, trustingly, closed her eyes, and fell asleep in no time at all.

He sat there beside her in the lamplight for at least half an hour. The protective little black cat had nestled itself against Aveline's head, purring. Graham looked in his journal at her sketches and read her words, over and over again. The way she had produced the drawings so quickly amazed him, and her command of words was excellent. A most unusual child. He would have to look for her family, of course, but he'd keep her here in the meantime.

Which meant he would have to have a word with his men.

He left the room, closing the door behind him. In the main room, Graham gathered all the officers together. "Some of you know MacFie and I found an abandoned wee lassie yesterday," he said. "Today I brought her here. She is, for all practical purposes, to be treated as my daughter. She will stay here while I look for her family. You need to know she has been raped and cannot speak. I expect you to protect her, make sure those under you are informed about her. If any man tries to seek favors from her, there will be hell to pay. Consider yourselves warned."

A murmur of assent went up.

"There's more," Graham went on. "Concerning the man who raped her. She says he was German, big, with a moustache. Somehow, he has been wandering around behind our lines undetected, and we need to find him. I believe he may have killed this girl's older brother. MacFie found a man we think is her brother dead in the cellar of the house. The German may be a deserter, or a spy. Whatever he is, he must be captured before he does any further harm."

He dismissed them and moved to go upstairs.

"Jamie!"

He turned. His brother George stood a few steps behind him.

"Yes, George, what is it?" Graham asked, weary.

"Will she be all right? Are you all right?"

Graham sighed. "I suppose. It's a wee bit uncomfortable for me. But more so for her."

George opened his mouth to speak, but Graham raised a hand to silence him. "Tomorrow, George," he said, turning toward his room. "I'm pure done in."

MEMORIES

IN THE MORNING, Graham woke early as usual. He washed and shaved and thought of the pale, vulnerable lassie, probably still asleep in her bed, as he dressed for the day. He speculated again what kind of depraved beast could violate a child. She had no womanly beauty yet to recommend her; it had been purely a play of power. He understood longing for sex—he missed his wife terribly—but he couldn't imagine, in a hundred years, being so motivated by animal lust that he could force himself on a defenseless wee lassie to get satisfaction. There was something beyond unspeakable in it. Aveline hadn't wanted it, hadn't asked for it, and had a lifetime ahead of her during which she would undoubtedly relive the event hundreds, maybe thousands of times.

Power and violence were all too familiar to him, from a childhood full of cruel authority figures. It made him uncomfortable to remember the roughness of the adults in his younger years, and he generally did not let himself think about it. But this horrific rape made him remember it, in spite of himself. He knew what it felt like to be kicked around, and it increased his unexpected sense of kinship with the child.

He shivered involuntarily, remembering her words. *He muttered at me. I don't know what he said. I don't know German.* Into his mind came the nasal shouting of his primary school headmaster, shouting abuse with each blow of the cane on his backside. Caesar, that man had called him, scathingly sarcastic. "You going to play your flute while Inverness burns, Caesar? How about you pay attention to your real studies instead? Dinnae think your father's name's going to help you get ahead if you dinnae work harder!" He had understood those words. He wished he hadn't.

They always got to him most, the words. He would have taken beatings over the head a hundred times without complaint, if only his father and headmaster and bullies would have stopped using cruel words. The words cut deep in a way no physical blows ever could, cut straight through and left his soul bleeding and raw. He'd wanted to be loved, appreciated. His mother was only marginally interested in him; his father openly hated him.

He was so lost in his thoughts that he jumped when MacFie came up behind him.

"The men are waiting for you, my lord."

Graham turned to MacFie, shaking his head as if to clear it. "Coming," he said.

STRANGE MEN

AVELINE EMERGED A little later. She stood in the open door of her little room, hardly more than a closet, the black cat in her arms. Her alert eyes and ears scanned for her hero. She was still very sore, and she didn't want to move much. She sat carefully on the floor and leaned her back against the edge of the doorframe and waited. She didn't want to wander around without her capitaine there to protect her. She didn't know her way yet, and there were an awful lot of men here. Something withery twisted inside her at the likelihood of meeting a man with whom she could not speak, whose language she did not know. Probably they would not try to harm her, but she couldn't be sure. Not anymore.

She couldn't remember her own father, who had died before she was born, but she liked to imagine he'd have treated her as well as Capitaine Graham did. Her mother she *almost* remembered, the way you try to grasp at a dream after you've awakened. All she'd had since Maman died was Armand, her big brother. Armand had been her entire world. He had always protected her. But close to two weeks ago, he too had vanished.

This Capitaine Augustus Edmund James Graham, Earl of Inverlochy, was the kindest person ever. He had been so gentle with her when he took her away. He would surely do all he could to help her find Armand if she asked him. And if Armand couldn't be found, well, she would stay right here with her capitaine.

Sweet Sylvie, she tried to say into her kitten's head, but no sound came out. She missed her voice. Would it ever come back?

She sat there some time until Graham appeared, searching for her. "I'm glad you're awake. Come along with me, lassie," he said, beckoning. He didn't smile, but his voice was kind.

ARMAND

AVELINE MOVED SLOWLY, and Graham let her set the pace to his office, where he gave her a seat beside him so she could conveniently write her answers for him.

"Would you mind telling me what were you doing in the barn when the German came?"

I was playing with Sylvie. I was tired of being in the house all the time. In the barn, I could have fresh air but not be rained on. Not that the fresh air is much better outside than in. Everything always stinks since the war came close to us.

"I see." He leaned his elbows on his desk. "Will you tell me about your life on the farm?"

What do you want to know?

"Anything. Perhaps start by telling me, what did you do every day?"

As if she hadn't heard him, she quietly sketched chickens and cows and then drew little gravestones beneath each one. *We used to take care of our animals. Until we ate them.*

"Who was Armand? I saw his journals in the desk too."

My brother.

"And why was he not fighting in the war?"

He got lame when he was a boy.

"And your parents?"

Dead.

"And you never had anyone to help you on the farm? How did you live?"

Armand couldn't afford to hire help because he was saving all our extra money so we could move someplace else sometime. Once a week, he went to town for supplies.

"He could walk, then?"

Oh yes. He limped, but he could walk into town all right.

Two miles a day he could do; more than that left him in a lot of pain. He did odd jobs for people in town to earn money, and I helped by taking care of our house.

"Did you ever attend school?"

No. Armand taught me. He was older than me. Twenty-three. He wanted to be a doctor after the war.

"And did you have any friends you visited, or who came to visit you? Go to church?"

No. Armand did not believe in God, so no church. Nobody ever came to our house, and nobody invited us to theirs.

"Why was that, do you know?"

Armand said it was better for us to keep to ourselves, and he would explain it to me someday.

Graham sighed. Saving things to explain for later was always convenient for adults, but not so much for children.

I think it was something to do with our mother.

"What do you know about your mother?"

I don't remember her much. I was not yet three when she died. But I know her name was Marie-Claire. There are photographs at the house, in the secret drawer in Armand's desk.

Graham looked meditatively off into space for a few minutes. She was drawing again, and a face emerged beneath her pencil: a strong, bearded face with piercing eyes and crowned with unkempt hair. She lovingly smoothed out the shading with one fingertip and smiled at it. Graham, watching, became more certain than ever that the dead man in the cellar was the same man in this sketch.

"Is that Armand?"

She nodded.

"And when did you last see him?"

Almost two weeks ago. He just vanished. He never goes anywhere without telling me where he'll be. So I have worried.

"You woke up one morning, and he was gone?"

No. We had eaten lunch, and after we washed the dishes, I went outside to play with Sylvie in the barn, and I fell asleep in the hayloft. It was hot and stuffy, and it made me sleepy. When I woke and came inside, Armand was gone. I thought he went to town. We needed food. But he never came back. It was scary to be all alone in the house that night. But he always told me never to leave the farm alone, so I stayed put.

"Do you have any ideas where he might have gone, if not to town?"

She considered a moment. *I don't know. I was excited, hearing those footsteps from the barn yesterday. I was sure it was Armand coming home. I ran to the door to greet him and then stopped short because the stride was wrong. Even before I saw the German, I knew it couldn't be Armand, because there would have been the step-pause-drag in the gravel. The German's step was heavy and steady.*

Two tears dropped onto her hand, and she sniffed. *I want my brother. Could we go back to the farm and see if he is there? He will worry if he comes and finds I'm gone.* She lifted her twilight eyes to his, and his own eyes filled at the sight of her tears.

Graham laced his fingers together and rested his chin on them. He knew how he'd have felt at thirteen if anyone had told him his own beloved brother George was dead: desolated, possibly even suicidal. But he would not lie to this girl. Something about her demanded straightforward honesty. "Sweetheart, Mr. MacFie and I found a man dead in the cellar of your farmhouse. His hair was the same color as yours, and he wore a blue linen smock over his trousers, similar to your dress. Does that sound like what he wore the last time he was home?"

She stared at him, her eyes glazing over in denial.

You mean he was right there all the time, and I never knew?

"I'm afraid so."

She dropped her pencil and shrunk into herself, shaking her head as if, by denial, she could make it untrue, her lips moving in a vain attempt to speak. He held out his arm to her, and she climbed onto his lap and sobbed into his shoulder for at least ten minutes.

Finally, she calmed, wiped her nose on the back of her fist, and reached for the pencil again. *Did he fall? Why did I never hear him call for help?*

"It's not pretty, Aveline. Are you sure you want me to tell you?"

She scowled. *I'm tired of people not telling me things. Look where it's gotten me!*

Graham sighed deeply. She had a point. "He'd been murdered, Aveline. Someone stabbed him, threw him down the stairs, and left him there to die." His words were carefully even and controlled, but she read distress in his eyes at having to tell her this. "Do you have any idea, any at all, why anyone might want to kill your brother?"

She shook her head. He recognized the question was more than she could handle now and changed tack.

"Is there anything you want to ask me, Aveline? Anything I can tell you that you want to know?"

She thought a minute, obviously hesitant. She glanced into his eyes as if deciding whether she would continue putting her trust in him. Her pencil hung over the paper a long time before she wrote again.

I want to know what the German did to me. Will I die too?

How to explain it without scaring her? Well, she'd experienced it. To understand it might help her be less afraid for the future. He wished again his wife were here; frank talk never was a struggle for her. He did not like discussing these sorts of things, but he knew he did, at the very least, need to find out if Aveline had any chance of being pregnant.

"No, what he did to you will not make you die. Tell me, though... have you—have you started your courses?"

She looked at him blankly, and he elaborated, "Do you have bleeding every month? Many girls around your age do."

She shook her head. *I don't think so.*

"You'd know if you had. It's normal. If you haven't yet, that's all right. It's good in your case. It means you won't—um—you won't have a baby."

Her forehead puckered in concern.

I don't follow, Capitaine.

He leaned his head into his hand and closed his eyes a moment. "I'm afraid I'm explaining all this badly. Well, first of all, the act the German committed on you, it is called rape, and it is a perversion. What he did to you should never happen to children. It is meant to be beautiful and lovely, and it *is*, if both parties consent. It's the way husbands and wives make babies together. But nobody should do it at all if both people do not want it. To force it on someone, as was done to you, is criminal."

Her little shoulders trembled, and she wrote with a shaking hand. *Then why did he do it?*

"I don't know. Some men are not men. They are beasts. In my opinion, the evil bastard doesn't deserve to live who would do this to anyone, especially a child." His fist clenched as he spoke. He had often, as a boy, wished his father would die and leave him in peace. How much more any pitiful excuse of a man who assaulted little girls.

She looked pale, and she closed her eyes and rested her cheek on the notebook.

"You should rest," he said, laying his hand on her soft hair gently and realizing, to his surprise, that it did not seem at all awkward to stroke it. "This has been a lot for one morning."

She did not move, but she scrawled lazily: *I'm hungry. Can I eat lunch first?*

He had to smile at that. The girl's appetite was clearly healthy.

"All right," he agreed. "Lunch first." And the girl took his hand, and they walked side by side, him shortening his steps to stay beside her, to get her something to eat.

APPLE CIDER HAIR

MME BLANCHARD WAS a warm, exuberant person, and welcomed Aveline with enthusiasm when Graham brought her into the kitchen.

"How have you lived so close to me all this time, and I've never known about you?" she asked. Aveline shrugged, suspiciously sizing up the woman and shrinking back behind Graham.

"Her brother kept her rather secluded," Graham explained. He rested his hands lightly on the lassie's shoulders. "You're one of the few women she's seen since her mother died. She's hungry."

"I can take care of that," Mme Blanchard assured briskly. "Come, sit, little one."

Graham squeezed her shoulder gently, to reassure her. "Make yourself useful, Aveline. I'll come back for you later, after I've taken care of a few things."

The lady sensed the girl's fear of being left behind, and in moments, she had distracted Aveline and set her at her ease, feeding her, fussing over her hair, and setting her to work. Still, when Graham walked in an hour later to fetch her, Aveline's face lit up like the sun with relief. It was a sweet face, a bit puckish, her skin clear and pale and her nose sprinkled in freckles like nutmeg on custard. She sat near the window, where the sun lit her apple-cider hair to its full brilliance, and he stared at her intently while she turned her eyes back to her task and finished peeling the last two potatoes for Mme Blanchard.

George appeared at his brother's side, slinging a casual arm over his shoulder, and looked at the girl. "That hair," he mused. "It's like...Mademoiselle Leclair's, isn't it?" He glanced at his brother.

"Yes," Graham answered, guardedly. "I thought the same thing, only I tried *not* to think of it."

"Sorry," George said. "I shouldn't have mentioned it."

Aveline looked up again, and Sylvie, curled at her feet,

opened her eyes and hissed at George. Graham beckoned Aveline, and she came slithering over to him, dodging out of George's reach as George tried to pet the top of her head.

"What's the matter?" Graham asked Aveline, guiding her out to the great room and sitting with her on the sofa. Her glowering in George's general direction was all the answer he needed.

It had never occurred to him that someone could mistrust or dislike his lovable, charming little brother on only a few minutes' acquaintance. Not that George was a paragon of virtue by any means, but Graham also knew George was rather a favorite among children in general. "He won't hurt you. He's my brother, you know. He has four girls of his own. My boys like him."

Aveline snatched a nearby newspaper and scribbled, *Sylvie doesn't like him*. Then she threw her pencil across the room and hid under the afghan on the sofa, and Graham left her alone.

He went back to the table where George had tipped back in a chair with his feet up, hat over his face and a floral kerchief tied about his neck. "Get your feet off the table, George," he scolded sharply, startling George so his chair tipped the rest of the way to the floor, and he landed with an undignified crash. "And how many times must I tell you that kerchief is *not regulation?*"

Graham sat across from George, who brushed himself off, attempting to recover his injured dignity. "I can't get any naps in around here," he complained, reluctantly removing the kerchief and folding it to fit into his pocket.

"Maybe you should go to bed before midnight occasionally," Graham shot back.

"You're cruel." George feigned despair.

Graham, unmoved, no longer heard George. He was remembering Mademoiselle Leclair, the governess with the hair like Aveline's. It was impossible, of course, that Aveline could be related to her, but nonetheless, the uncanny similarity of their hair forced Graham to confront childhood memories he'd tried to purge from his brain for almost thirty years.

PART THREE

1880-1888

Inverness-shire, Scotland

THE EARL'S SONS

DONALD GRAHAM, TWELFTH Earl of Inverlochy, worked up the ranks to lieutenant-colonel with the British army in India, beginning in 1854. He came back to Scotland in 1879 to marry Lucy Cameron. He was forty-six; she was twenty-two. The marriage had been pre-arranged by their families. The Camerons had money and plenty of it. Donald Graham was only minimally involved in the arrangements; he wasn't exactly in dire financial straits, but he didn't mind being sure it stayed that way. Besides, he needed an heir.

Once wedded, Donald Graham stayed in Scotland only long enough to impregnate his wife and be sure of his heir—happily for him, he got two at once, which saved him having to stay any longer to produce a spare. Augustus and George arrived on a frigid January night in 1880. Seeing they were healthy, Donald Graham returned to India as quickly as possible, and for the first five years of his sons' lives, he thoroughly enjoyed his military life, ordering people around and pursuing his favorite hobbies: seducing pretty maidens and rarely writing home. In 1885, he contracted a severe case of malaria, which so weakened him that he was sent home to recuperate.

A telegram preceded the earl, and his staff welcomed him home with all the pomp and ceremony they knew he would expect, but since he was still weak from his illness, he was brusque and uncourteous to them, and he stalked inside, leaning on his walking stick. His wife and sons stood dutifully in the great hall to greet this virtual stranger. George flashed on his father his winning smile and stuck out his hand. "Welcome home, Father," he said, pouring on every ounce of his natural charm. "I'm George. How do you do, sir?"

Donald Graham paused. Shook the five-year-old's hand. "Miserable as usual," he said gruffly. For him in his current state, this was outright friendliness, but Augustus Graham had no way of knowing it. He bristled that anyone should be less than genial to his George. Their father fixed his eyes on his elder son, expecting a similar welcome from him.

Graham's eyes flashed. He forgot what he'd been instructed to say. "Why can't you be nice to George?" he asked, sharply. "He was nice to you."

His mother hissed, "Augustus! Apologize at once!"

"No," said Graham clearly. "I will not."

Graham got his first glimpse of the old man's quicksilver temper then. His father gave him a whack against the shoulder with his walking-stick. Graham, who had never in his life been struck with anything more threatening than an occasional hair-brush to the backside, gasped and stumbled to his knees, and his eyes filled and spilled over with tears as his father's tirade went on. "Oh, that's how it is, is it? You talk saucy to your father and cry when you get what you deserve?" He shook his fist inches from Graham's face. "Get me away from this miserable child, woman. I'm tired. I want you to come tuck me into bed. And also explain this lack of discipline."

His mother, pale and trembling, cast an anxious parting glance at her sons, and George and Graham watched as their parents disappeared up the stairs. George, speechless for once, reached over and took his brother's hand and squeezed it. He didn't say a word, but Graham understood.

THE EARL'S WIFE

GRAHAM AND GEORGE'S existence prior to that point had been relatively dull, but pleasant enough. Lucy had always left them primarily in the care of their capable nanny and the nursery maids. But she was not an unkind mother, and she did particularly spend time with Graham, teaching him how to play the flute after he expressed interest. She made it a point to walk with her boys each afternoon if the weather allowed, and if it was too cold or stormy, to spend at least an hour with them indoors. All days were the same: mostly unmemorable, a pleasing stream of orderly nothingness.

But after her husband returned from India, Lucy became increasingly withdrawn. At meals, she had always presided over the table with grace and dignity, but the very first evening Donald was home, he displaced her, sending her to the foot of the table. He instructed Graham, as eldest, to sit on his father's right, and George on his left, and neither the boys nor Lucy were allowed to speak unless spoken to. From that day forward, Lucy meekly fulfilled her duties from her place as the lowest of the low, saying as little as possible, hardly ever smiling. To her husband, Lucy was a possession, an object—not a cherished companion. She was the necessary instrument through which the family line continued, and beyond that, her value was limited to being ornamental and a perfect hostess. She could be these things, but the boys sensed, behind the charm she put on for guests, something terribly sad about their mother and the changes in their lives. But the boys, in their isolation, did not know there was any other way families could be.

THE ELDEST SON

BEFORE HIS FATHER'S return, Graham had never given much mind to the obligations of being the eldest. He was only five, after all, and his mother was not even remotely interested in mapping out every detail of the boys' futures. His father, however, had his own plans. Graham was daily reminded he was The Heir, and therefore, his career must be The Army, as it had been for all his ancestors before him. A mere thirty minutes of time and a quirk of fate had prevented George from being born first, and although he sometimes resented the new load of obligations, Graham was glad the estate would someday be his. A military career did not appeal to him at all, however. He didn't know what he wanted to do yet, but it wasn't *that*.

Graham's disinterest in the army was not the only thing his father found irritating in his son. George had everything their father deemed of value. He was the handsome, sturdy one, brimming with charm and charisma, boundless energy, gracious social skills, and not at all interested in art and music; Graham was too thin for his height, too solemn, too prone to losing himself in the private and inaccessible world of his imagination, and very inclined toward art and music.

FRENCH GOVERNESSES

ONE OF THE first things the Twelfth Earl of Inverlochy had done upon his return home was engage a young French governess for his boys to replace the harridan—his word—who had been their nanny from infancy. The boys were sorry when Mrs. Alexander left; they had liked her, even if she was strict and dull.

The pretty new governess was twenty-five, animated, a bit scatterbrained, and given a higher seat at the table than Lucy. The boys weren't sure what to make of her. All the same, she took care of them all right for a year, until one evening the boys came in to dinner to find she had gone. No explanation was ever given, but within a month, an even prettier French girl of twenty-one replaced her. She lasted seven months before she too inexplicably vanished.

After her, there was no governess for some time. Then, shortly before Christmas in 1886, right before the boys' seventh birthday, Mademoiselle Leclair walked into their nursery. She was seventeen, and more beautiful than anyone Graham had ever seen up to that point. She had clear pale skin and hair like apple cider, and she never was as much a governess as a big sister to them, so young she was and full of amazement.

The boys began to notice a pattern in their father's behavior with their governesses. As with the others, he came to the nursery "to make sure all was well" with Mlle Leclair. Then his visits would lengthen and become more frequent; as with the first two he gave the girl one or two extravagant gifts. The others had disappeared shortly after the gifts.

Graham and George liked Mlle Leclair and didn't want her to leave like the others, and in bed at night, they plotted how they might keep her from leaving, but weeks drifted into months, and they never came up with anything concrete, and then summertime came.

One July afternoon, George was busy at some play Graham deemed uninteresting; he wanted only to steal away someplace and practice scales and exercises on his flute as his mother had taught him. He knew the perfect place. High in the west tower was an unused room, said to contain a ghost and, therefore, respectfully left alone. Graham didn't believe in the ghost, and he wasn't afraid of it anyway, and he knew nobody ever went there. In that room, he would at least be safe from reprimands by his father for disturbing the peace of the castle.

He climbed the twisting stairs of the tower, blissfully dreaming of the afternoon of music ahead of him, when an unfamiliar sound sent a prickle down his spine, coming from the very room he sought. He poked his head around the doorframe, gaping in shock, rooted to the floor, watching in disgusted fascination. Then, realizing he did not want to be caught watching, he stepped backward into the hall and ran for his life.

Moments later, George came skidding in, alarm on his face, to find Graham sitting on the edge of his bed, his hands still gripped around his yet-unplayed flute.

"What's the matter?" George asked, breathless from his hurry.

"What made you come in here just now?"

"I was in the kitchen tasting strawberries, and got a feeling. Tell me what's happened."

At first, Graham wouldn't say, but George pressed him to explain.

"What would you do if you saw Father do something very, very bad, George?" he asked at last, slowly.

"I don't know," George said honestly. "Why?"

Graham shuddered. "Because—because I just saw Mlle Leclair and him in the ghost room, and she had no clothes on, and he was sitting on her, and making terrible noises, and she sounded like she was crying. It scared me. I don't know what to do. Should I tell Mother?"

George stared wide-eyed, mouth open. Finally, he spoke. "I wouldn't tell her," he said. "What good would it do? Father does whatever he wants anyway. And he'd have you thrashed for watching and shout at Mother too. Better let it alone."

Graham looked at George with tears in his eyes, and he whispered fiercely, "I hate it here. Father hates me. I wish I'd never been born."

George hugged him. "But then I'd not have you for my brother. It'd be better if *he* hadn't been born. Or if the malaria had killed him. Don't cry. He'll get caught someday. Bad people always do in books."

George's confidence marginally cheered Graham. "It was disgusting," Graham said again. "I wish I could forget it. I shouldn't have told you."

"I don't mind," George said. "I already knew he was a louse."

There was a long pause before Graham spoke again. "George," he asked, "do you have any idea what 'fucking French cunt' means?"

George didn't. But he stored the words in his brain for later.

THE EARL'S RIDING CROP

ONE DAY, SIX weeks afterward, their father took it into his head that the boys needed his assistance to ride better. George realized this was part of the pattern. After the gifts to the governesses—Mlle Leclair *had* received a diamond pendant two months ago and a silver watch soon after that—their father would unexpectedly become keenly interested in bettering his sons' skills at something or other which had never much concerned him before *and* always took them well out of the way of the house.

George was putting it all together in his head when his broodings were interrupted by his father scolding Graham for some trivial error in horsemanship. George, to diffuse the situation, jumped in and asked cannily, "Father, will Mlle Leclair be gone when we get back to the house?"

The distraction worked. Graham gaped at his brother, astonished at his deduction, amazed he hadn't thought of it first, while their father fixed George with a Look. Graham was all too familiar with that Look, but he had never seen his father give it to George. He opened his mouth to rescue George from certain doom when George went on cheerfully, and a bit too loudly, "I guess you get tired of fucking French cunts, eh, Father?"

The ferocious and terrible look on the old man's face might have been funny in other circumstances. He jabbed his riding crop in George's direction. "Don't you *ever* say that again!" he warned, hoarse with rage.

"Why did *you* say it then?" Graham threw in. He would not let George get punished for this. George glared at him, but before he could interrupt to redirect his father's attention, Graham went on with angry tears in his eyes, "I *saw* you! Is that what you do to all our governesses? Is that why they always go away?"

The crack of the riding crop against Graham's face echoed off the stable wall. He fell off his horse, stunned by the pain, and landed so hard, he was sure he would be sick. His father kicked him in the ribs, hauled him to his feet, and held him by the collar.

"Why would you *do* things like that?" Graham asked, his voice high with distress. His father laughed uproariously, and a stream of profane details about sex poured out of him. Graham tried not to listen, tried to squirm out of his father's strong hand, but he couldn't help hearing.

"I will never do that to a woman," Graham gasped out at last, his voice trembling in terror and anger. He got whacked in the ear.

"Oh, you think so? You'll change your mind. You will. You'll spill your virginity fast enough in a few years."

"I won't," Graham said, trying to dodge a blow to his other ear and failing. "I won't be like you."

His father pinned him against the stable wall. He looked absolutely insane with rage. "I've a mind to make it happen, find an old whore someplace to do you over. You don't deserve to enjoy it with a pretty girl, that's for sure."

"You're disgusting, and I hate you," Graham said, his voice thin and ice cold, his heart numb with the terror that his father might actually make good this vile threat. He couldn't wipe away his streaming tears or defend himself from the knocking about; his father had his wrists pinned in an iron grip.

"Let him go."

George's voice was quiet and authoritative, but his eyes were wide with fear as they met Graham's. He laid a light hand on his father's tense arm. "Let him go, Father."

The old man did as George asked. He seemed to have forgotten George had set off this fight in the first place. He stalked away, leaving George to take care of Graham, who had slid jelly-like down the stable wall to the ground and, hugging his knees, buried his face in them and sobbed shamelessly. George crouched next to him, laying a gentle hand over his brother's shoulders, fighting back tears of his own. "I'm sorry," he whispered. "I didn't mean for him to go off on you."

"Well, I did," Graham said flatly. "You didn't deserve a

beating like this."

"Neither did you," George snapped. "He wouldn't have done this to *me*. You should have stayed out of it. Haven't you gotten enough beatings for nothing?"

It was the closest they had ever come to arguing over anything that mattered.

"Let me have a look at your face," George said, his tone gentler, and Graham looked up obediently. His ears throbbed, and a bloody line crossed his cheek where the crop had broken through his skin.

"It's beastly unfair," George said angrily. "I wish I could stop him for good, but I don't know how."

"I'm bigger than you, and I can't stop him," Graham pointed out. He sniffed. "If I could only keep my mouth shut. But I can't let him say horrible things either."

George slumped, looking uncharacteristically depressed, reaching for his brother's hand. "What's a whore?" he asked at last.

"I have no idea," Graham replied, although he did have an inkling. "And I don't want to."

For ten minutes, they sat there quietly, hands clasped on the ground between them, staring out over the yard. Then George stood. "Come on," he said, helping Graham to his feet. "Let's get you washed up. Baggett!"

The young stableboy materialized before them. His eyes widened at the sight of Graham's face. "Are you all right, Lord Kirkhill?" he burst out.

"No, he's not all right," George said evenly. "I'm taking him to the house. Please, take care of the horses, would you, Baggett?"

"Aye right. Straightaway." He watched with concern as the two lads, only a few years younger than himself, made their way slowly across the grounds, one supporting the other.

THE TYRANT AND THE COWARD

GRAHAM DIDN'T WANT to come to dinner that night. His face and much of the rest of his body were a mess of bruises, and he hurt everywhere. George had tenderly washed the place where the crop had broken his skin, but there was no hiding the evidence of the altercation. Although Graham particularly was not hungry, they both knew he must appear at table. Despite his injuries, he entered the dining room straight and proud. He would not let his father intimidate him.

His mother gasped at the sight of her mild-mannered son's face when he came to stand behind his chair, and George tried to smooth things over with a preposterous excuse. "We were fighting." They never fought, and their mother knew it.

Graham locked eyes with his mother, pleading silently. He knew she was not as blind as she pretended to be to his father's character. Perhaps this time she would interpose in his defense?

She did not. Her gaze faltered, and she looked into her lap at her hands, tightly twisting her omnipresent handkerchief.

Graham sat in his place, and his shoulders drooped. It was all he could do not to cry. Merely being in the same room with his tyrannical father made his stomach knot together. Never knowing what would set the old man off was the most terrible thing. Not having the only other adult in the family stick up for him was the next most terrible thing.

Two not-quite-eight-year-old lads against a tyrant and a coward did not stand a chance.

Mademoiselle Leclair did not come to table. They never saw her again.

THE DRIVER

THE NEXT MORNING after breakfast, the butler, Bates, interrupted Graham's flute practice in his room.

"Your father wishes to see you in his study, my lord."

Donald Graham, writing at the desk, did not look up as his son came into the room, and the boy stood there for five minutes, waiting, before his father spoke.

"Augustus," he said casually, "in one hour, you will be driven to the station and put on a train to Inverness. I have arranged for you to go to school there. Bates has been instructed to pack your bags."

"George too, sir?"

"No. Just you. Be ready promptly. In the hall in one hour."

"Yes, sir," Graham said, his voice scarcely audible. He turned and left the room and ran like the wind, looking for George.

But George was nowhere to be found. His mother, writing letters of her own in the morning room, acted surprised at the inquiry. "Why, George is off to market with the gardener this morning, don't you remember?"

Graham slumped and walked away. It was so deliberate, this prison of solitude. What explanation had been given to George for going to market alone? They loved market day. Ostensibly intended as practical training in bargaining and working with money, to the boys, it was a reprieve from their bleak home life. Whatever George had been told, Graham was sure George had no idea his brother was leaving home. His father acted as though nothing had happened, as if banishing his son to boarding school were as ordinary as sneezing. He went to his room for his coat and hat and gloves and waited in the great hall by the door, looking the picture of misery. Neither of his parents came to bid him farewell. The butler, Bates, brought him his valise.

"Is my flute in it?" Graham asked, plaintively.

Bates laid a gentle hand on the lad's thin shoulder. Speaking in undertones, he bent close and answered, "Aye, it is. I shall miss you, Lord Kirkhill. Take care of yourself."

Bates handed Graham up to the driving board beside the waiting driver, and Graham sat stiffly, clutching his valise on his knees. They didn't speak until the castle was out of sight around a bend in the drive, and then the driver spat off to the side of the road. "We saw what happened yesterday, me and Baggett, and you did good standin' up to the old bastart. Pardon me, my lord, but that's what the old Earl is, a right bastart. The village folks all says it was the malaria what turned him mad, but I says the malaria is an excuse. He's always been a fearsome madman, except before he married your poor mum, he had nobody weaker to bully but the housemaids, and he was hardly home to bother *them.*"

Graham didn't answer. He didn't know what to say. The happenings of yesterday seemed like a bad dream, what with his parents appearing to have forgotten it altogether. Only his battered face and aching body proved for certain it had been real. He kept his eyes straight ahead. He tried not to think of George, blissfully unaware of his brother's departure. Would George know he was in trouble and come looking for him, as he had the day Graham had seen his father with Mlle Leclair?

The driver too fell into quiet contemplation, whistling softly. Graham knew the song well, and the words rang in his head:

And adieu to all I love, bonnie lassie, O!
To the river winding clear,
To the fragrant-scented breer...

INVERNESS PROPER

THE DRIVER WAITED on the platform with the boy and made him repeat back all the instructions about where to change trains until satisfied that Graham would not forget. He saluted the boy, and Graham waved back at him until he vanished from sight. Then he sank back into his seat. He watched as everything familiar drifted away past his windows, and unfamiliar scenery took its place. In the pit of his stomach, he felt ill, as though his father had punched him there, and tears welled in his eyes.

He contemplated what awaited him at the other end of the line. Strangers, a strange place. He briefly considered running away to sea instead of changing trains, but he didn't want to go to sea, and he didn't know what else he could run away to. Join the traveling tinker folk? There was an idea. They would be far kinder than his own people. He and George occasionally sneaked off to play with the children of the ones who came through in the summer.

He daydreamed of the carefree Travellers all the way to Inverness. Their colorful, adventuresome life was not easy, but he would exchange the bleakness of his privilege for the security of love in hardship any day, given the choice.

But he did not run away to join the Travellers. He waited at the station until a cab driver came to collect him, and all through the grim and dusky streets, Graham longed intensely for the open spaces of his home.

Term had not started yet, and for two weeks, he was put to work helping to clean the gloomy schoolrooms. He didn't mind much. It distracted and tired him, and he slept well at night. But when the other boys began to arrive, Graham felt uneasy at the sight of them. He had seldom interacted with other children, and these were hardened and rough, and he shrank from them.

On the first day of school, the headmaster addressed the assembled students and singled out Graham. "And this," he said, with theatrical sarcasm, "is young Augustus Graham, Lord Kirkhill, gracing us with his presence as a result of behaving unpardonably to his father, Lord Inverlochy. You must treat him with all due respect."

Graham looked at his hands and tried not to cry, but he couldn't stop a few spiteful tears from sneaking out. A few boys close to him tittered and passed on the news to their neighbors. Before the day's end, he had become the object of everyone's scorn. Spying his not-quite-healed face, a few of the bigger lads tried to pick a fight with him.

"You look like a fighter," one lad taunted. "Is that why your father sent you here, 'cause you can't keep your fists to yourself?"

"No," Graham said. He didn't want to whimper, but he was unable to control it. "My father hit me."

The boys guffawed. "And the Queen's me mum," one of them said. "Well, as long as you're already bruised, a couple more won't show much." And he punched Graham in the face and walked off, his boisterous pals laughing with him, leaving Graham where he had fallen in a puddle of water, his nose bleeding.

Graham couldn't escape the taunting. From one building to another, he would walk alone, followed or encircled by thugs.

"Make way for Lord Kirkhill!" they would cry with exaggerated bows as he passed.

"He's not here 'cause he's a fighter after all. He's here 'cause he's a bloody *crybaby*!"

"Who wets his bed," sneered another.

"And plays the flute like his mummy. Mummy's boy misses his mummy, aye!"

Graham did his best to ignore them, carrying himself with as much dignity as he could muster, but it was impossible not to cry about their cruelty.

The headmaster—an old friend of his father's—also apparently considered it his duty in life to make young Lord Kirkhill's school life as miserable as possible. He caned him, called him Caesar, made a public example of him, humiliated him constantly, and there was nothing Graham could do.

Except to find refuge in his music whenever he could, although it became harder and harder each day to find places to practice where he would not be overheard and taunted. All through September and October and November, Graham counted the days until the Christmas holidays when he could go home and see George.

PSALMS

ONE DAY IN November after classes, pursued by the usual gang of bullies through the narrow lanes of the school grounds, Graham slipped into a side door of the chapel, out of the icy whistling winds. If he hid here awhile, they might let him alone. Perhaps the presence of the vicar would deter the bad boys from even coming in. He settled, sniveling, onto a pew in a corner and hugged his knees to himself, deeply engrossed in bitter self-pity at the unfairness of life. Quiet reigned here, a hush not as much silence as an absence of distress. It calmed him, took the edge off the nastiness of the lads outside. At last, he glanced at the pew beside him. A Psalter lay there, and he took it in his hand and opened it.

The Scriptures were not familiar to him. He had heard them read in church on Sundays, but he had never paid much attention. His family did not even pretend to be religious at home; their church attendance was an obligatory nod to tradition, not a devotion from the heart.

The Psalter fell open, and Graham's eyes widened as he slowly sounded out the words on the page.

Save me, O God;

for the waters are come in unto my soul.

I sink in deep mire, where there is no standing:

I am come into deep waters,

where the floods overflow me.

I am weary of my crying: my throat is dried:

mine eyes fail while I wait for my God.

They that hate me without a cause

are more than the hairs of mine head:

they that would destroy me,

being my enemies wrongfully, are mighty—

He looked up, startled. It was as though this had been written with him in mind. He was half afraid to keep reading. But he did.

> *Hear me, O LORD; for thy lovingkindness is good:*
> *turn unto me according to*
> *the multitude of thy tender mercies.*
> *And hide not thy face from thy servant;*
> *for I am in trouble: hear me speedily.*
> *Draw nigh unto my soul, and redeem it:*
> *deliver me because of mine enemies.*

He lowered the book to his lap, shaken through. He didn't understand all the words he read, but he'd comprehended enough. He wanted in that moment to have God on his side, felt convinced God wanted to be on his side. He found himself kneeling, staring toward the cross at the front of the church. He folded his hands over the open book and whispered, "I don't know much about you, God, but I am tired of crying and being scared, so please, do what the book said and come near and deliver my soul from mine enemies. My father might not get me here, but all the lads can, and the headmaster—and thank you, sir."

He didn't know what to expect to happen next, but he stayed on his knees, rested his cheek peacefully against his folded hands, and fell asleep.

"Are you a' right?" a voice said, the accent of Inverness thick in it. A gentle hand touched his shoulder, and Graham jumped, fearful. Then he relaxed. It was only the vicar.

"Who are you, son?"

"Augustus Graham. Lord Kirkhill, sir. My father is the Earl of Inverlochy." He might as well let him know right off that he was the boy everyone hated.

The man considered him a moment, seeming untroubled by Graham's identity. "Tell me, laddie, do you sing?"

"I suppose so." Where was this going?

"I've had a few lads come down with measles the past week, and my choir is short for the service on Sunday. I'm trying to help the choirmaster find some boys willing to fill in. It isnae so easy as ye'd think. This is a tough lot of lads, and most of them dinnae want to have anything to do wi' church, let alone choir. If you're willing to sing, it would be a great help."

"I'd be glad to try, sir. Would we practice here in chapel?"

"Aye, we would."

"I would do *anything* to keep safe in here, sir. Anything you ask," Graham, said, face pale and earnest, as he clutched the Psalter to his chest.

"Well, stay close. He'll be alang in a moment, and we'll see if he thinks you a good candidate."

Graham waited, and soon the choirmaster and several other boys filed in, and the vicar introduced him to them.

"Let's hear what you can do," the choirmaster said and handed Graham some music. It looked intimidating, but he could read music a little, thanks to his mother, and he gave it his best shot. He listened while the boys sang through it once, following along quietly. The second time, he threw himself into it, and the choirmaster and vicar exchanged glances. At the end of the piece, the choirmaster looked at him hard while he and the vicar had a conversation in whispers just out of earshot.

"Young man," the choirmaster said at last, coming close to Graham, "what would you say to voice lessons and the lead part in the Christmas service?"

Graham's face lit up. "Oh, yes, please, sir!" He was wanted for something, something that would keep the thugs out of his hair. Being wanted was all that mattered. They gave him a stack of music to study and instructions on when to come for his lessons.

"Can I take this with me?" he asked the vicar as he left to have his dinner. He held out the Psalter.

"Aye, I expect you will take care of it."

He put the book and the music inside his coat and went to dinner. Afterward, he curled into his bed, opened the Psalter again and read what it fell open to.

When the LORD turned again the captivity of Zion,
we were like them that dream.
Then was our mouth filled with laughter,
and our tongue with singing:
then said they among the heathen,
The LORD hath done great things for them.
The LORD hath done great things for us;
whereof we are glad.
Turn again our captivity, O LORD,
as the streams in the south.
They that sow in tears shall reap in joy.
He that goeth forth and weepeth, bearing precious
seed,
shall doubtless come again with rejoicing,
bringing his sheaves with him.

Graham was sure it was a miracle, and from that day forward, he never doubted the existence of God. In his bed, he folded his hands on his chest and sent up a silent prayer. *You heard me. You heard me. Thank you.*

Outside of chapel, life didn't improve for Graham. The gang of school bullies still mocked and tormented him, called him a sissy and beat on him. But now—and he never understood exactly how—a peace stayed inside him that they could not touch. The more he read in the Psalter, the surer Graham became that God was on his side. God had given him a refuge in the chapel. It was as if he had only been waiting for Graham to ask for it.

Every spare moment he had, he spent in that refuge. In the chapel, he could play his flute or sing his heart out, and nobody mocked him. He also began to learn to play the piano. On half days and Saturdays and Sunday afternoons, when the rest of the lads ran outdoors like freakish colts, hitting things with sticks, Graham stayed in the chapel making music of one sort or other. His voice was a power held within himself, something bigger than his body, something thrilled to be let out to play in the spacious church instead of staying trapped inside. Graham's voice was his and his alone; he could learn to train and control and modulate it at will. It was always there for him, even in the absence of a piano or his flute.

The choirmaster was strict and not quick to hand out compliments, but Graham could still tell his progress pleased the man. "You've a cartload of raw talent, my boy," he said. "In a year, you'll have already learned everything I can teach you, I'm afraid. But I've a friend in Inverness who could take you further."

Graham glowed inside. Kind words gave him wings, damped the meanness of the other boys. He had found another bit of Psalm he repeated to himself over and over: *The LORD is on my side; I will not fear: what can man do unto me?* Fear and anger at the unjust treatment had not left him, but the belief that One greater than his problems watched over him brought quietness to his troubled heart.

CHRISTMAS

T HE MESSAGE TELLING him which train to come home on had not yet arrived, but still the Christmas service was the happiest day of Graham's life to that point. He sang well, and he knew it, and it made him warm inside to know he could do something to bring joy to others.

Afterward he returned to waiting for a message from home. But no word came, and Graham realized, sinkingly, that nobody would send for him, and he would spend the Christmas holiday alone at school while everyone else got to go home. In one sense, he didn't mind the reprieve from the taunting and misery of all the other boys picking on him, and he certainly was in no hurry to see his father. But he did want his brother. He missed George so much it was painful.

He sat on his bed with the single letter from George that he'd gotten since he came here. It had arrived almost at once. The page, a characteristic mess of flourishes, careless spelling, and inkblots, comforted Graham enormously.

My Brother,

I was mad as a HORNET wen I came home from market & found you were gone. I asked father why & he said you were a bad inflooince on me & it was time for a sepper ration. I told him that was beestly unfair, but he said I'll get a privit tooter this year.

It IS beestly unfair! Here I am, trapt like a butterfly in a jar. A very big stone jar, with towers & a mote but a jar any way. A Prison! I don't have any one to play with now! & you'd be happy to stay here in the quiet, & I'd love to have all your school mates to be frends with. BEESTLY UNFAR.

Wen you rite don't menshon this letter, cos father dosnt know I'm sending it. I'm sneking it out throo Bates. Father's told me I'm not to rite you. So wen you rite be a pal & act like you have n't herd from me or I'll get into trubbel. I'll rite agen if I can get Bates to sneek another note out for me.

George

After that, there had been no word from George at all. Graham wrote weekly dutiful postcards to his family, but never received any response, not even a Christmas greeting. Yes, this would be a miserable Christmas indeed.

The choirmaster took pity on him and gave him new music to learn over the holiday—two of the contralto solos for Handel's *Messiah*. Graham had not heard them before, and the words so moved him that he wept.

> *He shall feed His flock like a shepherd,*
> *and He shall gather the lambs with His arm,*
> *and carry them in His bosom,*
> *and gently lead those that are with young.*

> *He was despised and rejected of men,*
> *a man of sorrows and acquainted with grief.*
> *He gave his back to the smiters,*
> *and his cheeks to them that plucked off the hair;*
> *He hid not His face from shame and spitting.*

He sat in the chapel a long time after the choirmaster left him alone, and when the vicar came in, Graham held up the music and asked, "Please, sir, tell me who these are about."

The vicar looked at the music and back at the boy. "Why, these speak of Christ, son."

"Who is Christ?" Graham asked. Many of the lads used that name when angry, but the vicar spoke it with reverence. "If he was so gentle, why were people cruel to him?"

"Christ is another name for Jesus, laddie. Have ye nae heard of Jesus? Here," and the vicar pulled an old book off a shelf nearby and opened it. "Both o' those are frae Isaiah. I'll show you."

The grey head and the gleaming chestnut one bent over the pages in the dim light, and the vicar read aloud the words to the boy, who drank them up and asked to hear them again so he could savor them and store them in his head. The vicar told him to take the book back to his room with him, and Graham sat awake late into the night, reading. Much of what he read did not make sense to him, but he found much that did. He fell asleep at last with the book still open in his hand.

MUSIC

WHEN SCHOOL OPENED again, the boys had new things to torment Graham about. Now he was more than a soppy mummy's boy; he was a preacher too. They threw his old borrowed Bible into a puddle, and Graham spent hours in the vicar's room, peeling apart the pages and drying them before the fire.

Not a word did he hear from his father all the rest of the school year. At the end of it, he received a telegram saying he might come home for the summer.

Finally reunited with George, Graham was blissfully happy for several hours. George came with the driver when they met him at the station, and the boys hugged and spun in circles before jumping into the carriage.

"It's horrible," Graham said. "School is. It's as bad as home. Maybe even worse. Here, it's only Father who treats me like rubbish. There, it's everyone but a few people."

Graham's initial joy ended at dinner. He was careful to behave properly, greet his father politely, and do all he knew he ought. But it made no difference in his reception.

"You look like you've spent the last nine months in a dungeon, Little Caesar," his father remarked coolly. "Aren't Master Redmond and the school treating you well?"

"Master Redmond treats me as if I am his own son," Graham said, unable to conceal the venom in his voice as he quoted the headmaster's favorite phrase.

"Excellent. I knew I could trust him to see to it you didn't get spoilt there."

Graham did not—could not—answer. He stared at his plate, all appetite lost. He had been elated to come home, but now he was here, he knew that anywhere he could possibly go would be full of heaviness.

His father's attitude did not surprise him. Being away from George for so long, however, made Graham acutely aware for the first time of how different they were. Graham was quiet and reflective, sensitive and highly opinionated, while George rolled along with whatever life brought, always game for mischief and fun. Although he hated the way his father treated Graham, George seemed less willing now to throw away outright the comfortable security of his favored position by speaking up.

Also there was George's perpetual untidiness. Graham requested that his mother let him have a room of his own, and she consented. They made the change quietly, lest his father should object out of sheer cussedness.

The summer passed, and Graham left for school again. He had said nothing to his father or his mother about his voice lessons, preferring not to tell them until he had to.

But during his second summer home from school, his dedication to practicing won out over his dedication to secrecy, and his mother, impressed with her son's talents, informed the local vicar of her boy's voice. The vicar asked him to sing the next Sunday, and Graham said yes, in spite of the fact that his father would now know all about how his heir had been "wasting his time".

He sang for God alone that Sunday. After the service, as he came down the aisle to meet his family, a look of euphoric serenity touched his face that not even his father's disapproval could remove. In fact, he didn't even think about the old man at all for the first five minutes of the drive home. He was still lost in his own little world, at peace.

His father broke into his reverie, his tone a mixture of astonishment and disgust. "What the devil did you have to sing like that for? You sounded like a blooming *girl*."

Graham blinked, slowly comprehending he had been spoken to. "The vicar asked me to sing, sir." He wouldn't incriminate his mother in the transaction.

"Well, it is disgraceful."

"I like to sing, sir." Graham kept his voice low and respectful.

"I expect you'll grow out of it soon enough," his father replied with unexpected mildness. After a few minutes, he added, "All that music stuff is fine for women and the scrapings of society, but you will be an officer in Her Majesty's army. Don't forget it."

Graham did not answer. He had drifted away again, melancholy about the fact that his father could not grasp the thrill of art in any form. He did not appreciate the exhilaration of standing in front of a full church on a Sunday, of singing a solo and having to project himself above the organ. It was the only kind of power Graham cared about: the power to brighten the world with beauty.

His mother understood, he was sure. She was musical, and quietly pleased with Graham's singing. But she said little, and Graham suddenly recognized his father's latest insult could have been meant to hurt her as much as him. He felt sorry for her, newly aware that she was not as self-centered as he had previously judged her. Perhaps all she did—fussing over her appearance and her wardrobe and distancing herself from her sons—was her way of protecting herself from the harsh reality of her loveless marriage to a man twice her age and the children she hadn't much wanted but had been expected to produce.

Graham resolved to be sympathetic. He supposed being married to a tyrant was even worse than having one as a father. Children could grow up and leave their homes; wives were trapped until they died.

PART FOUR

10 November 1916

Allonville, France

CASUALTY CLEARING STATION

ESTELLE WAITED, LONGING for another small glimpse of her beloved's eyes, unspeakably worried. He had opened them once after she'd arrived at the hospital this morning, and seeing them had given her hope, even if they did not register recognition. He had not opened them again since; his fever still raged. It was all she could do to get water and broth into him to keep him alive. Occasionally, a nurse came around and gave him a shot of something "to help him sleep it off," the woman explained to Estelle.

To distract herself, Estelle looked through the pile of drawings she and George had taken from the wall of Jamie's room. Drawn on scraps of all kinds, from newspapers to empty envelopes, they told Jamie's entire life story prior to the war and much of his and Aveline's shared life this past summer. One of the sketches was even of her, she knew, due to the caption underneath in Aveline's tidy printing:

Who is she that looketh forth as the morning,

fair as the moon, clear as the sun,

and terrible as an army with banners?

It was Jamie's favorite scripture to quote to Estelle, especially when she was in one of her ranting moods, and it warmed her to know he had taught it to Aveline as well.

She put the drawings away and opened his journal. She'd already read it through once, and she had started over again. There wasn't much else to do.

GRAHAM'S JOURNAL, 3 JULY 1916:
CULLODEN

Sometimes I cannot grasp why I am still alive. I have been deeply troubled by this question since last night when MacFie brought me the report of British casualties from the first day of the battle. We have lost more men in the last two days than we lost throughout the thirteen days of fighting at Loos last autumn. I shall not be able to bring myself to tell Estelle any of this, at least, not yet, so I will record all my thoughts here instead.

I am going to write about Culloden. I saw more of Culloden than I cared to as a lad. Stepping onto that moor always sent chills through me, as if ancestral memory could have tugged me back in time and demanded my life of me there. Every 16th of April, Mother dragged George and me there to put flowers at the Cameron memorial. Some of my earliest memories are of my mother by her clan's stone, silhouetted against the sky, playing "The Flowers of the Forest" on her flute, the wind ruffling her hair. She was so beautiful and carefree in those days before my father came back home.

She still made the journey after he rejoined the family, but Father always refused to go along. There was always a contentious argument before and after the visit, about the Graham and Cameron ancestors and which had been on the right side in 1745. Mother said if the Grahams had sided with Prince Charlie, maybe Culloden would have turned out differently, whereas Father insisted Culloden was folly no matter who fought, because the Scots had lost the battle already and should have surrendered before wasting all their blood there. If the Grahams had been Jacobites, he said, the entire family would have been driven out, their place and estate lost, and we'd all be coarse and vulgar Americans now instead of the Glorious Scots we still are.

Mother couldn't ever win the argument; it was an undeniable historical fact that the only reason she was still in Britain was because some English souls had taken in the fatherless Cameron children and housed them in exchange for service as maids and stable boys. When they grew up, the Cameron children returned to the forever-changed Highlands and married, living humbly and slowly rising back to better society. My mother's marriage to my father was condescension on his part, but her sterling reputation, her father's money, and the fact she was pretty were sufficient recommendations.

Now I think of it, it must have meant a good deal to her, Culloden. She never dared to argue with my father about anything else.

Anyway, reading the casualty list from today was like a hefty smack in the gut. These were men I had helped to train and gotten to know as if they were sons or brothers. I could put a face to almost every name listed.

Buchanan, married eleven years, whose wife was finally expecting a baby. Young Cameron, who had postponed going to university to join up. Campbell, who, like George, had left a flourishing career in law; MacBride and MacPherson and Menzies, all engaged to lovely young ladies back home. Munro and Warbeck and Wilson were, like me, family men with wives and children at home. And others. Dozens and dozens of others.

All I can think of is having to write condolence letters to all these families and of the scene at my own home if my family received one of these terrible letters.

Estelle would be devastated. *Not hopeless; she is too independent to ever be hopeless, and I did put everything in order before I left so she would never want for anything if I die out here. She'll never lack for anything, but she would be devastated nonetheless.*

All of these men dead—and for what?

The first day's slaughter here at the Somme seems as suicidally pointless and ill-managed as Culloden, and it makes me sick. I cannot help but feel as if I will never escape the ever-present beckoning of death which Culloden Moor instilled in me from my earliest memory.

Will I make it home?

There I go again. Fear, the monster, always with me, gnawing at me like rats. I desperately want to stop being afraid. It is easy to be brave with Estelle at my side. It is not so easy when she is six hundred miles away.

PART FIVE

31 August - 21 September 1916

Somme, France

CHÂTEAU BLANCHARD

GRAHAM FOLDED HIS latest letter to his wife, precisely matching the corners and creasing the folds uniformly flat. He sighed as he sealed the envelope and addressed it, then took his candle to look in on Aveline.

He was glad to find Aveline and Sylvie lay sprawled peacefully out on their cot. She must have felt safe, to sleep like that, instead of curled into a resistant ball.

He couldn't remember a time in his own youth when he did not feel safest curled into a resistant ball. At home. At school. In the army. Everywhere. Until he married and finally felt safe enough to relax.

Looking at the sleeping child reminded him of her dead brother's journals, still in his bag. He had not had a chance to look at them. Now would be a good time. He returned to his desk and opened one, patiently scanning each page for information, hoping to find names or family history.

There was disappointingly little in this vein, but toward the end of the last journal, one passage caught his eye.

A man came here last night after Aveline was asleep. He spoke terrible French, but he made it clear he wanted food. Had little to offer of course, but he insisted on coming in. I let him but told him to be quiet. Aveline's door was open, and he saw her sleeping there. He stared at her. Made me uneasy. I beckoned him away. Gave him the last food on the shelf, two tins of beans (he did not know about the reserves under my bed). He paused at Aveline's door again on his way out. He pointed to her and asked how much for her and held out a gold coin.

More money than I have seen since the war came here. But I have not kept her hidden away for the last ten years only to subject her to that now. Not for a million gold coins. "No," I said. "Never. Go." He left, but he looked angry.

Have not let Aveline out of my sight since. I want so much more for her than to repeat the miserable life our grandmother and mother knew. Nobody must lay a hand on her. Once I save enough money, I can get us away from this town's gossip and prejudice, to a place where we can have a new start, and I can help Aveline get an education and marry well. I have our grandmother's earbobs, and those pearls. I have been unable to find a way to sell them for what they are worth. In Paris, perhaps I could. Too many people know us here.

Might be wise for Aveline and me to clear out in case that man comes back. We need food, but I cannot leave her here alone for hours while I walk to town and back, not now. Have wanted to evacuate, but it is hard with my bad leg since the horses were taken. Aveline is sturdy but stubborn; she would want to bring that cat, and I'd need her to carry things, not drag along another mouth to feed. I have not been up for the fight. But our days here are numbered. I will have to take her to town with me on my errand, and not tell her we are not coming back. She will not ask to bring the cat if she believes we are coming home afterward.

Poor Aveline. She knows nothing of this. I have tried hard all these years to protect her from other people, the taunts and judgments and prejudice against our mother—I do not want these to dog her steps all her life. Perhaps I have sheltered her too much, but what else could I do?

That was the last thing Armand had written, on the night before Aveline said he disappeared. Graham looked up from the book and tried to piece together the scant facts he had to figure out what happened to Armand.

The German must have come back to try again to buy

Aveline the next day, and when Armand refused, the German killed him. But why such a savage killing? One bayonet stab would have sufficed. Perhaps Armand had fought back, and the German did not want to risk a gunshot.

Then, obviously, the German had not found Aveline that day; she'd said she was sleeping in the hayloft with Sylvie. Why had eleven full days passed before he did find her? He must have had duties somewhere that kept him occupied, and he had come back at the first possible opportunity.

Why, though? There were whorehouses close by. Graham did not go to them, but plenty of other men did. Surely *they* would have taken this man's gold. Why pick on a little girl?

And these jewels Armand mentioned. These might be worth killing for, but it seemed doubtful a stranger would know about them. Where would Armand have hidden such a treasure? Graham determined to return to the farmhouse and look as soon as he had the opportunity. Aveline should have her grand-mother's jewels.

Graham swept the books impatiently aside, blew out his candle, and went to bed. He needed sleep.

FROM THE WINDOW OF CHÂTEAU BLANCHARD

THERE SEEMED TO be hundreds of men swarming about the place, Aveline thought, if you counted the ones camping outdoors. She watched them from the window in Capitaine Graham's bedroom, where she spent most of her time hiding after he and Mr. MacFie vacated it each morning.

The men were always busy. This afternoon, they had tapes and flags all over the grounds and appeared to be attacking an army of invisible foes, and it amused her immensely. Armand had told her stories of playing at soldiers with other boys when he was little, before he went lame, before their parents had died, and she imagined it must have looked something like this—on a smaller scale, of course. And with no actual lives at stake.

She stayed far enough back from the glass so nobody glancing up would catch sight of her. She was not one bit interested in being Seen. In the two days since Capitaine Graham had found her, she had hid in this room alone, or with him in his office, or in the kitchen helping Mme Blanchard—anywhere she could avoid being generally Seen. She still didn't want to move much, and it hurt to sit, so she spent a good deal of time lying down or standing.

She couldn't altogether avoid being Seen, of course. Capitaine Graham's brother George was determined to befriend her, and the more he tried, the less she liked him. It was nice, she supposed, to know someone else could speak French with her, but she wasn't used to people who talked endlessly about nothing. He had given her a gift, a notebook of her own which fit nicely into a pocket, which she *did* appreciate in spite of herself. She had sketched in it a little, but she mostly wanted only to be still and quiet.

The thing most preoccupying her mind was that in a few days, Capitaine Graham would go back to the trenches with his men, and he wanted her to stay with Mme Blanchard. She did not like that idea at all, but she had not yet decided what to do about it.

She flopped onto one of the beds and rested her head on Sylvie, as if the cat was a pillow. Sylvie made a small protesting noise but didn't move, and Aveline set to forming a plan.

4 September 1916

My darling Jamie,

Send the girl to me! If she truly has no family, I mean. I suppose you are in the trenches now. Perhaps you may not get this as quickly as usual. I hope Aveline is faring well with the Blanchards. I worry terribly about you.

My bed takes so long to warm up at night without you. I picture you there, camping in the outdoors, cold and wet, and I try to be thankful for what I have. But I still wish you were here instead. It has been too long since you had your leave in February, and I hate thinking it might still be months before you get leave again, but remembering those few days we had is a great comfort to me nonetheless.

Estelle

TO THE TRENCHES: 8 SEPTEMBER 1916

GRAHAM PUT AVELINE to bed and gave her strict instructions that under no circumstances was she to leave the house. He charged Mme Blanchard with her care until his return, and then he vanished into the busy crowd of his men. He didn't give Aveline another thought all through the long hours of marching in the dark to the trenches.

When they arrived, Graham and MacFie went down several steps to their dugout in the rear trenches. There were two cots in it, two crates for chairs, and a board on top of another crate to serve as a table. The floor, covered in boards, was little better than the ground itself, now that so much mud had been tracked in on top. Graham heaved a sigh. The smell was appalling, and it was close and dark and damp, but those things were nothing in comparison with the filth. The conditions always assaulted his senses, no matter how many times he came to the trenches.

Graham fancied he could detect fleas and lice already crawling on him, despite his only having been here a few minutes. MacFie remarked dryly, "Nae self-respecting tinker would ever live in muck like this."

Graham laughed humorlessly. "You may as well make up your mind to enjoy your moment of glory as the earl's honored guest."

"His lordship needs to find better accommodations," MacFie quipped.

"At least we appear to have this one to ourselves?" Graham said, grasping at any small blessing. "Last time, we had five of us in a space this size."

MacFie shrugged. "My family and I always sleep in a space this size."

Graham had to admit that was true. War was a great leveler. "But your tents are clean," he said.

MacFie gave a sage nod and said no more.

Meanwhile, Willie Duncan and George Graham found their hole in the dirt. As bleak as their captain's, it lacked only the luxury of crates to sit on, and they did have to share with another lieutenant and his man. George flopped onto his cot to have a nap. Willie decided to walk. He lit a cigarette and strode along the trench. The men of the division settled in, amid colorful epithets about the conditions, and the men they were relieving marched out. All was quiet on the other side of No Man's Land.

A small, dark, furry thing flashed past, brushing against his leg. Willie frowned, hoping it wasn't a rat. He hated rats. Secretly, he feared them more than being shot, or going over, or being on a patrol. He remembered last fall at Loos how George had woken with a rat sitting on his face, and the beastie's feet had gone into George's mouth as the creature scrabbled to get away. The mere thought of it still made Willie shudder.

Then he glimpsed something else slinking along the inner wall of the trench, pale against the muddy sandbags, in the same direction as the furry thing had gone. He struck a match and, in its light, discerned a face he'd only ever seen skulking in shadows at the Blanchards' or peeking from behind Captain Graham. He couldn't remember the face's name, and he took her wrist to keep her from running away.

"What are *you* doing here?" he hissed at last, forgetting she could not speak English. He tried to string together the correct French words, but they came out in a tangle.

She squirmed out of his grasp, turned up her nose a bit in defiance, dug out a piece of charcoal from her pocket, and wrote on a nearby board. *Je veux Capitaine Graham.*

"He's no going to be happy you're here," Willie Duncan said grimly, but he jerked his head beckoning her to follow. "Come alang."

He held up a hand to her to wait while he poked his head

into a little room. "Captain Graham, sir, I've found a wee lassie lookin' for you."

Graham leapt to his feet in the flickering light as Aveline peeked around the corner. He spluttered a moment, absolutely furious, before repeating Willie's own earlier question, but in proper French. "Aveline, what the *bloody hell* are you doing here?"

She came in, planted her feet firmly on the floor, chin up, mimicking the lads standing at attention. It was so funny, Willie laughed aloud, and Graham himself had a difficult time not joining in, in spite of his anger. "At ease, Perrault," he said with a sigh of resignation, seating himself again. "Come, tell me what you think you're playing at."

She plopped onto his lap instead of the crate he indicated, helped herself to the pencil she knew he kept in his pocket, sharpened it with the penknife in her own pocket, and turned to write on the paper.

I came in one of the supply wagons. It was dark, and nobody could tell I wasn't actually a sack of potatoes. I told you you weren't going to go off anywhere without me.

Graham narrowed his eyes. Armand had not exaggerated about the tenacity and persistence of this wee lassie. "So *that* is what happened to my knife." He held out his hand for it. "I suppose the cat came too?"

Of course. She's here someplace. She did not like being in the sacks with me. She ran off as soon as I unburied us.

Graham took off his cap and rubbed his forehead as though he had a headache. "And what do you suppose Mme Blanchard will do, Aveline? Have you thought of that? She will be upset in the morning, to find you escaped her."

I left her a note telling her I came with you.

"I am not one bit pleased with this, Aveline. Not one tiny bit."

She looked crestfallen, but she didn't budge.

"Do you have any idea what danger you're in out here?"

No more danger than you're in. We will take care of each other.

He didn't have a ready counter for that. He looked at Willie. "Duncan, find MacFie, and tell him to come here." Graham ran his hand over the back of his head, flustered.

I WON'T GO. She wrote the words big and bold and underlined them twice.

A GIRL IN THE TRENCHES

A FEW MINUTES later, MacFie ducked into the room. He was surprised at the sight of Aveline, and Graham said, "Sit down. We need to have a talk, the three of us. Shut that blanket by the door first."

He brought MacFie up to speed on the situation, and the three men sat quietly a moment.

"Perhaps I can take her back in the morning, sir?" Willie Duncan offered.

"She won't go without a fight," Graham said, "and I'm concerned she won't stay if we do take her back. She's in danger here, but she'd be in more danger wandering the roads trying to get to us again, and I've no doubt that's exactly what she'd do."

"Maybe if she was willing to be one of the lads..." MacFie suggested. As one, they looked at the girl with her lovely wild hair flowing free.

"If she looks like a girl, and a man who's not one of ours finds her, he might try to—" MacFie let the unfinished sentence hang a moment. "And if a Dread Staff Officer graces us wi' an unexpected visit, he'd have us all for letting her stay here. But if she looks like a lad, nobody will notice one extra."

"She could do lots of things for us here, no doubt," Willie put in, warming to the idea of putting anything over on the Dread Staff Officers.

Graham looked at Aveline and considered. "We'll be here ten days. Two weeks at most. A long time for her to be here, but a long time for her to be alone among strangers too."

"She's safer with you, Captain. You're the only one she trusts yet," MacFie reminded him. "We found her only three days ago, after all. I'm in favor of her staying with us, this time. By the next time we're sent down here, you'll have either found her family, or she'll realize she's better off wi' the Blanchards."

Aveline, who could not understand the men's words, met

Graham's gaze steadily when he turned to her, but despite the determined set of her mouth, her eyes were shadowed with fear. She was terrified of being sent away, and he knew it. His mind went back to the morning when he had been sent to boarding school without a farewell from his parents or brother and never summoned home for Christmas. He felt a pang even yet at the memory. What would he have chosen, were he in Aveline's place? Stay in the face of death with someone who loved and cared for him, or be cast alone into a realm of strangers? When Armand had died, he took with him the only world his sister had: himself. She was more truly alone than anyone else Graham had ever known.

He dragged his crate closer to her and gently lifted her chin. She did not flinch, but he could plainly read in her eyes the plea, *Don't send me away*, and he knew what he had to do.

"Aveline," he said, speaking softly in French. "In this place, there are explosions and noise, lice and floods of mud when it rains, and you cannot be with me all the time. If you change your mind, we can't easily take you back. It would be best for you to return to Madame Blanchard." He paused, waiting for a reaction, but Aveline's gaze did not waver. "If you *must* stay," he went on at last, "it is particularly not safe for you to be here as a girl. None of my men will harm you, but other men might, if they see you. I do *not* want anyone to hurt you. If I allow you to stay with me, you will be safer if you look like a boy. We can find you clothes easily enough, but we'd also have to cut your hair. Would you let us cut your hair?"

She hesitated only an instant before nodding assent, and he seated her nearer the light. She held perfectly still as he tied her hair back and chopped the tail off to save it. He handed her the lock of hair, gleaming and beautiful, and they exchanged a glance of sadness. "It will grow back," he said, sure it was not the right thing to say. She only lifted her chin resolutely and sat straighter. Graham handed the comb and scissors to MacFie and stepped back to sit on the bed and watch.

The shears sounded sharp and harsh to her ears as they took off her hair, and felt ice-cold against her skin. MacFie cropped it close on the sides and back, leaving it only a little longer in front. By the time he had finished, Willie Duncan had returned with the smallest clothes he could procure. They were still too big for her, but she turned up the cuffs of the tunic, and MacFie added a few new holes in the leather straps of a Sam Browne belt and the kilt, and Graham gave her a holster, which she wore on her left hip like he wore his.

"We are going to teach you to shoot," he said. "Since you're here, you need to be useful, and hitting a target is useful. Besides, you'll want to defend yourself against any more Germans..." He saw her eyeing the empty holster suspiciously and added, "You get the gun *after* you have learned to use it."

MacFie handed her a small mirror, and her mouth dropped open at the sight of her incredibly boyish reflection. Willie Duncan, who had disappeared again, returned with a tam, and while she put it on, Graham quietly gathered up the wrinkled pale blue frock she'd been wearing since they'd found her and took it outside to throw it away.

He sent Willie Duncan running back to the big house to assure the Blanchards that Aveline was safe. "Carry the girl's hair with you, put it in my room to save it for her, and don't come back until it's dark tomorrow," Graham instructed. Willie leapt up the steps and disappeared into the darkness.

KILTS ARE NOT SKIRTS

AVELINE WAS UTTERLY unperturbed by the stir she had caused. She was far too busy getting used to her strange new clothes. She kept raising a hand to her cropped-off hair and running her fingers over it. How did these men live their whole lives with their hair so short? Didn't their heads *freeze*? She pulled down her tam as far as it would go, but her head *still* felt cold.

The kilt was not as strange. Despite Capitaine Graham's lecture yesterday about not laughing at the noble tradition of kilts and that they were Not Skirts, privately she remained unconvinced. It looked like a skirt to her, and she considered it preposterously silly that any man would choose to wear such a thing, let alone be proud of doing it. The Scots must be a most unusual sort of people.

Graham collapsed, exhausted, onto his cot while she still stood fussing in front of the tiny mirror. He hadn't told her where she should sleep, but she resourcefully solved the problem all by herself. There wasn't another blanket for her to sleep on the floor, so she climbed in beside him, tam pulled over her ears, Sylvie curled at their feet, and went straight to sleep.

RAIN AND LICE

THE WARM WEATHER intensified the horrible smells of the place, and after one reasonably dry week, it rained, a relentless drizzling which made the conditions even more torturous. The snipers and the listeners in the saps were soaked through from the rain dripping off the rims of their helmets. The room where Graham and Aveline and MacFie worked and ate and slept together was dark and cheerless and damp. Mice and rats invaded everything, despite Sylvie's best efforts, and all the humans had lice within days of being there. It was unpleasant, but nothing could really be done until they left the trenches, and even then, they could never fully eradicate them. The rodents were flea-ridden, and Sylvie scratched constantly, trying to get fleas out of her fur. Aveline wrote a complaining note to Graham.

Capitaine, these Not-Skirts we are all wearing, they are perfect dwelling-places for lice. Have you looked at your pleats lately?

"I have not," he said, pulling a face. Were the ones on his head not bad enough? "I will take your word for it."

He watched her as, methodically, she dug one louse at a time from her kilt and dropped each one on the candle-flame. Dozens and dozens of the little bugs went up in smoke that night, but there was no winning the battle against the lice. He could only hope the British Army would be more successful against the Germans.

10 September 1916

My darling wife,

Aveline was not being facetious when she said she would not let me leave her alone. She followed me to the trenches. So—here she is. MacFie cut her hair, and we gave her a dead boy's clothes. Scant protection, perhaps, but the best I can do. She will not go back to the Blanchards until I do. We had a long discussion about it.

I will keep her in the rear trenches with me as much as possible, but of course, she is everywhere and into everything all the time. There is no controlling her. She is like a feral cat; her lack of companionship, outside her brother's, has ill prepared her for ordinary life, I am afraid. She was so shy and retiring at the Blanchards', I was honestly a bit surprised she came here. Now, though, she seems to feel safe. Imagine feeling safe in the trenches, of all places! Perhaps it is the clothes. They are a shield of sorts, like an actor taking on another personality with a new costume.

Her manners need work; she tends to ignore anyone she does not wish to acknowledge. I am trying to break her of this and teach her to respond politely to everyone, and she is, to her credit, trying to comply with my wishes.

Aveline's talents are raw things, but her talent for art particularly is so obvious, I long to give her the chance to develop it. She asked me to send you this sketch she made of her cat Sylvie, with her greetings. I encourage the drawing. It is the only way I can be sure she stays in one place for any length of time. I also plan to put her to the task of writing letters to the families of the men who die. Her handwriting is much better than mine, and I hate writing them, and there are many to send. I made her a template letter so she can learn what all the words mean before I let her write actual letters. She also helps the medical officer at the aid post; no amount of gore appears to trouble her, odd as that sounds. She did mention her brother wanted to be a doctor. Perhaps that has something to do with it.

You are right, February was a long time ago. I would welcome another chance to sit at your feet and let you pick nits out of my hair. Alas, all your hard work was in vain—but at least I had a few days free of the things. I suspect, next time, you will be required to immerse all of me into a kerosene bath, however, not just my head. I will exchange the danger of being shot or shelled for becoming an incendiary myself.

Your Jamie

Estelle smiled through tears as she lay the letter to rest on her lap. He was trying to make light of the emotionally fraught reality of that February leave, and she loved him for it, even while wishing she could shake him.

She'd been gloriously happy when she'd met him in Dover that afternoon, and at first he hadn't appeared so very changed. They'd had a lovely dinner and a long walk along the beach before going to the room she'd found for them to stay in.

The sight of the room seemed to alarm him somehow. Although he didn't say anything, his eyes betrayed his unease. But she had a solution. "I brought this," she said, smiling, and handed him his flute case. His expression softened, and she settled into a chair with her knitting, knowing he'd be beyond her reach for hours. But it would be worth it if it brought him back to her in the end.

He was a bit rusty, but it wasn't long before he was serenading her beautifully with all her favorite songs. She beamed at him over her knitting, and he beamed back.

At nine o'clock he reluctantly put the flute to bed, lest the other occupants of the place complain, and Estelle changed into her nightclothes and prepared for bed as well.

Jamie did not. He stared out the window, straight and rigid, toward France. When she touched his arm, he startled, turning empty eyes to her. She shrank back slightly, but did not leave, just held his gaze, until he stepped forward and gripped her shoulders, seeking her mouth, but stopping short of actually kissing her.

"I want to make love to you," he said, his voice an odd, husky whisper. "But what I need is sleep. Days and days of sleep."

"Come sleep, then," she urged him. "The bed's comfortable."

"It's not that simple." His breath came shallow and quick, and he turned from her, circling the room with lighter in hand, until every lamp in the place blazed with light.

Estelle followed him, listening to his low, expressionless words. "I need something I cannot explain, something I don't understand myself. I'm going quite mad, Estelle." Again he stared out the south window, hands deep in his pockets. "They're still there."

"Who's 'they'?"

"My boys. George. MacFie. I should be with them."

"Jamie-love, they don't mind you being here," she said, gently, even as fear stabbed her heart. He resumed his pacing, and she thought, *This war is tearing at his sensitive, gentle soul—unravelling the man I love.* Tears pricked at her eyes, and she ran to him and slipped her arm through his. "If you must walk, let me walk with you. Talk to me, darling."

He didn't seem to hear her, but he did not object to her suggestion, and eventually began to speak, to let out the horrors— endlessly, disconnectedly rambling.

About a corpse whose empty chest he'd accidentally stepped into, and the rats which ran out of the body at his footfall. About the foul language and the noise and the filth, and the Protestant chaplains who, unlike the Catholic ones, were too cowardly to come to the trenches. "The boys come to me, if they want prayers and counsel," he said. "It's not my job. I have too much to do already. But I can't turn them away, those boys whom I'm praying with and then sending over the top to be massacred."

Estelle listened silently. "And MacFie," he went on. "MacFie keeps me steady. He's imperturbable. Covers for me when I quail. He'd take a bullet for me, he would, but he mustn't—I need him—"

Several hours later, he at last exhausted himself enough to collapse onto the bed and sleep like the dead. Estelle extinguished the lamps, carefully covered him with a blanket, and nestled close enough to lay her hand on his and watch his pale, thin face, distressed even in sleep. As horrendous as were the things he'd told her tonight, darker things yet lurked in the wildness of his eyes, locking her out of his deepest counsels. It tore at her heart to see him so changed, so barely holding himself together.

She was thankful for MacFie's watchcare, at any rate. He'd never spoken anything but praise for the man, and Estelle longed to meet him and thank him. She had an unsettling suspicion it was really due to MacFie that Jamie hadn't already completely lost his mind.

In his sleep, Jamie muttered words she couldn't quite make out—names of fallen comrades? Estelle laid a light hand on his hair, greyer than when he had left home, and stroked it, making a mental note to comb out the nits in the morning. His hand sought hers and clung tight, and he snuffled softly. *Like a little boy*, she thought. *He never got to be carefree as a boy. He still can't be carefree, and it's destroying him. Lord, please deliver him from this life he hates so.*

In the morning, Jamie rose subdued but more himself, daylight having driven away the ghosts.

"Shall we have breakfast?" she asked, holding out her hand to him.

"I only want you," he said, and he pulled her into his arms, giving her the kiss he had been unable to manage the previous night.

Estelle was happy to comply, although even his lovemaking also felt different—uncharacteristically desperate, slightly clingy. "I need you," he kept saying. "Need to run home with you and never leave again—please, darling, don't let go of me."

"I'll never let go, Jamie."

But she wondered with trepidation whether he would still be sane when he finally did come home. She would never stop loving him, fighting for him, but she did fear what she saw— feared the implications for their sons, particularly. They needed their father, and he had enough trouble being a father as it was.

Estelle scanned the letter once more, folded it back into its envelope, and tucked it away safely with the rest of her letters from him. Since he'd found Aveline, Estelle had sensed a rallying in her husband, and it had eased her mind. She wanted Aveline safely out of France, but in the meantime, she was grateful the girl gave Jamie a reason to keep going.

GORE AND GUNFIRE

GORE DID NOT trouble Aveline. Guns did.

Well, *German* guns, at any rate.

She did learn to use the pistol that went in her holster. She learned quickly, and only three days after her capitaine started teaching her, he allowed her to carry it about.

The firing back and forth between the British and the Germans terrified her. Her capitaine would not let her come to the front trenches, and after the first thirty seconds of firing, she did not argue. She darted into their dugout and cowered there weeping, often under the bed, clutching Sylvie, every time the firing went on. She understood that Capitaine Graham had to be out in the fighting with his men, but it frightened her. Each time a shell exploded, her active imagination drew all sorts of horrible demises for her beloved capitaine.

She and Armand used to watch the explosions of shells and flares at night from the farmhouse windows: a terrifying sight, yet eerily beautiful as well. The Germans' rockets were especially lovely—greeny-yellow like Sylvie's eyes and very bright—but it was different right in the heart of it, right where the explosions shook not merely the earth, but the people standing on it as well.

She learned just how different it was when she woke in absolute quivering terror one dark night while shells exploded outside. Her dreams had been troubled, and she clung to Graham, sobbing. How could he sleep through this as though he were deaf?

He held her lightly in his arms and murmured to her.

God is our refuge and strength,
a very present help in trouble.
Therefore will not we fear,

> *though the earth be removed,*
> *and though the mountains be carried*
> *into the midst of the sea;*
> *Though the waters thereof roar and be troubled,*
> *though the mountains shake with the swelling*
> *thereof...*

His voice trailed off into silence, and so did the guns, and soon she was asleep once more.

TERROR AND SORROW

AVELINE WOKE QUIET and subdued, overwhelmed by everything. It had been a lark the first few days, pretending to be a soldier lad at war. But as her capitaine had tried to warn her, the shelling and machine-gunning were proving too much. She wrapped a groundsheet around herself tightly and sat on the cot, her back pressed into the corner. She'd had her chance to go back, and she hadn't taken it. She would stick it out. Somehow. Could she? Her natural stubbornness had shrunk into a small and fragile thing.

"Are you all right, lassie?" Capitaine Graham asked her as he prepared to leave the dugout. "I can't stay here with you, but I want you to be all right."

She stared blankly, much like how she had stared the first time he'd seen her. He went to her and lifted her chin. Tears stood in her eyes, but she pulled away and nestled into the cot in her groundsheet cocoon.

He turned and left her to herself. She felt utterly miserable, a small and insignificant figure in this man's world of war. If anything happened to her, if she were to die, would anyone be left who cared?

WILLIAM DUNCAN

A VELINE WAS AWOKEN around noon by a playful whistling near her ear. She turned her head. The young man
called Willie Duncan bent over her, smiling.

"Captain Graham's buried in paperwork and asked me to
bring you lunch and make sure you were all right," he explained,
in thickly accented French.

She sat up, slowly, brain dull from too much sleep and
sadness, and took the food and water he handed her.

He did not leave straightaway, as she expected he would.
Instead, he settled onto a crate, folded his arms, and waited
for her to finish. She watched him out of the corner of her eye,
sizing him up as she ate. She'd seen him at the Blanchards',
of course, and on the night she came to the trenches. He was
young, younger than Armand, she guessed, lean and tanned. If
it weren't for the neatly trimmed moustache, she'd have sworn
he wasn't much older than she was. She decided she liked him.

She slid off the bed and walked to the table and wrote in her
little notebook, tore out the page and handed it to him.

How old are you?

He laughed, and she liked the sound of it. Then he leaned
forward to whisper, "Sixteen. But that's a secret. Dinna tell, aye?
I'm supposed to be twenty here."

She cocked her head, assessing him, and nodded her agreement. Satisfied, he went on. His French was flawed and halting,
but she got the gist of it. "Everyone calls me Babyface around
here because they say I dinna look a day over fifteen. I get asked
all the time if I bribed the recruitment officers to get in. But
I've always been tall for my age. The recruitment officers get
paid per recruit, and they dinna care. I told 'em I was eighteen
when I signed up. I grew the moustache to look older, but it's no
helping much. Captain Graham's brother says it adds a whole
year to my looks. He knows my real age, but he's kept mum. I
dinna ken if the others suspect I'm too young to be here, but I've

pulled my weight, and nobody has questioned it." He gave an exaggerated shrug, and a smile crept over her face.

Thank you. Tell my capitaine I am all right.

His expression turned serious, and he leaned closer and asked her, earnestly, if she truly *was* all right.

She met his steady gaze, and then her eyes fell to her hands, folded together in her lap. She didn't know what her capitaine had told his men, but she suspected they all knew what had happened to her. The idea made her flush deeply in shame. Still, Willie Duncan sat waiting for her answer. At last, she took her notebook and wrote, in tiny printing: *I am not all right. But I don't want to talk about it.*

She liked Willie, but she wasn't ready to trust him with her secrets. Not yet. Maybe later.

He nodded, gave her shoulder a gentle squeeze, and left the room.

QUESTIONS

THAT NIGHT, AFTER they had eaten their tins of beef and carrots—heated over MacFie's ingenious little burner, which he had invented out of old food tins, whale oil, and worn-out puttees—MacFie went out to do his time on watch. Graham and Aveline shared the little excuse of a table so she could draw, and he could write home.

"Duncan said you were still rather blue when he brought you your lunch. Are you better now, lass?"

I guess, a little. I was scared and sad. I don't know why. I wish I were brave and not scared of the explosions.

"I'm terrified of the shells," Graham said.

But you slept through them last night. Except for the bit when you told me poetry.

"I don't remember," he admitted, with dismay. What else did he say in his sleep? "You are braver than I in other ways. I could not help the medic the way you do."

You helped me.

He blushed. "I did because I had to. But truthfully, if I'd had a choice, I'd have made someone else do it."

Well, I am thankful you were there. And that it was you and not someone else.

"I'm glad you feel that way." He went back to his letter, and she added more to her sketch of him writing, then paused to stare at him.

What is your home like?

He did not look up. "I live in a castle in Scotland."

Are you a king?

"Hardly. I'm only an earl."

What's an earl?

"It's someone with a title. Exactly halfway down the peerage ladder. I fall in place under dukes and marquesses, and above viscounts and barons. A bit like your old system of princes and comtes and so forth, when you still had a king."

She looked at him wide-eyed. *Am I supposed to bow or anything?*

"No," he said, meeting her eyes with a crooked smile. "No need for that. I'm Lord Inverlochy, the thirteenth to have the title. But Capitaine is sufficient. Here in the war zone, I am just another officer, another person."

This was true, she knew. He always shared the food parcels his wife sent him with all the other men, scarcely tasting any of the contents himself. He treated all his men with respect, even MacFie, whom many of the men looked down on as one might look on a dirty beggar, because he was a—what did they call him? A Tink? She wasn't sure what it meant.

What's a Tink?

Graham sighed. "Didn't take you long to pick up on *that*, did it? Don't ever let me hear you using it. It's a word people use to refer to Traveller folk. People think they're dishonest. But MacFie's family are good, hard-working people, not thieves."

Armand said people assumed things about him and me because of our mother. Is your brother an earl too?

"No. He has no title and never will unless I and all my sons were to die. Only the eldest son has a title."

That seemed odd, but she didn't trouble herself further over it. *Have you always lived in a castle?*

"Aye, my family has lived in the same castle for at least four hundred years. I was born and grew up in it. I will likely die in it if I survive the war."

Thirteen is bad luck.

"Somebody has to be thirteenth. I'm not superstitious. Anyway, I haven't died yet. Lucky for me, I didn't live in France in 1793, or your ancestors would have had my head."

She did not take the bait. *Being thirteen has been bad luck for me. I can't wait to turn fourteen. Tell me about your family?*

"Well, you know George."

She made a face. *Besides him.*

"George isn't all bad," Graham said, contemplatively. "But he isn't so good either."

Does George have children?

Graham hesitated before he answered. "Aye. He has five."

That's a lot.

"I only ever had George, myself. He'll show you pictures of the children if you ask him. But don't ask to see a picture of his wife. He doesn't have one of her."

I want to hear about your family. Your children.

He smiled again. "All right. There's my wife, Estelle. She is half French, spunky and independent and self-reliant. I never worry about her. But I miss her tremendously. And my three sons. Peter is nine, Thomas eight, and Vincent going on seven." He paused, then switched topics. "Do you have any relatives, Aveline?"

I had a grandfather in Paris. Armand said he was not nice to our mother. I've never met him.

"Do you know his name?"

Armand-Marceau Perrault. But I do not want to find him, and anyway I am sure he is dead.

"Did your parents have any brothers or sisters?"

Papa had one brother, Philippe-Marceau Perrault. I only know of him because there was a photograph of them together as boys. I don't know where he lived. Maybe Paris too. Maman's family came from around here, I think. She had no father, her mother died when she was my age, and grandparents raised her after that, an orphan. Armand said she was a kind mother.

"I see," he said, musingly.

Can I go home with you when you go?

"Perhaps." He couldn't make promises, not yet, no matter how willing Estelle was to have her. Not until he'd settled the matter of her relatives.

Everybody has a story, don't they? I've never met so many people in one place ever before, and they all have stories, and I want to know them all. Her mind drifted back to Willie Duncan's laughing blue eyes. She particularly longed to know his story. Why had he come here, underage, if he didn't have to?

"Well, ask them. I am sure they'd all be glad to talk your ear off if you'd let them."

Maybe I will. Only, most of them don't know French. She used the tip of her grubby finger to blend the pencil strokes of her sketch. Willie Duncan had enough French to talk with.

Graham replied absentmindedly, "Duncan's French is decent enough, if you can get past the Shetland accent. Thick as day-old porridge, it is..."

She shot him a startled look. Had he read her mind? She swiftly changed the subject. *What are you most afraid of?*

"Not getting home," he said after long reflection. "Dying out here and never seeing my family again."

For me, it's being left alone. I would sooner die than be alone again.

Graham reached out and squeezed her hand briefly. All her life, she had been deserted. By her parents, by her brother. She had nobody else. He felt a pang in his heart at her profound loneliness. He'd been abandoned and unloved all his life, even with his parents present. What must it be like to have had a brother you loved looking after you and then lose him, the only family you had left?

What is the first thing you remember?

"My mother playing the flute," he said promptly. "She would practice in the nursery from the time I was born. I loved listening to her play. She said I could carry a tune before I could speak words."

I remember Armand tossing me in the air and catching me again.

"I could almost toss you into the air still." He winked at her. "Bed, lassie. No more questions tonight, or I'll never finish this letter."

She grinned at him, but she did as she was told. She lay quietly on the bed, her eyes fixed on him but looking into some other world, and slowly they closed. Soon Sylvie appeared, and in her sleep, Aveline embraced the cat. Graham smiled fondly at the two of them and went back to his letter.

11 September 1916

My darling Estelle,

I am glad you want me to send Aveline to you. She is a handful, I must warn you. I fear she and Vincent may overturn society once they are together. I've had to answer at least thirteen questions in the time it's taken me to write this paragraph, and I've had to banish her to bed so I can have a few minutes' peace to finish.

Not much has happened today or yesterday. I got two memoranda from two separate Dread Staff Officers this morning. One urgently needed to know how many tins of raspberry jam we were issued, and I urgently replied that we've never been issued raspberry jam, only ever the blasted plum-apple, except for one time when it was gooseberry. The other reminded me that the unit we came to relieve did a lousy job of inventory report and how he hoped I would Try To Be Accurate with my own report when we leave here. I have set George to the task of keeping track of all the stores, ammunition, and equipment and everything else. He and I have been making an exhaustively precise inventory list at the end of each day, not only of what we have left, but also what we used over the course of the day, and sending a copy by runner back to him. I hope the D. S. O. will enjoy digesting it all as much as we enjoy compiling it.

I am fortunate in the sense that I don't generally have to be out in the thick of things. I'm too busy being buried alive under the Himalayan range of paperwork falling to me. I have to work out schedules only a day in advance. It's like as not the people I assign to tasks will die before their turn comes anyway. I've been giving George plenty of terrible jobs to do, partly because he needs a dressing-down, but mostly I don't want anyone to accuse me of giving him preferential treatment for being my brother. I am glad he's here, though. Much as he irks me at times, it is oddly comforting to know he's with me, where he has always belonged.

George is still writing to Alice. He's not admitting it, although it's my job to censor the men's mail, and I know. I can't bring myself to read the letters. I expect the fear that I might read them is enough to keep him from saying anything incriminating or overly demonstrative. You know, he may genuinely love the woman. It hurts my heart to think of it. There is no easy way out of this mess for him. He will have to make a choice sooner or later, and I pray with all I have it will be the right choice. This I will give him: he does not go to the whorehouses in town when the other men do. By his own admission, it is a definite break from the pattern he's established over the last fifteen years or more. He will have to work out his future and his consequences himself, though. I cannot do that for him.

I do hope Aveline will learn to not be so single-mindedly devoted only to me. She does like MacFie all right, and the medic, and she has taken a fancy to young Willie Duncan as well. He has a little French, as George and I have been drilling it into him since the day we met him. But she's wary of everyone else. She says she's not afraid of them, and they all are very protective of her, but she doesn't interact with them if she doesn't absolutely have to. Ultimately, every day, it is me she shadows, not MacFie or the medic or Duncan. Am I, or have I been, so suffocatingly attached to you?

Your Jamie

14 September 1916

Dearest Jamie,

I am positive that no child could be more trouble-some than Vincent. I am up for the challenge. When will you know if we can bring her home? I do wish you could at least convince her to go back to the Blanchards'. It makes me uneasy knowing she is right in the thick of things. Of course, I don't want you there either, but it's not right to have her there. I know you feel the same way. I wish I could be there to care for her.

Tell George I said for him to stop behaving like a philandering, unattached seventeen-year-old and stop creating children with other women. No, don't actually tell him I said that. But it's true nonetheless. Have I told you lately how much your unimpeachable constancy means to me? You have your insecurities and occa-sional black moods, and your maddening tendency to fall into reveries and no longer hear anything around you, but I've never once had to worry you might have a wandering eye. Alas for us women, poor Maggie is not the only ill-done-by wife in Britain. I'm afraid it's a disease among men, dissatisfaction with what they have. Many of my friends know their husbands do exactly what George has done, and I think it's jolly good Maggie has had the mettle to put her foot down. If more women did, there might be fewer men like George.

"Suffocatingly attached," my foot. Seriously, Jamie darling, you DO have the most odd ideas sometimes. (And I love them. Don't ever stop sharing them. Please.)

Oh, if I were only with you now, how I would suffocatingly attach myself to you with kisses.

Your Estelle

GEORGE

AVELINE WANTED TO say hello to Willie Duncan, but when she poked her head into the dugout, only George was there. Aveline wasn't sure what it was about George that made her suspicious of him. He was cheerful and carefree, and he did try to be friendly to her.

"Looking for Duncan?" he asked, and she nodded. "He's meeting the supply wagon with some of the other men. He'll not be back for a while. Come, see a photograph of my girls," he said, beckoning her closer to him. She took a few steps toward him, and he handed her a picture. It showed his four daughters in matching frocks and hats. She turned it over and read *Susan, Amanda, Mildred, Beatrice. Easter, 1914.*

"Susan is twelve now. I don't hear from them." Although he sounded casual, she detected an undercurrent of sadness. He chattered on about them for some time while she continued studying the photograph, half-listening, wondering about the girls' mother. "Don't ask to see a picture of his wife," Capitaine Graham had said. "He doesn't have one of her."

Don't they have a mother? Aveline wrote on a scrap of paper.

George fell silent for only an instant before he had come up with a reply. "Of course they have a mother," he said, with forced cheerfulness. She wasn't fooled. Her quick eyes scanned the dugout and lighted on a tiny frame by his bed.

Capitaine Graham said you didn't have a photograph of your wife. So who's she? She indicated the tiny frame and looked challengingly down her nose at him. George opened his mouth to answer and closed it again.

"Oh," he said, again trying to seem unconcerned. "That's... Alice."

What about the fifth child? There are only four here. She jabbed a finger at the photograph he'd handed her.

He stared at her in momentary shock, as if the fifth child

were a surprise he'd not yet heard of, but in a moment he'd collected himself enough to reach into his inner breast pocket and take out a photograph of a smiling baby boy, with *Baby George* on the back in a neat woman's hand. He looked much like his father, she decided, glancing from the photograph to George and back again.

"My brother doesn't keep my secrets very well, does he?" He didn't sound angry. He tried to ruffle her hair, but she ducked out of his reach.

George had a glint of fun and mischief in his eyes, not unlike the glint in Willie Duncan's eyes, but it was out of place in George, who was so much older. *A older man should be more serious*, Aveline thought. *He should be able to answer questions without being evasive.* That annoyed her. If she'd asked Capitaine Graham the same questions about the children's mother, he would have told her the truth straightaway, not tried to distract her.

Probably George was not a bad man, but he was not at all like his brother. Not one bit, not in looks or in character. He certainly talked too much.

She dropped the photograph back onto the crate George was using to write at and turned around, leaving the dugout without another word. He could keep company with his own voice, and she would walk along the communication trench to the place near her old house, where Willie would be helping to unload the wagon loads of supplies.

15 September 1916

Sweet Estelle,

My father used to frequently speak with pride that he was unencumbered by human emotion (and it was true in his case), but he also used to say true military men were too tough and hard for tears. He was wrong. I find I am not the only emotional man in the British Army. In fact, we are all moved by things here. So many of our boys gone. Too many ugly realities we have to confront. Morale among my men droops more each day we are in this trench. For the most part, we hold our positions where they are. Once, maybe twice, a week, we fire at the enemy or they at us. But most of the time, we are sitting here, just... sitting. We know what awaits us when we come here; we have seen it all before. But each time it seems worse. Many of the men smoke like chimneys, and I know why. The nerves wear thin with idleness. I would take up smoking myself if not for fear of it ruining my voice. There is simply nothing much to do in between battles. In the morning, there is an attack planned, and I pray we are successful. This endless stalemate of entrenchment, Estelle, it is hell. It is the never making real progress that gets to a man.

I am exhausted, and I have nothing even remotely cheerful to say. I have too much time to dwell on all my failings, and I feel as though my life, especially the portion of it in which I have been a father, has been a howling void. I wish I could try again. I want our boys to respect and love me, I want to be for them what my own father was not, but I have no examples to look to, and I don't know where to start.

Aveline is teaching me there is more to being a father than I imagined. I've not honestly tried to know our boys, and I suppose I haven't needed to. They have a nanny, after all. They are a mystery to me beyond the superficial, and I feel terribly guilty for not ever having recognized them as people. Aveline requires looking after for her safety and survival. It has fallen to me to be that person to her, and I had no idea children were so very, very demanding. I suggest you arrange a raise in pay for Jeannine, and do tell her I now have some idea what she is up against.

(I suppose I've also been so afraid of hurting them that I have swung far opposite of my father's methods and distanced from them, which is not what I want either.)

Aveline's hunger for love is intense, and I don't know how to respond to it. If I make it home, I want to be a better man, a better husband, and a better father. Otherwise, I will leave a legacy of unhappiness where there should be love and joy. I want my boys to weep for me when I am gone, instead of merely feeling relief as I did when my own father died. They would miss you. I know they would grieve to lose you. But I don't know if my absence makes any hole in their lives at all, even now. Does it, do you think?

Why is there so much violence? Seeing the violence done to Aveline makes me realize that whether one is knocked about and hardened over years, as I was, or in mere moments, it is no less terrible an evil, and it has shaken me to my very core.

I do not want our boys to fear us. Respect us, yes, but not fear us. You know yourself how I cannot lay a hand to our boys, out of pure terror to strike them, even if they require discipline. My father got pleasure out of hurting people. I can see myself going blind with rage indefinitely if, only once, I let it out. The mere thought sickens me, that I could be capable of such harm.

I'm scared, my love. Scared and feeling my weakness. I wish you were here; I am always sure everything will be all right when you are near me. If anything happens to me tomorrow, please, know I loved you, and tell the boys I loved them too.

This is a miserable excuse of a letter.

Your Jamie

AID POST

WHILE THE MEN fought, Aveline spent the day at the aid post with the medic. The wounded ones brought in by the stretcher-bearers were terrible to behold, but she had a stomach of iron. The medic could speak a little French, and in previous days, during lulls in the care of the wounded, he had taught her the English names of things so she could bring them when he called for them. He'd written the words for her in her notebook, and she'd drawn pictures of each thing to help her remember.

Today, though, there was no time for English lessons. Scores of men came through, and Aveline cleaned and dressed many of the lighter cases all on her own, leaving the medic more time to tend to the worst cases. She picked bits of shrapnel out of limbs, held the heads of a few men who required immediate amputations, and wrote out the instructions dictated to her. She did this phonetically, but considering how many men in the army were all but illiterate, nobody further up the medical chain questioned the unorthodox spelling on these diagnoses. She had never dreamed there could be such a lot of injuries in such a short time, but she did not flag until the last man had been tended to and sent on to the advanced dressing station. Then she sank to the floor, overwhelmed, and hugged her knees to herself.

THE PROMISE

IT WAS LATE when she summoned the strength to walk to the dugout and wrapped her blanket around her shoulders like a shawl to combat the damp night air. Capitaine Graham, looking haggard and beaten, slumped down on his crate-chair, his back pressed to the damp wall. MacFie wasn't there. She hoped nothing had happened to him; she knew how fond her capitaine was of his man.

More than fond, really. She sensed something deeper between those two, almost as if Capitaine Graham *needed* MacFie in much the same way she needed Capitaine Graham.

She rallied herself at the sight of Graham's exhaustion, lit MacFie's little stove and heated their dinner, but it took him a long time to be ready to eat it. When he finally did, she watched him with some concern and decided he needed distracting. She wrote:

Tell me again what it will be like to go home.

"Back to the Blanchards?" he asked.

No. Scotland.

He swallowed his last bit of dry biscuit and apple-plum jam, then collapsed onto his cot with a groan of exhaustion. She sat beside him, smoothing his hair off his forehead; Sylvie jumped into her lap and began to purr, trampling her mistress' kilt with her little paws. Aveline took his hand and waited.

When he spoke at last, his voice was thick with sleepiness. "We will go home to Inverlochy Castle, and I will walk with you to the top of the mountain where you will see the whole estate spread out around you under your feet like a carpet. The heather will glow purple in the afternoon sun, and the flag will fly from the roof because I will be home, and you will be my own daughter and wear a skirt of my tartan. You will have a wonderful mother and three little brothers, get the education Armand would have wanted you to have, and you will never have to be alone any more..."

His voice trailed off, and his hand in hers went slack. Just like that, he'd fallen asleep. Aveline leaned down and kissed his face, scratchy with a day's worth of beard, but he was dead to the world and did not stir. Sylvie still slept in her lap, and Aveline did not want to disturb her. She stretched to snuff out the candle, nestled deeper into her blanket, and daydreamed of this family she had acquired but had yet to meet. Estelle had even sent a letter, specially for her. Aveline had read it so many times over the last week, it had already become dirty and worn.

She pictured the look Capitaine Graham got in his eyes when he spoke of his wife: a look she couldn't comprehend, but it sent a pang of longing through her entire body to glimpse it. He must love Estelle very much indeed. Would any man ever get that look in his eyes thinking of *her*?

Her capitaine wanted her, really wanted her, to come home with him. She believed with all her heart she had found a real family at last, and she too fell asleep, trusting and content, warm and happy.

Graham woke two hours later from a dream of Estelle. Aveline still sat up beside him, snoring softly. He got out of bed carefully, laid her down in his place, lit the candle on his desk again, and scribbled furiously.

16 September 1916

My precious,

Today was positively hellish. I am exhausted, and my own mortality stares me in the face constantly. Always, always there is but a step between me and death. Today, our division as a whole lost over two hundred men; over a thousand were wounded; hundreds of others are yet to be accounted for. And my field telephone is blasted out of operation yet again, which means I was besieged by runners with stupid directives and irrelevant memoranda from the Dread Staff Officers. Don't the D. S. O. know we're trying to win their war for them out here? They don't bloody care. We are expendable. They ought to be required to spend at least a week out here to know what it is we actually do, what we put up with. As for the men for whom I am directly responsible, I lost fifteen. Two officers (not George, thank God). MacFie was almost shot. This is easily the fifth time I have seen a bullet miss him by a hair. He must be charmed.

It was more successful than many of our battles have been, despite the losses. We did take two trenches, a road, and a good number of prisoners. Many of our lads are out working on consolidating our newly gained ground. MacFie is on watch tonight, so Aveline and I are alone here at the minute. She's sleeping.

I was on the front line today as well, helping to keep things running smoothly. It took a long time to get things under control after most of the work was done, and I collapsed to sleep here shortly after I got back to our dugout. Poor Aveline, she wanted to talk, and I couldn't keep my eyes open another minute. I have only slept for two hours, but what woke me was a most lovely dream of you, you and I tangled in the sheets together and your soft and yielding warmth filling my arms. Then I woke up, and I was still here, in the dark and the cold, and you were not. I want this damned war to end so I can come home to you.

I will come home.

And when I come, I will sweep you upstairs and convince you to allow me to ravish you. I have so much lust inside me, and it is all for you—

Graham threw down his pen and crushed the letter in his hand in frustration. He half wished he would be wounded enough to be sent home but not so badly that he died from it. He wanted his wife. Only sometimes did his desire for her consume him as now; usually, especially in the trenches, misery and survival instincts obliterated any other emotions.

But the dream. It had been so vivid.

In his head, he could hear Estelle's voice as clearly as if she were in the room with him: *You won't have to convince me. I will be so willing, you won't know what hit you.*

She would be too.

He squeezed his eyes closed and let out a shaky breath.

One day at a time. One moment at a time. This war could not last forever. Could it?

He hid his face in his fists and whispered, "God, let this end. Let me out of here before I go mad." For a moment, he waited, as if he expected an audible answer, but he heard nothing but the sound of scrabbling rodentia in the shadows. Aveline made a sharp, silent sound in her sleep behind him. He glanced at her, and he said to himself, *Until I get her out of here, I have to hold on. God help me hold on for her. Hold thou me up, and I shall be safe.*

He rested his head on his arm, repeating that last bit of Psalm like a litany until calm came back into his heart, and in a moment, he had fallen dead asleep.

17 September 1916

Jamie-love,

You are the bravest man I have ever known. Don't let anyone tell you otherwise. To have been treated as your father treated you and yet not be bitter about it is bravery.

Strength is not defined by how well one stands up to beatings or whether one can prevail over another. Strength is defined by how one treats the weakest of the weak. Your kindness to Aveline is not weakness, but proof of your strength.

You should write to the boys when you write to me. They would love it. They always ask me to read them your letters. And yes, I do believe they miss you. They don't say it in as many words, but Peter especially often asks when you will come home.

He does want a horse of his own dreadfully. Peter, I mean. It is all he talks about from the moment he wakes. Yesterday, all three boys went out to pick up stones in the new oatfield going in next year. I paid them so much per cartload, and Peter wants to go out tomorrow again and the next day and the next, until he has enough for his horse. Thomas and Vincent are less financially ambitious, but they go along for the company. Thomas is more interested in the rocks than the money. He kept a heap of them for himself, saying he wants to crack them open and find out if there is any-thing interesting inside. I do wonder what in the world will he be when he grows up? Such a strange child. He went out with Peter again today with notions of excavating the entire field, confident there are fossils or dinosaur bones out there, but I am sure he will not find anything of that nature. And Vincent—well, Vincent is Vincent. I do believe he will drive me to an early grave. He decided this morning to worm his way into the hothouse to steal grapes. Thomas helped him, and Peter kept watch, but Vincent was the mastermind behind the plot. I gave them a choice between a birching and forfeiting the latest day's stone picking pay, and they all chose the birching.

Your Estelle

21 September 1916

My dear boys,

I thought I would write a little bit to you along with a letter to your mother. I long to come home and see you all again. Your mother tells me you all have been stone picking. I am glad my boys are industrious. Please stay out of the hothouse, though, and tell Mother I said you may have grapes once a week so you are not tempted to thieve.

Peter, perhaps you could spend some of your time making sure my horse gets plenty of love and carrots and exercise? Tell Baggett I don't want to come home and find Altair has become fat and lazy in my absence.

We came back from the trenches on the 19th. We are all exhausted, but "rest" in the war doesn't mean what it does at home. We still have plenty of work to do.

Aveline is sending you a few pictures she drew. One shows our view from the door of the dugout. The trees have no leaves in this area anymore. The other is of the paperwork which rains down on me. She finds it considerably funnier than I do.

I hope you will write to me and tell me what else you have been doing.

Father

PART SIX

1892-1899

Eton College, England

ON A TRAIN IN SEPTEMBER, 1892

LIKE THEIR FATHER and grandfathers had done over the last two hundred years, Graham and George were bound for Eton. Despite the fact that their separations had sharpened the differences between them over the last several years, Graham was beyond relieved that, for the first time, he could go to school with his brother. He had survived five hellish years in Inverness, and although he anticipated the next few would be no less grueling and miserable, he would have at least one ally in a new world of strangers.

After all his years of private tutoring, social butterfly George was keen on the prospect of being among other boys. He spent the first hour of the train journey chattering about how fantastic it would be to have *friends*. "Father doesn't like me playing with the village children," he said.

"You just want people to worship you," Graham said.

"I'll settle for some mild admiration. Anyway, you'll still be able to have music lessons! You said yourself you'd outgrown the teachers at Inverness."

"Do you think Father will mind me taking music lessons?" Graham asked. He held his battered leather flute case in his hands—it was never far from him.

"Just take your lessons and don't mention it to him," George said. "If he finds out, play it down as routine. Lots of boys have music lessons. I've had piano lessons! Hate 'em, but Mother made me swear I'd keep going at Eton." He sighed melodramatically. "Father's awfully old, anyway. Maybe he'll die before we finish school, and then you can do whatever you want."

Graham felt guilty for wishing this would be the case. He shouldn't want his father to die, but he knew that until that day, the heavy weight of his father's existence and expectations, oppressive as if he were being sat on by an elephant, would never lift. It had been hammered into Graham's head from the day his father returned home from India that his future career was inflexibly destined to be in the army. Graham couldn't imagine anything he wanted less for himself, but he did not argue. It would have been pointless.

George, already bored of sitting still, restlessly drummed his fingers. "Anyway, just think, now there'll be a long train journey between you and him!"

It was true. Even in Inverness, Graham had never felt perfectly out of the old man's reach. It was not inconceivable Donald Graham could have turned up one day and caused mayhem, but his father wouldn't make a casual trip to Eton. Not in a million years.

THE HIDING PLACE

A T FIRST, ETON seemed huge and intimidating. His school in Inverness had been much, much smaller. Even George was a little awed by the new surroundings. But it didn't take long for him to adjust and befriend every lad in their house, including the older boys. Graham, meantime, was glad that thus far, nobody had bothered him. He was wary of making friendly overtures; that had never ended well at Inverness.

He quietly went about, staying as inconspicuous as possible, doing what work was required of him without complaint, so he would have his free hour in the afternoons, sitting in the chapel.

As at his boarding school, Graham found his favorite refuge at chapel—not as much during the formal services, but in the afternoons when it sat empty, and he had God all to himself. From his pocket, he took the precious old battered Bible the vicar at Inverness had given him and paged through it. The stories of David and the Psalms were still his favorite. He liked that David was such a friend of God, he could say anything to him, even question him or be angry, and God never struck him dead with a thunderbolt for doing it. Instead, always, in the end, God brought comfort to David—a dynamic Graham envied and wished he could have with his father, even though he knew he never would. He thought of Esau's plea: *Hast thou but one blessing, my father? bless me, even me also, O my father.*

Graham wondered what God might look like. He didn't believe the old painters were right, showing God as an ancient man with a big white beard. If God truly had no beginning or ending, He should look wise and beautiful and ageless, not frightening and old.

He stared at the carved ceiling, its patterns fanning out between the windows like the trains of two rows of brides in fine gowns. He closed his eyes, and let the familiar warm and holy hush of the chapel fill him.

He that dwelleth in the secret place of the Most High
shall abide under the shadow of the Almighty.

This is my secret place, he decided, looking around in the comforting silence. *I will be good and quiet and work hard and mind my own business, and if I have trouble, I will come here and tell it to God like David did.*

THE ORGANIST

GRAHAM ALWAYS CAME to chapel armed with his flute and, when he was alone, would stand in front of an imaginary crowd of adoring people who loved him so much they would listen to him play the dullest sets of scales and exercises. Other days—Mondays, Wednesdays, and Fridays— an organist came to practice his art, and Graham would sit there listening, enthralled. He didn't particularly want to play the organ himself, but he was entranced by its power and majesty, and the obvious delight of the man who coaxed beauty out of it. The deep thrumming vibrations filled Graham with awe and a sense that he could do anything.

Graham had thought he was inconspicuous, but the organist had noticed the solemn lad with the anxious eyes lurking in the shadows watching him. One day, without turning in his seat or stopping his playing, the organist called out in a lilting, melodious voice. "Come here, young man."

Graham emerged obediently and went to stand beside the organist, eyes anxious.

"Who are you?" the man asked.

"Augustus Graham, sir."

"You like music, Master Graham. I've heard you playing in here before."

Graham blushed.

"Nothing to be ashamed of. You play well."

"Aye, sir. I have to have music."

"Do you sing?"

"Aye, sir."

"Sing this with me." The organist turned to another piece and nodded. Graham looked at it. It was familiar to him, although he had not sung it himself before. He hadn't sung much at all since coming to Eton, but he did his best.

Where'er you walk, cool gales shall fan the glade;
Trees, where you sit, shall crowd into a shade.
Where'er you tread, the blushing flow'rs shall rise,
And all things flourish where'er you turn your eyes.

"Your voice is changing," the organist observed.

"Aye, sir." That was the reason he hadn't been singing much. It made him self-conscious.

"It happens to us all. You're going to make a fine baritone. I hope you are taking voice lessons here?"

"Aye, sir." Not *quite* a lie. He hadn't started yet, but he wanted to.

The man smiled. "'Aye, sir, aye, sir.' Surely, you can say other things."

"Aye, sir—I mean—" Graham caught himself. "What's your name, please, sir?"

"Davies. Peter Davies."

"I like to listen to you play, Mr. Davies."

"You are drawn to music like filings to a magnet."

Graham nodded.

"You like the way music fills you, is it?"

Graham's eyes lit up. "It does, sir! How did you know?"

"I've seen you close your eyes while I play, hands resting on your knees palms up, soaking it in. And I've seen you in here playing your flute when you thought you were alone, pouring out your soul. As if the music is sacred to you—an act of worship. Or perhaps I'm only projecting my own feelings onto what I observe in you." He finished the piece and reached for his hat. "Come have tea with me, young David."

They left the church together. Graham was tall and slight, nearly as tall as the man beside him. Mr. Davies, despite being about seventy, was as energetic as if he were thirty years younger, and Graham had to move quickly to keep up with him.

They walked to a tea shop and sat by the window, where Davies asked Graham to tell him all about his musical background. Graham timidly told him about his mother and the flute and his voice lessons at Inverness, skipping over everything to do with his father. Davies listened, attentive, then took Graham's hands and looked at them appraisingly. "You have fine, strong fingers on you. Do you play piano, too?"

"I do."

"Good lad. You're Scottish?"

"Aye, sir."

"Tell me about your people. Besides that your mother plays the flute, you've not mentioned them at all."

Graham hesitated. He did not like to mention his father was the Earl of Inverlochy, even though the mere fact that his presence at Eton at all made it likely his family had either money or privilege. Nevertheless, through tactful questions and an endless supply of music-related stories, Davies drew him out, and before long, Graham chattered away comfortably to his new friend.

A FATHER'S OPINIONS OF MUSIC

GRAHAM SPENT TIME with Davies every chance he got. The two of them were seen together often, walking the streets of Windsor, one sharing his wisdom, the other drinking it in like a sponge. He often came to the chapel when Davies came to play the organ, to listen or sing along, and every Sunday they walked to church together. Graham was delighted to discover that Davies not only shared his love of music, but a deep faith in God as well.

At other times, he went to Davies' tiny flat, which was crowded with a collection of musical instruments from all over the world, including a fine Welsh harp that had belonged to Davies' mother. Peter Davies knew the rudiments of playing most of them; but he mostly loved having them around him.

"Where did they all come from?" Graham asked, staring in wonder, the first time he visited.

Davies laughed. "I've nothing else to spend my money on, and my more adventuresome friends who travel bring me the exotic ones from abroad. Help yourself to any you want to experiment with."

Graham did just that. His favorites were the wind instruments, but he was also inexplicably fond of the xylophone, simply for being completely different to anything he'd tried previously.

"Here's one you can take with you wherever you go." Davies handed Graham a little black box. A beautiful gleaming harmonica lay on black velvet inside. Davies did know how to play this one and began teaching Graham, who delighted in its compactness. He did carry it everywhere.

Toward the end of the school year, Graham came to spend a Sunday afternoon with his friend, gloomy about his impending departure.

"Why so despondent?" Davies asked, passing a teacup to the boy, who sat at his feet. Graham took it, letting the warmth soak into his hands, and watched the man pour his own tea without answering the question.

He was silent so long Davies had to prompt him.

"I haven't told you about my father," Graham said.

"You told me he's the earl of Inverlochy." Davies sipped his tea, eyes steadily fixed on Graham.

"He doesn't like music," Graham said. "He doesn't like me. I dread going home. He'll ask what I've done this past year, and he'll beat me for having less than the best marks in everything, and he'll make fun of me because I love beauty and music. He doesn't understand me. I think he actually hates me."

He set aside his teacup and turned his face away to hide the tears that were springing to his eyes.

Davies leaned forward toward the miserable figure on the floor before him and laid a hand lightly on his shoulder. "I suspected there must be something amiss at home, or you wouldn't always have the look of a hunted fox in your eye. Except when you sing. It disappears when you sing." He turned Graham's face gently back so their eyes met. "As for your father, you're in good company there. Handel's father hated music and wanted him to be a lawyer. Handel tried, but his heart wasn't in it. Fortunately for us, he used the gifts the Lord gave him, and you should too. You don't have to let your father silence you forever. Even if you do have to join the army for a time, don't ever give up your music. Cling to it as a dying man to oxygen. If you let it slip out of your grasp, the part of you that is essentially you will starve to death."

"You think so?"

"I know so."

After a long silence, Graham murmured words so low Davies couldn't make them out. "What did you say?" he asked.

Graham looked up, his face stained with tears and his dark eyes glistening. "I was remembering Jeremiah. The prophet. He said, 'I will not make mention of him, nor speak any more in his name. But his word was in mine heart as a burning fire shut up in my bones, and I was weary with forbearing, and I could not stay.' And I feel like that about music. I don't think I *could* give it up, even if it would make my father love me, or even just tolerate me, which it wouldn't. It's like you said, like breathing."

Davies nodded. "Respect your father always, lad, but stand your ground too." He sat back in his chair and nodded toward Graham's abandoned teacup. "Drink it up, before it gets cold."

Graham obeyed, and after a long silence while he finished the tea, decided to ask a question of his own. "I've always wondered—were you ever married, sir?"

Davies shook his head, and his eyes went soft in contemplation. "I loved once. A lovely, lovely girl named Clara. We were engaged to be married, but there was that epidemic of cholera in '48, and I lost her." He absentmindedly turned a ring on his finger as he spoke.

"Was that her ring?" Graham asked.

Davies smiled, wistfully. "It was. I got it back from the engraver's two days before she died. I never had a chance to show it to her." He took it off, and Graham looked at the inside. "*Ti a Fi am byth.* It means 'you and me forever.'"

Graham handed back the ring and stared at him anxiously. "Is it hard, being a bachelor?"

"Not so hard. I've become used to it."

"That's what I want to be."

"Do you now?" Davies asked, a smile breaking over his face at the boy's earnestness. "And why, pray?"

Graham didn't want to talk any more about his father, or dredge up the story of what he had done to Mlle Leclair, and he fell into deep reflection on how he could answer without giving any details. Finally, he said, "I don't ever want to hurt any girls."

Peter Davies smiled and laid a hand on Graham's shoulder again. "I don't think you have it in you to hurt any girls, lad." He shook his head. "You'll find a fine wife someday, and be happy together, you and she. I know it."

HOME

GRAHAM FELT AS if he were leaving his left arm behind when Davies waved goodbye to them from the station platform.

"He's the best man I've ever met," Graham said, mostly to himself.

"He must be, you spend enough time with him," George said off-handedly. He strained to see his reflection in the dirty train window, tweaking at a particularly ugly pink paisley necktie.

"And why shouldn't I have one friend?" Graham snapped defensively. "You've got dozens."

"Don't be cross," said George. "Maybe I miss you."

Graham knew he was an expendable part of his brother's social circle, but he didn't care to discuss that, so he changed the subject. "That tie is atrocious."

"Got 'em all back this morning," George responded cheerfully.

Graham sighed, remembering the day George, flighty and impulsive as always, bought himself a dozen noisy neckties from a market stall in Windsor and, for the next month, wore them at every possible extra-curricular opportunity.

Until he grew too bold and went to morning chapel in a particularly vibrant purple one and got called for a visit with the head.

"I've got an extra fetching orange one you can have if you want," George added generously.

"No," Graham said. "Quit being such a *peacock*, George."

The boys got home late the next afternoon. Graham became uncomfortably aware, as they stood before their parents, that the differences between him and George were starker now than ever. Their mother actually smiled at Graham. "You've got such a lovely grown-up voice," she told him, with more warmth in her tone than he had heard from her for years. "And you're so tall. I hardly recognize you."

Graham suspected his father was aware that he, and not George, was currently more of a man, but couldn't bring himself to admit it. Something flickered in the old man's face—recognition, Graham thought, that his own quiet dignity was superior to George's flamboyant clownishness. The look did not last. Donald Graham turned away and marched out of the room without a word.

Nothing had changed at home. Graham went to his room with a heavy heart and a longing for Peter Davies.

THE EARL'S OPINIONS OF MUSIC

GRAHAM SEQUESTERED HIMSELF away as much as he could with his flute, or at the piano, or singing his heart out in the solitude of the estate's chapel. At least three hours each day, he spent with his music, perfecting everything he had learned over the last year. He felt ridiculously pleased with the way his new voice sounded, rich and deep and unexpectedly powerful. He did not have it under control yet, but he knew that would come with time.

Halfway through the summer holiday, Graham's father came into the drawing room where Graham was playing the piano and launched into loud shouting.

"Augustus, I've told you a hundred times to stop leaving your blasted music lying about!"

He had not, in fact, ever said anything about it before. There was no need—Graham meticulously kept his precious sheets contained and in perfect order. He turned toward his father, not meeting his eyes, and said, "Where, sir?"

His father swept the music off the rack on the piano. It fluttered in pieces across the floor, and he stabbed at it haphazardly with the point of his walking stick. "This," he said. "I'm sick of it. Get it out of my sight."

Graham quietly got off his bench and knelt to gather together his violated music. His silence further angered the old man, who came down on his back with the stick, hard. Graham gasped and flinched, the pages falling to the floor again.

"Pick that up," his father said. Another blow, brutally hard. This time he was braced for it, but tears sprung to his eyes all the same. He collected the rest of the music as quickly as he could, but not before he'd received a dozen more whacks and jabs.

Graham managed to limp to his room and flop to his bed on his stomach. George, sensitive as usual to his brother's distress, came to his side in minutes.

"What did he do to you now?" George asked.

"He thrashed me for leaving my music lying about."

"But you don't leave your music lying about."

"I don't," Graham agreed, sniffling. "But he threw it all over the floor and shouted at me anyway."

George lay beside him and stroked his brother's hair. "Keep your hands well out of his way, all right? You have to protect them." He sounded unusually serious, and Graham, touched by the concern, hid his face in George's shoulder and wept again. George let him cry, and then he said, "I forget what a good person you are until we're home, and I see the way he treats you. I shouldn't begrudge you your Mr. Davies. I'm sorry."

Graham didn't say anything. George went on, "You know what I wish sometimes? I wish we were the other kind of twin and looked alike. Just imagine the mind games we could play with the old man and the havoc we could cause!"

"Aye, *you* would," Graham agreed. "I'd be no good at being you. He'd still know which of us was which."

THE MUSICIAN AND THE CLOWN

IN HIS SECOND year at Eton, Graham threw himself seriously into the study of French and Italian, encouraged by Davies, who had, over the summer in his frequent letters, mapped out for Graham what he needed to do to be ready for a music career. "Prepare for it as if you're going to do it," he advised. "Your father might change his mind."

"Or die," Graham said, bitterly.

"Or die," Davies agreed, calmly. "My point is, you need to prepare now. In a year or two, you might apply to conservatories in Paris, say. You have much work to do to get ready. A lot of study. You read music well, but you need to study the science of it. You need to know the languages most of the music is written in. Now tell me about your holidays."

Graham's face darkened even further. "I got beaten up, just like I told you I would."

Davies looked up sharply. "How badly?"

Graham shrugged. "The usual. I couldn't sit down properly for a day or so."

Davies sat back in his chair, stroking his beard, contemplative. He didn't say any more about the beating. Instead, when he spoke, he said the last thing Graham might have expected.

"I want to meet that brother of yours."

"Must you?" A pang of fearful jealousy stabbed his heart. He did not want to share Davies with George.

Davies gave him a Look, and Graham looked at his feet and said, "Aye, sir." But he didn't want to do as he was told, especially as George had been particularly freakish lately.

George greatly enjoyed the newfound sense of power which came with no longer being a first-year student. He filled jars with spiders and earwigs and let them loose in the rooms and beds of the first-year students. He told gruesome murder stories when dessert was served until some of the boys had lost their appetites and he could have their portions. He sang loudly and deliberately off-key to Graham's flute playing, claiming he was trying to improve his brother's ear.

Graham blushed deeply at his brother's behavior and muttered, "*Do* grow up, George!" at least once a day. The idea of presenting Davies with his perfectly embarrassing brother made Graham wince.

All the same, the next Sunday afternoon, George came to have tea with Graham and Davies. Despite Graham's stern lectures about not behaving like an absolute *goon*, George was as lively and charming as Graham had expected he would be. Graham gradually relaxed, however, as he saw that Davies gave George no special attention. He should have known Davies would not be so shallow, but now he felt reassured.

"He's not much like you, is he?" Davies mused after George had taken his leave to meet friends elsewhere.

"Not much," Graham admitted from where he sat, raptly absorbed in the xylophone's bell-like tones. "But mostly I'm glad to have him. Especially at home. He tries to stop my father…"

"I'm glad of that," Davies said.

"Here at school, he hasn't much need to stand up for me, so he acts like an idiot instead."

"He still *looks* like a boy," Davies agreed. "But I'd say in some ways he's more mature than you are."

Graham made a dismissive noise.

"Don't make those Scottish noises at me, my boy. I know it is very difficult for you to speak as freely as George about anything, even to me, and I dare say you talk to me more than you do most people." He watched Graham as he picked out *Arrival of the Queen of Sheba*. "I don't think you're naturally so shy—you've learned to be, haven't you? Shut yourself in like a turtle, because it's the only way you've found to protect yourself, is it?"

Graham stopped mid-phrase and looked up. It was true; he was.

Davies stood up and paced the room, his hands clasped behind his back. "I hate to think of you trapped at home with that man. It's not just that he can't see your potential, that would be bad enough, but to think of him *hitting* you—" Davies stopped abruptly, distress in his face. "He's your father, I know, and you must obey him however terrible that may seem, but he's cheated you out of love and kindness, which are the most important things he ought to be giving you. You cannot allow yourself to believe that you're not worthy of those things. He's starving you, leaving you all stunted inside."

Graham laid down the mallets and stared at Davies, astounded at his perception. He could never have articulated it himself, but the observation was dead accurate. Davies came to him and laid a hand on one of his.

"You'll be all right, lad. You're capable of moving higher than your father's narrow dreams for you. And he's given you *some* positive things. You're organized and determined like he is. Used in the right way, those are great assets."

"Maybe," Graham managed. He bit his lip and turned his face away from the warm smile Davies gave him.

"Perhaps we appreciate each other more because of what we haven't had," Davies said. "I've always wished—" he paused and walked to the window, as if hesitant to voice his thought, and when he spoke again, Graham had to strain to hear. "I've always wished I had a son. I wish there was anything I could do to make your life easier for you. I even wish you *were* my son. You'd be a good deal less well off, but—"

"I wouldn't care," Graham interrupted impulsively, stepping toward Davies. "I would rather be poor if I could be loved." He had often wished Mr. Davies could be his father. Was it wrong to wish that? He had the babyish urge to climb into the man's lap and be held. Instead, he knelt before him and bowed his head as if waiting for a blessing. Davies laid a hand on his head and lightly ruffled his hair, before lifting the boy's chin so their eyes met.

"There now," Davies said, a touch of sadness in his smile.

"I'll teach you what I can, and whatever you can do with that, I'll be proud of it. You'll be mine that much at least."

Graham nodded. He did not trust himself to speak.

THE PARIS CONSERVATORY

THE FOURTH SUMMER home, Graham and his father had a row about Graham's music. Graham asked, timidly but with impeccable politeness, if he might apply to attend the Paris Conservatory.

"Are you a fucking girl?" his father exploded. "You will not go to any fucking conservatory in fucking Paris. You're going to Sandhurst. They'll turn you into a man. Much better for the world than another utterly useless opera singer. What makes you think you can get into some fancy place, anyway, when you barely manage to pass any of your classes? Look at George. *He* gets top marks in everything. Do you have any comprehension how much it costs to send you to Eton? Soft as a girl, you are..."

Graham did not bother to respond. He had never really been soft. He'd stood up to the disconnected attitude of his mother and abuse of his father with Spartan calm—at least on the outside—for the last twelve years. He wasn't afraid of working; he just didn't want to do the work his father envisioned for him. Davies often told him it showed greater strength to stay quiet than to lash out in retaliation, and that was the kind of strength which mattered. He stood straight and looked down at his father, who could no longer use his height to intimidate Graham, but he did not meet the old man's eyes.

He remembered the xylophone and a most outlandish idea popped into his head. He said stubbornly, "I'll go to South America and join a dance band."

"I'll disown you."

"Try," Graham muttered. He turned on his heel and left the room.

He did not apply to the Paris Conservatory.

WHAT GOD LOOKS LIKE

THE FIRST THING Graham did upon returning to Eton for his final year was run to Davies' house. Davies opened the door, and his face lit up as he welcomed him in, only to grow sad as Graham poured out his tale of woe. The two of them talked for hours.

"There is still time," Davies said, trying to reassure him. "You have at least one more year to fill your head with music. Use it."

The last four years, Graham had invested every moment he could into training his voice, improving his flute-playing, being in the orchestra, contributing to school concerts and church services and any other musical event he could find to participate in. He redoubled his efforts for his final year. He even found time to give two recitals in February, one for voice and another for piano and flute. The enthusiasm of Graham's listeners sparked vivid daydreams about performing for packed houses all over the world. He'd show all the mean, cruel people that he was better than they'd thought. Even his father would see his genius and admit he'd been wrong. It would be a Most Satisfying Thing.

One Friday afternoon in March, Davies did not come to chapel to play the organ as he always had. Concerned, Graham hurried to his flat and let himself in with the key his friend had given him. Davies wasn't there either.

Graham panicked. This was wrong; Davies was as predictable as the sunrise. As surely as George always knew when something was wrong with Graham, Graham now knew that something had happened to Davies. He sank into his friend's chair, feeling as if he would suffocate.

After a few minutes, he had the presence of mind to go knock on the landlady's door, to ask if she knew of Davies' whereabouts.

"Oh, lad," she said, looking stricken. "He's been taken to

hospital. He took a fall a few hours ago, down the front steps. Hit his head something fierce. You can see the blood yet."

Graham felt sick and numb. He did not pause to ask any more questions but took the front steps two at a time and ran along the street until he found a cabbie who would take him to the hospital. There, he searched anxiously until he found Davies' bed. A nurse stood beside him, and Graham asked, voice trembling, "Will he be all right, sister?"

She looked at him with thinly veiled disdain. "Who are you?"

He hesitated only an instant before answering. Usually he didn't like flouting his title, but this time he knew it would be to his advantage. "I'm Lord Kirkhill," he said, twin tears rolling from his eyes. "I'm here to look after him."

The nurse shot him a skeptical look, but decided it was safer to assume he was telling the truth about who he was. "I don't know if he'll be all right," she said brusquely. She turned and left, and Graham knelt beside the unconscious Davies. He leaned close to him, listening to his heart beating.

As long as he could hear that sound, there was hope that Davies might wake again. He had so much he wanted to say to Davies, things he wanted to ask him. "You have to wake up," he whispered, his thumb stroking the rough, friendly face, slack and pale in unconsciousness. "Please, wake up. Don't leave me."

Two hours went by. Davies did not wake, and although Graham sat up eventually, he made no move to leave. He did not remember or care that he might miss classes or supper. He held one of Davies' hands and sang softly to him the song they loved best.

Where'er you walk, cool gales shall fan the glade;
Trees, where you sit, shall crowd into a shade.
Where'er you tread, the blushing flow'rs shall rise,
And all things flourish where'er you turn your eyes.

Sometime in the third hour, Davies' heart stopped. Graham's own heart lurched in denial and disbelief. He forgot where he was and climbed on top of his friend, framed his face with his hands, and kissed his mouth lightly. *Wake up*, he thought again. *Please wake up.* He gazed intently, waiting for those pale blue eyes to open and the familiar fond smile crease his face, but nothing changed, and Graham sank in despair to Davies' side and wept into his shoulder until he had no tears left. He closed his eyes and wished he could die too.

He jumped when a hand touched his arm. His housemaster and two nurses looked at him, faces solemn. "Come, Lord Kirkhill," he said gently. "Your brother's frantic. He told us to look for you. Come away now. There's nothing more we can do here."

Graham's tears started again. It took the combined efforts of the three adults to pull Graham away from Davies. Once they had him on his feet at last, he bent, as if to kiss the dead man's hand, and then Graham unresistingly let the housemaster guide him out into the night and into a waiting carriage. The housemaster said nothing on the drive home, and Graham stared dumbly into the street ahead of them.

On his finger, he turned and turned Davies' ring. Was he a thief?

He didn't care if he *had* stolen it. It was his.

ACQUAINTED WITH GRIEF

IN HIS INITIAL hours of grief, Graham had not considered how Davies' absence would affect his daily life. He felt as bereft as if someone had chopped off one of his feet and left him to crawl along as best he could all alone. All Saturday and Sunday, Graham refused to leave his room.

George, unusually patient and sober, came and sat with Graham every spare moment he had, trying quietly to get his brother to eat, or talk, or sing, or anything besides sitting in his chair sobbing silently or lying on his bed staring at the ceiling, lost and directionless.

Any time he thought of going out, he remembered Davies was gone, and it hit him like one of his father's punches to his stomach. Never again would they meet passing in the street, or make music together. He wouldn't be there to rejoice with Graham when he graduated in a few months, nor to advise him about music, or simply be proud of him. Davies wouldn't be there to help him navigate his future, would never help him choose a wife or become an honorary grandfather to his children. There seemed absolutely no point in going on living when the only person who seemed to care about him was gone.

Their housemates, under strict instructions from George, likewise reined in their usual noisy banter. Graham was an odd one, not easy to get to know, but the younger lads, especially, all respected him. He had an air of authority without bossiness, and although he didn't talk much about anything besides music or religion, his sorrow affected them all more than he would have guessed.

"What's the use?"

George jumped at the sound of Graham's voice, coming hard and sharp from the bed. Graham did not sit up, but he added, "What's the use of *anything* when the only person who cared about my interests and me is gone?"

"He's not the only person who cared about you. Don't be ridiculous. I want you to have your music career. Mother does too. She just can't say it."

"Damn."

Again George jumped. Graham never swore.

"Damn, damn, *damn*."

"Graham—" George said, but his brother was off his bed now and ferociously ripping his precious music books to pieces and throwing them to the floor. "I hate everything. Everything. *Everything*."

George leapt to his feet and tried to catch Graham by the wrists. "Stop it," he said, shaking him. "Look what you're doing!"

Graham wheeled around and struck him in the face.

George staggered backward, stinging less from the blow than from the fact Graham inflicted it. Clearly, his brother had taken complete leave of his senses.

"And I hate you too!" Graham said. He swung at George again, but George ducked out of his way. "I hate your smug, arrogant face. Tell me again you want me to have my career. Tell me again Mother cares, you spoiled *baby*."

Graham had never known such rage, such an urge to inflict pain. He was crying again, hot tears this time, and he knocked George to the floor and sat on him while he swung at him with his fists.

Had Graham been a fighter, George would have fared badly indeed, but he was not, and the housemaster, upon hearing the ruckus, came rushing in and separated the boys before Graham could do much damage.

"I *hate* you," Graham screamed after George as the housemaster took him out of the room, and he threw his heftiest music book at his brother's head. He missed.

He kept on shouting hysterically until, a few minutes later, the housemaster returned. He threw a glassful of cold water into Graham's face, and Graham gasped and stepped backward, silenced and dripping. "Enough," said the master sharply. "Sit."

He gave Graham a severe and ominously soft-spoken lecture about his behavior and its consequences. Graham would eat and attend classes the next day with no fuss if he didn't want trouble. He complied but with no enthusiasm. He barely touched his food.

Each afternoon, he came back to the house, having been forbidden to go anywhere but classes for a full week, and he lay on his bed, perfectly silent. He did not play or sing.

On Thursday, he went to his room to find all his music neatly stacked on his desk with a note on top.

Dear Graham,

You are correct. I am a damned spoiled baby, and Mother probably doesn't really care, but this pile of paper is your future, and I won't let you give up your dreams just cos somebody died. He'd want you to keep on, and you know it. Anyway you do believe you'll see him again, don't you?

Some of these I could mend, but I had to buy new copies of some that were pretty bad, and Cunningham and me have spent every spare minute copying over all your annotations for you.

"It is vain for you to rise up early, to sit up late, to eat the bread of sorrows: for so he giveth his beloved sleep."

Love, George

Graham sank to his bed and, for the first time since the fracas with George, he let himself weep. George was being terribly sporting, and he'd even quoted a psalm, no doubt the only time he'd ever voluntarily done such a thing in his life. He'd had to take time looking for exactly the right one too.

When the time came to lower the coffin into the ground at Davies' funeral, Graham held up the proceedings by leaning on it as though he wished he could join the dead man in the darkness of death. George, who had heroically foregone a cricket match to be with him, had great difficulty in pulling his brother away.

Now, instead of going to the chapel for his hours of quiet, he would sit with his back against Davies' modest headstone and play for him. It was far easier to play through streaming tears than to sing. People passing by the churchyard regularly became used to the mournful ballads coming from the unseen player among the tombs. His grief was something he didn't have the words to share with anyone, not even George. He felt terribly, utterly forsaken.

When I'm lonely, dear white heart,
Black the night or wild the sea,
By love's light, my foot finds
The old pathway to thee.

Vair me óro van o,
Vair me óro van ee,
Vair me óru o ho,
Sad am I without thee.

He learned a few weeks later that Peter Davies had made him heir to everything he possessed. It was unexpected: his friend had really, truly loved him.

George had been right. Graham determined he would not disappoint Davies' dreams for him. He would not forsake his own dreams.

Lord and Lady Inverlochy did come to Eton for the end of year concert and the boys' graduation. Graham suspected they only came for George, but it no longer mattered. He sang his heart out. There were better pianists and flautists than he at Eton, but nobody questioned that, for vocal talents, he was the best the school had.

When they got home, while George prepared for Oxford, Graham begged his father one last time for the desire of his heart and got struck over the shoulder with his father's stick for his trouble, so hard that it might have cracked his skull had it made its target, but Graham ducked away just in time. The mark stained his shoulder for weeks afterward.

LUCY, O!

G RAHAM WENT TO his room and played his flute for hours every day over the next weeks. His mother would come to sit with him and listen quietly to his music. She spoke not at all, and looked so tired and pale and sad he wanted to cry. He wanted to comfort her but could not imagine how to comfort a woman he scarcely knew. One afternoon, he did the only thing he *could* think of, which was to play her favorite song. He watched her as he did so, and tears slipped out of the corners of her eyes and down her cheeks. She made no sound, no movement.

"Sing it to me, son," she whispered when he finished. "But instead of 'lassie,' say, 'Lucy.'"

He dropped on one knee before her and took her hands in his while he sang.

> *Though I dare not call thee mine, bonnie Lucy, O,*
> *As the smile of fortune's thine, bonnie Lucy, O!*
> *Yet with fortune on my side,*
> *I could stay thy father's pride,*
> *And win thee for my bride, bonnie Lucy, O—*

She took his face in her hands, silenced him with a kiss, and left the room. He stared after her, perplexed, but he did not follow. He was used to abrupt dismissals and desertions; he decided she had simply become tired of listening.

She did not come to dinner, which did not surprise anyone; she mostly took her meals in her room these days. But very early in the morning, a sharp rapping at his door woke him. His mother's maid stood there, ashen-faced and hysterical.

"Come quick, Lord Kirkhill, your mother—" was all she could choke out. "We're feared of his lordship, please come!"

He leapt past her, down the hall and into his mother's room.

She lay on the floor with a bottle of laudanum near her. He tipped it. It was empty. Her other maid ineffectively bent over Lucy, and Graham spoke sharply to her, "Get up, girl, and go call for the doctor!"

She ran from the room, leaving Graham staring at his mother's agonized face, white against the dark hair tangled around it, and she clutched for his hand, babbling incoherently, her voice high and so weak, he had to stoop close to make out her words.

"He used to sing that to me, just like you did, Lucy, O!"

"Who did?" Graham asked. Surely not his father!

"I hope he has happiness. I never did. I had to marry the earl. I didn't have a choice. You can't fault me for letting someone show me kindness, for taking scraps of happiness—" She gasped, and he lifted her in his arms to help her get a breath. "It's all my doing, I couldn't stand up to him. I tried once, and he beat me for not beating sense into you. He raped me or hit me any time I questioned him. He started in on me the very first night. He said I wasn't a virgin, but it wasn't true, and..." Her voice trailed off, and he shook her slightly.

"Wake up, Mother," he said, urgently. "The doctor is coming. He'll help you."

"No," she rasped out. "Nobody can help me anymore. Your music helped me. He won't let you go to Paris. It's my fault, I was scared of him, I was afraid he would kill me. I wanted to see you grow up fine and— Oh, God, just awful. I am such a terrible mother." Again her words slurred, and she slumped, and again he shook her, forcing her upright. He couldn't speak.

"I failed you," she whispered. "Look at my back, and you'll see, you'll see I understood, really, always. I was so scared." She clawed at his arm, gasping for air again. "He would have killed me—that riding crop—I can't—"

Graham watched, horrified, as her lips went blue. He let her slide out of his arms to the floor and scooted backward, frightened out of his wits. Long after her heart stopped, her unnaturally dilated eyes stared at the ceiling. He could not bring himself to touch her, to try to close them, and he could not move. He half feared her dead body would leap up and claw at him again. Her words had barely made sense, and they chased each other about in his head.

George, true to form, appeared out of nowhere and sat beside his silent brother, quietly resting his head on his shoulder as, together, they stared at their mother: George with pity, Graham with numb horror.

"You always know," said Graham, with difficulty. "How do you always *know*?"

George didn't answer for a while. "Just a feeling I get."

"You're deeper than you let on," Graham whispered to him. "Thank you for being here." His teeth chattered from an inner chill, and George held him close trying to calm him.

The doctor arrived too late to revive his mother, but when he laid her out on the bed, Graham saw the marks she had tried to tell him about. Angry scars ran all up and down her back, and her arms covered with what looked like blade marks, some frighteningly recent, most faded to thin silver lines. Had his father done that to her, or had she done it to herself? He had never wondered why his mother always wore long sleeves and high collars, and he wanted to be sick, realizing the dark secrets she had hidden all these years.

"She never *would* let me look at her back," the doctor said, angry. "Now I know why. That damned father of yours beat her raw, and more than once from the looks of it. And not a blasted thing I could have done if I had known."

The cause of death given to the public was "heart failure." Graham mourned for his mother with the detachment one would use to grieve for a stranger, and with the guilty regret that, like Mlle Leclair, there had been nothing he could do to save her.

His father barely flinched at the news; Graham was sure his

father's eyes twinkled when he heard.

It was a sickening way to finish off the summer, but Graham was glad for any reason to get away from the castle, even if it was to the dreaded Sandhurst. He envied George for getting to do what he *wanted* to do, studying law. But mostly, he just missed him.

GOODBYE TO THE EARL

GRAHAM FINISHED AT the military academy in 1899 and went home for a brief visit before being sent to Gibraltar. George came home too, and the brothers spent most of their time out of doors, riding and sleeping under the stars, so as to avoid their father as much as possible. The old earl refused to speak to Graham at all.

The day he left, Graham debated whether to say goodbye to his father, remembering the day his father sent him away to Inverness without a proper farewell. He was still angry about that slight whenever he remembered it. He thought of Davies and how he had had no chance to bid farewell to a man he loved. He had no regrets there, not real ones; Davies had known Graham loved him, and they both believed in the resurrection. The parting wasn't permanent.

Supposing his father died as unexpectedly, however, Graham knew he could never live with himself if he did not give the old man the chance to be nice. He had no reason to believe he'd ever see him again in heaven. Graham wanted nothing said or done on his part he would live to regret.

He sought out his father, in his study as usual at that time of day. Graham looked at the man seated in the chair at his desk, as if he were seeing him for the first time in a long time. Donald Graham was no longer the robust lieutenant-colonel. He had shrunk—or perhaps Graham had just grown. How had this frail-looking man ever been intimidating? How was it Graham still felt sick quiverings inside him, merely being in the same room?

He swallowed his fear and hoped his trembling did not show. "I'm leaving now, Father."

As usual, his father did not look up right away, and when he did, at last, acknowledge his son, it was with a *hmph*.

"Goodbye, sir."

Donald Graham did look up then, and Graham locked eyes with his father, the first time in years he had dared to make full eye contact with the man. His father said nothing, and after a moment, Graham turned and silently left the room.

PART SEVEN

11 November 1916

Allonville, France

TERRIBLE AS AN ARMY WITH BANNERS

AFTER A DAY and night of sitting at her husband's side with no change in his condition, Estelle became restless and asked for work to do. She donned an apron, rolled up her sleeves, and pitched in alongside the doctors and nurses wherever they needed an extra pair of hands. Always, she longed for Jamie to awaken. She checked on him as often as she could. George showed up and took a turn watching over his unconscious brother.

By evening, Estelle was catching on that none of the medical personnel were paying any real attention to her husband.

"I keep asking why they haven't gotten to him yet, and nobody gives me a straight answer," she complained to George. "Every time he stirs the slightest bit and seems like he might wake, they come along and give him shots 'to help him sleep.'"

George raised an eyebrow. "I think you know as well as I do what that means."

Estelle narrowed her eyes. "Aye, there's something they're not telling me. *Well.* I have had enough of *that*."

She turned to go, and George called after her, "Want me to have a word with them?"

"I don't need a mediator," she said ungraciously and stormed off to confront the head of the hospital with her demand for an explanation.

"Who is your husband again, madam?"

She told him, and he shuffled through paperwork. He was obviously exhausted, but she felt too annoyed to be sympathetic. "I'm sorry, madam, but we are rather busy trying to save the lives of those we know we can save." He hesitated, and under her fixed stare, he caved. "Since you insist upon knowing, we do frequently administer morphine to patients with little hope of survival, to—to make it easier on everyone."

"So you're saying you're going to just leave him there to die?"

He looked uncomfortable, but before he could reply, she spoke again.

"LIKE HELL YOU ARE," she said, her fists clenched at her sides as she leaned over his desk. He looked taken aback at her language.

"I will *not* have you let my husband die while I am here watching what a terrible job you are doing. I'm his wife, and we have three young sons. Like *hell* you are going to stand by and do nothing! He's *not* a terminal case, or he'd have died already."

He stared speechlessly. "Mrs. Graham, I—"

"LADY INVERLOCHY TO YOU, SIR."

"I apologize, my lady," he murmured with a slight bow.

By odd coincidence, he managed to have Jamie looked at within half an hour. The doctor examined the nightmarish foot and ankle, puffy and crackling under his touch.

"He has a high fever," came the brusque diagnosis. "His foot is badly infected. Gas gangrene."

"Maybe if anyone had looked after it properly in the first place, infection wouldn't have had a chance to set in," Estelle said with crisp condescension. "I suppose next you'll tell me you have to cut it off."

"I'm afraid so, Lady Inverlochy. Perhaps you would like to go out for a while and come back when we have finished?"

"I will not leave. My faith in the trustworthiness of this establishment has been greatly undermined. I'd hate to come back and find you've cut off his head by accident."

The man in the next bed laughed aloud at her sarcasm, but Estelle did not release the doctor from her unrelenting gaze. George stood there, unusually silent, until the doctor glanced his way.

"Don't look at me," George said. "Do it because *she* tells you."

Another instant of silence.

"All right," the doctor agreed. "Come along with me. We'll do it right away."

She held Jamie's hand throughout the entire ordeal. Despite her earlier bravado, she could not bear to actually watch. It had to be done, or he might die, but she knew how terribly distraught he would be upon waking to find himself crippled.

If he ever woke up.

She didn't want to give any possibility to that horrible *if*. He must recover. He must; she couldn't bear any alternative.

Afterward, George sat with Estelle. At first, she was glad of his company, but after half an hour of listening to him speak every thought which popped into his head, she glared at him and asked, "Haven't you duties, George?"

"Of course I do," he said, breezily. "I've done them."

She closed her eyes and forced herself to stay calm. "Then please, do *shut up*, George. I don't want to listen to anybody saying *anything*."

"All right," he agreed, reaching out a hand to squeeze hers. "I suppose this is almost as distressing to you as to me."

She swatted his hand away and rolled her eyes. "How does Maggie put up with you, George?"

"She doesn't."

"Not anymore, anyway?" Estelle asked pointedly.

"You're a full-on tigress tonight, aren't you?"

"Will you *please* go away? You've hovered here for hours, and I promise I will love you dearly again later, but right now, you are more than I can bear, and I would like a little quiet space to breathe in, thank you." She waved her hand toward the door, and George, sensing his life might be endangered if he did not quickly obey, rose to his feet and bowed slightly.

"See you tomorrow, then."

"If I must." Estelle had already dismissed him. All that

existed for her now was Jamie, slumbering under the influence of morphine, this time with her personal sanction.

She sat by his cot until night fell, and they were left more or less alone. Then, in the darkened room, she climbed under his blanket with him and held him, carefully, snuggling close as she always used to do. He still burned with his fever, and sometimes he muttered incomprehensible things.

She murmured into his ear, "I love you. I love you, darling. We all want you home for Christmas. Please, Jamie, please. Live for me. I love you. I can't let you go. If you make it through tonight, we go back to Scotland tomorrow. Think of it. Scotland. Home."

MEMORIES

ESTELLE THOUGHT OF her three precious sons, safe at home and likely sound asleep in their beds by now, and smiled. She could picture them all. Peter, so like his father, cuddled up with himself like a hedgehog; Thomas still and straight as a log; Vincent upside-down or sideways in a tangle of blankets, snoring. She prayed they would never have to leave her to go to war. This war was supposed to end wars, people said, and she clung to that thin hope, however foolish it might be in reality.

She remembered all the evenings over the last year which she had spent playing her piano by candlelight, alone, and curling up in their bed, even more alone. She had the boys and Jeannine for company, of course, but it wasn't the same. It wasn't the particular togetherness she and Jamie had carefully maintained over the years, the intentional spending of time together, the effort made to keep their romance alive. It was of the utmost importance to him, he would say, that she not find reason to become tired of him or fall out of love with him. They often went riding or walking in the summer twilight and did not come back inside until well after dark fell.

Last July, right before Jamie left for France, he had been given a week's leave to come home before being shipped off. They hadn't been together in six months. That week, they had done their best to make up for lost time: immense amounts of cuddling and kissing, lingering touches, and musical duets. There was something so intimate about music, something magical and precious about listening to each other and working together to create a seamless union.

And, after the boys went to bed, he and Estelle went out walking every night. They had a number of places they liked to go. In cold or wet weather, they resorted to the haymow in the cowshed, or the hothouse, or a certain pillared folly; but when it was warm enough, there were outdoor places they favored to hide in.

Sometimes they would only cuddle and kiss, but that last night before his departure, both of them had wanted more. It felt like a farewell, with an ominous note of uncertainty pervading it. He might never come back. They both knew it, but neither wanted to acknowledge the possibility.

That night, they found themselves wandering in the direction of a particular heather-scented hollow a mile from the castle. Estelle leaned against him and held his hand tightly, and when they reached the hollow, he pinned her lightly against the massive old oak tree at its edge and bent to kiss her—a deep and leisurely kiss, so different from the shy, self-conscious ones of their early times together. She made a small appreciative sound.

"I wish you never had to go away," she murmured, her fingertips light as they stroked his hair, smooth and fine and flyaway.

"Don't talk about it," he whispered against her cheek. He drew her away from the tree. "Dance with me, my love." They waltzed slowly, his hands untying her sash and popping open the row of buttons down the back of her dress with a practiced ease and smoothness which always pleased her. "Tonight," he said softly as her diaphanous evening dress drifted and pooled at her feet in a dove-grey cloud, "I want to dance in the heather with my very own woodland nymph." He took all the pins out of her hair, and she shook her head, letting her hair tumble down her back.

She smiled, stepped out of her cloud and set to work on his clothing until he too stood bare. They pressed close, skin to skin in the thin misty air, fingers laced together. The moonlight and the scent of the heather diffused magically through the mist all around them; the trees about them loomed shadowy and mysterious. It was cool, but they did not care. They danced, barefoot, clinging closely, while he sang softly to her all her favorite songs, and her hands stroked his skin with a light touch that drove him wild.

He kissed her hand, her wrist, his lips brushing along her arm, and cupped her chin in his hand and bent to kiss her upturned lips. She knew she might never kiss him again after he went away tomorrow. She wanted to memorize everything about him, carry him in her heart all the way to the end if he should die in France. She dropped to the ground with him, and they did not say any more for a long time, only felt and dreamed and sighed in their delight.

When later they lay there cuddled close together looking at the moon, he sang again softly.

When the golden sun is sinking
To his home behind the hill,
And the zephyrs softly murmur
'Round the old and ruined mill;
When the birds have ceased their warbling
And the flowers have gone to sleep,
Meet me, Nannie, blue-eyed Nannie,
Where the stars their night-watch keep...

"A pity my own name doesn't fit the rhythm better," Estelle said. "Nannie, indeed."

He didn't seem to hear her. "I am so glad you married me," he whispered fervently. "I have never been as happy in all my life as I have been since we married."

She kissed his cheek lingeringly and turned to look into his eyes, her hand resting lightly on his chest. "I wish I could undo all the terrible things that were done to you."

"We can do better with our own sons, I hope."

"We can. We are." She petted him lovingly. Her mind was not on their sons.

He laughed softly. "I'm getting cold."

"You've nae meat on yer bony bones, that's why," she said teasingly, and climbed on top of him and snuggled there. "I'll be your blanket." He wrapped his arms around her tightly, and she sang back to him:

> *Come, sweet Jamie, softly whisper,*
> *If you love me still as true*
> *As when first our troth was plighted*
> *On the heather wet with dew.*
> *I am waiting for you, Jamie,*
> *By the tree we love so well...*

She let the words trail off, and he burst out laughing for real. She loved when he laughed; it was a rare treat.

They lay there a long time, opening their hearts to one another as they rarely had a chance to do. It seemed right to do it on this eve of his departure, to say all they might never have a chance to say again.

"You've become a much better hugger since the day you proposed to me," Estelle said mischievously. "Do you know you won my heart the moment you sang me 'A Red, Red Rose'? You made me think I was the only one in the room, and you were singing it just to me."

"You were the only one in the room for me. And I was singing it for you. Every song I have sung since has been sung to you, whether you could hear it or not. And when I danced with you, I wanted to kiss you, wanted to tell you how much I loved you. I couldn't make sense of what was happening to me."

"You *did* tell me you loved me."

"I did not!"

"You did too. *So fair art thou, my bonnie lass, So deep in luve am I.* I knew it came right out of your heart. Even though you looked as though you were making love to that potted fern on the other side of the room."

"Is there anything you don't notice?"

"Not much—oh, don't go all embarrassed on me, silly man! Anyway, I *knew* this angel-voiced officer with the worried face must be my destiny. I was dreadfully afraid you were already taken."

"And *I* am afraid you are going to put potted ferns all over the castle now solely to tease me."

"What a splendid idea," she said, giggling.

They wandered back to the castle an hour later. Jamie had brought an electric torch so they could make their way without stumbling, and when they got to their room, they dove under their silk eiderdown and made love again.

"How are we going to get along?" she asked the next morning, despondently, as she laid out his uniform for him and handed him things to pack in his kit bag.

"One day at a time," he said practically. But his expression was sad as he picked up his flute, which he had left out the previous afternoon. He fell into a dreamy world of his own as he played it for ten minutes, while she sat on the foot of their bed and listened. "I will miss this." He lowered the instrument and looked at it wistfully.

"Play for me before we go down," she begged, coming up behind him and putting her arms around his waist, leaning her ear comfortably against his back. She loved to stand like this while he played, letting herself be swayed along with him as he succumbed to whatever movement the music inspired in him. It was like a dance, and it made her extremely happy under ordinary circumstances. Today, though, it had a note of desperation in it, and the song he played was hardly cheering either.

When I no more behold thee,
Think on me.
By all thine eyes have told me,
Think on me.

When hearts are lightest,
When eyes are brightest,
When griefs are slightest,
Think on me.

When thou hast none to cheer thee,
Think on me.
When no fond heart is near thee,
Think on me.
When lonely sighing
O'er pleasure flying,
When hope is dying,
Think on me.

He put away the flute with the tenderness of a mother laying her baby in its cradle and snapped shut the clasps. For a moment, his elegant hands lingered there, spread over the worn leather, before he brought it to his lips, kissed it, and handed it to Estelle. He didn't need to ask her to keep it safe for him; he knew she would. Estelle buttoned his tunic and fastened his buckles, and he pulled her into an embrace so tight, the imprint of his buttons stayed on her cheek when he finally let go. They kissed passionately, both of them in tears.

"God go with you, my darling," she said, trying to smile.

"Stay safe, my love," he whispered back, laying his hand against her wet cheek.

She nodded. Hand in hand, they went to the waiting car. Again they kissed, although a bit less demonstratively, since the boys were watching. While he gave each of the lads a farewell hug, Estelle cut a half-blown rose and kissed it and handed it to him.

"Oh, my love," he said fondly, touching her face and kissing her mouth one last time, as he clasped the rose's stem in his free hand.

She smiled bravely, kneeling on the steps with her arms around the boys, as Jamie got into the car. One last wave, and the car was off, and a pang of loneliness settled over Estelle as it vanished into the distance. What if he never came back?

She turned and ran all the way back to her bedroom, where nobody would see her cry.

CONFESSIONS

ESTELLE REMEMBERED ALL those things as she lay there, drifting in and out of sleep until, late in the night, a young man appeared beside the bed, apprehensively turning his cap in his hand. She recognized him as the boy with the cat from the Blanchards' who had handed her the harmonica, and she sat up, struggling to pull herself together through the fog of her tired brain. Her fitful sleep made her even shorter on patience than she had been earlier, and she hardly felt in the mood for a visitor.

"Mr. Duncan, is it?" she prompted, less graciously than she would usually address a near-stranger.

"Aye, ma'am," he said. "Lady Inverlochy, I wanted to tell you what happened to your husband and to—to Aveline. If you want to ken, I mean. I've a couple of hours to myself, and I—I need to tell someone, see." He bit his lip as he looked at the floor. "It's all my fault, Lady Inverlochy, all of this."

She perceived how tightly he clutched his cap, how terrified of her he apparently was, how clearly he craved absolution for some perceived transgression. In a gentler tone, she assured him, "All right. Let's go outside, though. I don't think I can stay awake to listen in here." She stroked Jamie's face again, then reached for her coat. Duncan jumped on the opportunity to hold it for her, and she helped herself to a lantern.

He followed her outside, the frost whispering underfoot, and they found a crate near the stable. She sat on it with the lantern beside her and looked up.

"All right, Mr. Duncan, what exactly is troubling you? What is it you believe is your fault?"

He burst out, "If I'd done what I ought, Aveline would no hae been wi' Captain Graham the day he was injured, and—and she—" Here his voice choked up, and he dropped to his knees before her and hid his face in his hands. "Aye, it's my fault."

"I am not sure I follow you, Mr. Duncan," she said, laying a reassuring hand on his shoulder.

"I dinna want to be sent home," he said, raising his eyes to hers at last. She looked into them and read guileless honesty there, but it did nothing to clarify what in the world he was talking about.

"Whatever would you be sent home for? My husband always spoke so highly of you."

"I only comforted Aveline, I swear I didna do anything to her like what Captain Graham believes I did."

"What does he believe you did?"

"He thinks I slept with her, ma'am."

She had not expected this. Jamie had never so much as hinted at any such suspicions.

"He told me I was a disgrace because I joined at fifteen, wanting to be a man, he said, and now I'm in trouble, he says I'm trying to get oot of consequences by admitting I'm under-age," Willie went on, breathless. "He told me I had to choose between court-martial as a man and being sent home like a truant schoolboy. I dinna want to be shot, but going home to Shetland might be worse—"

"Perhaps you had better begin at the beginning, young man," she interrupted. "I haven't the slightest idea what you're babbling about, and I can't help you until I do understand. All I know about you is that you and Aveline were friendly."

"Oh aye, we were friends," he said earnestly. "And I fell in love with her, only I widna admit it, and I think she liked me too."

Estelle made room on the chest and motioned for him to sit beside her. "I will tell you all my husband told me, and then you will fill me in on all the details he left out."

PART EIGHT

23 September - 5 October 1916

Somme, France

23 September 1916

Estelle my love,

How it pains me that my family is all so far away in Scotland while I sit here in France, playing nursemaid to a lassie who is determined to not let me out of her sight, ever. The mere sight of your pristine handwriting makes me long for home, and this last time, there were letters from the boys too. I am glad they wanted to write to me. Peter's careful attempt to write perfectly shaped letters. Thomas' barely legible scrawling. Vincent's tottering printing cascading down the page. It makes me want nothing more than to hold you all in my arms right now and not let go for a long time.

Aveline has taken quite a fancy to Willie Duncan. Perhaps I mentioned that before. He can speak a little French, and he is a responsible young man. I do not mind her tagging about with him. He has a camera George bought him before we came to France, and has become quite a photography enthusiast. He has even set up a darkroom in the cellar here. (George really does throw money around as if it is nothing; how does he plan to manage after the war if Maggie doesn't take him back?)

After we came back to the Blanchards', Duncan took photos of Aveline and me, which I will send to you with this letter. I like the one of Aveline with her arms crossed. Such a typical stance for her. She is all at once defiant and vulnerable. Good food (well, not good, but better than what she had before, and certainly more abundant) and kindness have made for an astound-

ing change in her. She is becoming quite a young lady, filling out nicely, and several inches taller.

Aveline's innocence is bigger than herself. She has let it swallow whole all the pain and the evil that has been done to her. It can no longer be seen, but it sits heavy inside her like bad food, refusing to digest, causing her biting pangs of remembrance at inconvenient times. Even though we talked about it, I do not think she fully comprehends what was done to her. How could she?

Even though there is an unspoken Aveline Protection Alliance amongst the men, she is possessive of me, afraid to let me out of her sight, desperate for my affection and care. Why she trusts me so implicitly when all I did was find her and tend to her, I do not know, but I am careful not to break that trust, knowing it would take little at all to do exactly that.

She relies, it would seem, wholly on that cat of hers to decide whom she trusts and of whom to be suspicious. The cat has an all-out hatred toward George. I tried to explain that felinekind has never gotten along with George, and it has nothing to do with him personally, but she will have none of it. "What if Sylvie hisses at me one day?" I asked her, and she wrote, "She never will."

Pure luck, if you ask me. I don't need to tell you cats and I don't get along any better than cats and George.

She cries sometimes when she is alone; I know because when I come to say goodnight to her I hear her, and I go away until she is quiet again. She puts on a good front most of the rest of the time. Keeps those of us living in the château all vastly entertained with her wickedly accurate observations of the men, all their flaws and quirks, rendered in art and pinned to the walls. And she does all she can to be useful, uncomplainingly emptying slop buckets and washing dishes and lugging water.

I will let you know when you can come collect Aveline. I am still trying to determine if she has any relatives. Later this week (the 26th), we have leave to go to Amiens, and we are taking Duncan and MacFie along. It will be nice to have one day away from responsibility.

Your Jamie

GROWING UP

AVELINE WOKE WITH a start, thinking she had wet herself in her sleep. She leapt from her cot, switched on the electric torch her capitaine had given her, and gasped to see a glaring smear of red.

Her legs were stained with it too. Blood. She panicked at its metallic smell on her hands. This must be a terrible calamity, some hideously delayed after-effect of the rape. She stood there, forcing herself to be calm. Blood was just blood, after all. Wasn't it? She had seen enough of it at the aid post, but that was other people's blood. Her own was different.

She felt deeply, inexplicably ashamed. She didn't want MacFie to know, and she feared waking him if she knocked at her capitaine's door. She switched off the torch, covered the spot with her blanket, and ran down the hall and pounded on Mme Blanchard's door instead.

The lady came to the door, alarmed, and the hysterical girl showed her her bloody hands, and Mme Blanchard became even more alarmed. Aveline snatched a pencil and scrawled, *It is all over my bed. I think it is coming from me. Am I dying? Did somebody rape me again in my sleep?*

Mme Blanchard, who had raised three daughters of her own and was the only woman besides Aveline anywhere for miles, looked suddenly relieved and gave the girl a hug. "You're fine, my little one. Nobody did this to you. You're growing up, that's all. Come with me. We'll get you taken care of."

They went together into the bathroom, and Mme Blanchard helped Aveline clean herself up, gave her a clean nightgown and some towels and told her how to use them, and hugged her again.

"It might hurt you sometimes. That, too, is normal. Don't worry. And I'll come fix your bed later, so nobody else needs to bother over it. When you change out your towels, bring those to me too."

Aveline nodded gratefully and hugged the woman back. She padded back to her little closet room, clutching her stash of towels. She nearly jumped out of her skin when she ran into Willie Duncan, blushed furiously, and dashed into her room. She hoped he hadn't noticed what she held in her arms.

She sat at the foot of her bed with her legs crossed, hugging her blanket around herself and petting Sylvie, trying not to look at the blood on the bed, trying not to think that it was coming out of her.

She heard the sounds of breakfast being prepared, but she didn't move to help Mme Blanchard. She just sat, feeling lost.

Eventually her capitaine knocked on the door and poked his head in.

"Are you all right, lassie?" he asked, crouching beside her to get a better look in the dim light. "Not like you to not be underfoot in the kitchen at this hour."

She stared at him, her lips moving as if she wanted to speak, before jerking her head in the direction of the bloody blanket.

He saw it, but didn't react for a moment. He went off into some other sphere, remembering his naïveté. How, shortly after their marriage, Estelle had needed to explain menstruation to him. He had been perplexed by the whole idea of it, but mostly embarrassed. His ignorance clearly shocked her. It had rankled him a little that she knew more about the mechanics of sex and human bodies generally than he did, and she had no qualms about discussing it all over tea with him, educating him as casually as if it was weather they were talking about.

How would Estelle talk to Aveline if she were here? All *he* could think to do was issue the girl dire warnings to never let any man near her again, but he suspected she already wasn't too keen on that. He didn't want to scare her with harshness, but he needed her to recognize the potential consequences if she did, by some chance, have the urge to let any man be intimate with her.

Aveline wasn't sure what she had expected Graham to do,

but sitting there staring into space was not it. At last, when he came back to the present and held out his hand, she laid hers in it. He squeezed it, and his voice when he spoke was level and kind. "Aveline my dear, I have only one thing to say to you, and I want you to listen to me carefully. Now that your body has grown up this much, what the German did to you could make a baby if it were to happen again. You are far too young to be a mother. Do you understand me?"

She nodded, a little awed, both by the idea of having the ability to procreate and also by the dead-seriousness of his tone. He was not being one bit facetious. He meant it.

"Have you told Mme Blanchard?" he asked. She nodded, and he looked relieved. "Well, you ask her if you have any other questions, because a woman will be much better at this than I. Coming to breakfast?"

She shook her head. The hurting Mme Blanchard had warned her about had already started. She spent the rest of the morning curled on the bed, clutching at her stomach, tense and pale. It was the first time in two months Graham had been able to go anywhere without her at least asking to come along, and it surprised him, how accustomed he had grown to her ready presence. He certainly got a lot more work done without her hovering, but he was oddly cheered when she was once again getting underfoot later in the day.

TO AMIENS

AVELINE FOLLOWED CAPITAINE Graham to the stable and helped him get the horses ready for the ride to Amiens. By eight o'clock, they were on their way, the sky clear, the air warm, the countryside beautiful once one went far enough behind the lines. Aveline had grown up here, of course, and she wept silent tears as she watched it rolling past. How changed it had become in recent years. She could never go back to the life she'd known before, and her heart ached from not being able to speak her mind.

Her capitaine was not blind to her streaming tears. He put his arm around her, hugged her to his side and sang to her. She liked that. She pulled out her notebook and wrote: *I have never been so far from my farmhouse in my life. This is an adventure, isn't it?*

"Yes," he said. "It most certainly is."

They arrived shortly before noon and left the wagon and horses at military headquarters before walking off along the sunny street toward a café, where they had lunch before going to the cathedral, which Graham particularly wanted to visit.

"You just want tae hear your own voice echoing, aye," MacFie grumbled good-naturedly. He sat in a pew and folded his arms while Graham went to the front of the church and proceeded to give an impromptu recital to a few sightseers, who all clapped enthusiastically. He appeared to be enjoying himself immensely; Willie and Aveline took a stroll together around the vast room, looking at all the fine details and workmanship.

"He's got quite a voice, has he no?" Willie remarked.

Aveline beamed agreement.

"All the same, I'm hoping he doesna plan to stay here the rest of the afternoon. I want to take pictures! Maybe you should remind him he's the only one who really wanted to come to the cathedral..."

Aveline grinned. It was a shame to be indoors, even an indoors as grand as this, on such a clear and sunny day. She immediately went to her capitaine and demanded to go elsewhere. He scooped her up and swung her around with uncharacteristic exuberance, and the four of them left the place and walked along the street: an earl, a Traveller, a fisherman's son, and an orphan lass who looked like a boy, all thoroughly enjoying each other's unlikely company.

They went to a shop for some proper clothes for Aveline. She and her capitaine took such a long time, MacFie and Willie went outside to smoke while they waited.

"What do you want?" Capitaine Graham asked her. "Any frock you like, as long as it's suitable for traveling in. Estelle will take care of the rest of your wardrobe when you get to Scotland."

Aveline stared wide-eyed at the selection. She'd never had anything but the simplest clothes, and now before her was a feast of options. At last she chose a blue serge dress, sturdy and elegant, with lace at the collar and a plaid belt at the waist. He nodded his approval. They got a hat to match, and a pair of lovely black high-heeled boots with shiny buttons, and stockings and underthings.

When they came out at last, MacFie said, "All right now, let's find a pub, my lord?" He had such a patient persuasiveness in his tone that Graham actually laughed aloud and threw an arm around his friend's shoulder, and the four of them walked off again. Willie and Aveline followed a few paces behind. Willie carried Aveline's parcels for her, except for the shoes, which she insisted on taking herself. She was so full of joy at the sights of the city, and the shine in her eyes warmed Willie inside.

"It's nae wonder the Dread Staff Officers are clueless," MacFie remarked. He waved at the market stalls, the cafes, all appearing perfectly ordinary. "It's business as usual here. You'd hardly know there's a war on, would ye? And the portal of hell only a few miles awa'..."

WRITING BY BORROWED TORCHLIGHT IN THE WAGON ON THE WAY HOME

My capitaine is a grim sort of man usually, but today, I heard him laugh for the first time, quick and shy and full of light, and I am still glowing inside from hearing it. I think I will glow inside for days. Why does he not smile and laugh more? Is he worried about his family? He must be. And for his men and himself, and I suppose, perhaps, he even worries about me.

I wish I could properly tell him how precious he is to me. Dearer than anyone, ever. Even Armand. Armand loved me and did his best, but he didn't talk to me like an equal. I was just a baby sister to him. My capitaine treats me as if I am grown up. I like that.

He bought me new clothes today. I am a little scared of them. I have never seen such fine things, let alone worn any.

I know girls are supposed to look a certain way. Mr. George's daughters and Capitaine Graham's wife and the other women the men have photographs of, I have seen them, and I do not look like them. Dressed like I am, and with almost no hair! I never knew there was anything wrong or strange in my looks until I saw the men's photographs. But my capitaine does not seem to mind what I look like. I wonder if it matters, if it is wrong for me to feel I am safer and bolder when dressed like a boy. Maybe I will feel differently about it when I am in my new home.

Willie and Mr. MacFie came with us today. We had such a lovely time. Mr. MacFie is always quiet, and I never can tell what he is thinking, although he is always kind to me. Willie, though... When I look at him, and he looks at me, I get all warm. I am shy of him (sometimes), and somehow, I think I should be especially ashamed of how I must look to him, but as soon as he speaks to me, I forget that, and we have such fun together. It is as if he doesn't care what I look like, as if he likes me for being me. I like him. He took good care of me today at the cathedral and at the pub and everywhere in between, and now he keeps asking if I am cold and need a blanket.

I am sure I will like Scotland. It will be fine to go away from the noise of the guns and things. But also I know I will miss Willie. When I leave here, part of my heart will still be here in France with him, and that part of my heart wants to stay here and fight with him until the end.

DANCING AND OTHER THINGS

THE NEXT DAY, Capitaine Graham rode his horse beside the supply wagons and trucks, and Aveline sat behind him, her arms around him, laying her head against his back, quietly observing everything. She was glad they'd had their day in Amiens yesterday; today it was overcast, and occasionally it rained on them, but despite the clouds and damp, she liked this ride, just him and her. Restful and secure and safe. It wasn't convenient for her to write her thoughts to him while they rode, so she rolled them around her head, perfecting them like tumbled rocks until they returned home, and she could take out the notebook and share them with him: a sketch of some beautiful thing she had spotted that she wanted to remember, or questions for him to answer, or words she wanted to know in English.

When the supply runs had all been done for the day, Aveline sat on the floor of the great room at Graham's feet, leaning against his knees, listening as the men talked and laughed. Their words made more sense to her now, and she loved when they sang along to Graham's harmonica or piano playing. Another man had an accordion, another a drum, and several played pipes. There was something so intrinsically mournful about the sounds of all these instruments, no matter how lively the song, that her eyes would stream tears without knowing why. She ached to sing with them, to make any sound at all.

Willie pulled her to her feet and told the men to cheer up the music. "The lassie's to be a fine lady, is she no? Fine ladies need to learn to dance," he said. "Will ye play us a reel, lads?"

It worked. It was a perfect distraction. She learned quickly, and she liked being the absolute center of Willie's attention as he taught her the figures, and some of the others joined in.

After the rest of the men had all gone to bed, Aveline and Willie sat together while Graham finished a few tasks at his desk in the study.

Aveline pulled out her notebook and absorbed herself in sketching the lounging young man, lost in his own world on one of the long window seats with Sylvie curled up on him sleeping contentedly. She had to poke him to get his attention when she wrote, in a mixture of French and English, *Do you think I'm pretty?*

He considered a moment, watching the smoke from his cigarette rise upwards. "Aye," he said at last, not meeting her eyes. "Aye, you're bonny."

Even though I don't look like other girls?

He gave a small shrug, as if her looks were the least of his concerns. She sat on the floor, as close to him as she could get. *When I look at you, and you look at me, I get fluttery inside. I dinna ken why.* That was the latest phrase he'd taught her, and she was pardonably proud to be using it.

He still didn't look at her. "I ken," he said. "But Captain Graham widna like it if he heard you talk so."

Why?

He sighed.

"Avie," he said, turning and propping himself on one elbow, looking her straight in the eyes. Close enough she could feel his breath soft on her face. It felt very intimate, and she inhaled the scent of his smoke, closing her eyes in bliss. "Avie, you're no yet fourteen. I'm—well, no so much older than you really, but I'm supposed to be twenty. It widna be right."

I love you. I love Capitaine Graham more, but not the same way. I don't get fluttery inside when I'm close to him.

Willie laid one hand on her shoulder lightly. "Avie, it will be a punishable offense for anyone who tries to—to be intimate wi' you. Even if you want it. Captain Graham has made that clear."

But do you love me?

He returned to lounging, taking another deep drag on his cigarette. "I'm no answering that question. Dinna ask me. Please."

She perched on the two inches of window seat left between him and the edge, leaned over him, and touched his face. He was *so* good-looking. She felt very grown-up, and she wasn't fooled by his evasiveness. She knew he liked her.

"Please, Avie, run alang to bed," he groaned, turning his face away, but she leaned over him and kissed his cheek.

At that moment, Graham emerged from the study. Willie saw him before Aveline did. Aveline and Sylvie both tumbled to the floor as he shot to his feet, and Graham descended on Willie like a hawk. He got right in the younger man's face and hissed, "What the hell are you *doing*, Duncan? I've given explicit orders that nobody is to touch Aveline. She's vulnerable, and I will not have you seducing or manipulating her."

"Captain Graham, sir, let me explain—"

"I've half a mind to put you under discipline, Duncan."

"Sir," Willie said earnestly, "I will take any discipline you wish to give me, but I swear to ye I would never dream of harming her. Do whatever you want to me, but please, go easy on the girl. She means nae harm. She's just confused."

Graham glared grimly at him. Aveline tugged at his sleeve, and he brushed her away like a pesky fly. She didn't give up, though, and at last, he turned to her and she pointed to her notebook.

He didn't do anything wrong, Capitaine. It's my fault. He told me to go away, and I wouldn't. She looked at him, abject penitence in her eyes, and glanced apologetically to Willie.

Graham considered for a minute. "I'll let you off this time," he decided at last. "But don't let it happen again. That's an order."

"Understood, sir." Willie saluted smartly.

"Go to bed, Aveline."

She obeyed instantly, scurrying away.

Graham turned to follow her, but looked back and fixed Willie with a sharp penetrating stare. "Are you in love with her, Duncan?" he asked.

Willie's answer was a bit hesitant and evasive. He did not

meet Graham's eyes. "She's young, sir. I'm fair fond of her, of course. There's never a man here who isna fond of Aveline."

Graham continued to look at him. At last, deciding he would have to be satisfied with that, he nodded good night and went to say goodnight to Aveline.

He had no right to be *too* hard on Willie Duncan, he supposed. Estelle had been only two years older than Aveline when he'd met her. But the gap was far more frightening at fourteen and twenty than at sixteen and twenty-two, and Estelle had been nearly seventeen before Graham had kissed her, let alone talked of marriage with her.

He had no doubt Aveline thought herself capable of being in love, but the violence done her would likely lessen her inhibitions and blur her ability to make sound judgments. He supposed she could do worse than Willie Duncan, whose only real vice—if it counted as a vice—was smoking too much.

Graham went to Aveline's closet, candle in hand. She sat on her bed, hugging her knees, looking ready to cry. He beckoned her with his finger, and she came. He put his arm around her and said, "Give yourself a few years, lassie. I promise you'll be better off if you do. Don't let yourself get so caught up in Mr. Duncan that you forget you're going home with me."

Aveline didn't meet his eyes, only climbed into her bed, still holding his hand tightly. He sat beside her, waiting, until she had fallen asleep and he was able to extract his hand without waking her.

He sighed. It was high time she got out of here before anything further developed between her and Willie. Graham remembered the relatives of hers he was supposed to investigate. Sleep would have to wait; he went back to the study and made some telephone calls to Paris. Estelle had a cousin there who promised to check on the names Aveline had provided and get back to him.

THE REMAINING PERRAULTS

A FEW DAYS later, Estelle's cousin called back and said the grandfather, Armand-Marceau Perrault, had indeed died. But Philippe-Marceau Perrault, the other son, was still alive. He might want his niece. He gave Graham the address, and Graham sat down to write. He did hope the uncle would prove amiable, that all the rumors were exaggerated, and Armand's protectiveness of Aveline had been unwarranted. But he would proceed with caution. He found the idea of turning her over to a stranger distinctly unsettling. Buying Aveline new clothes had reinforced the idea that she was going home with him. Perhaps he should have waited—

Well, there was nothing to do now but write the man.

1 October 1916

Dear Philippe Perrault:

My name is Captain Augustus Graham. On 29 August, I found a girl in a barn on a deserted farm. Her name is Aveline Perrault. She will turn fourteen next month. She had been living on this farm with her brother, Armand, all her life until he was killed eleven days prior to my finding her. She kept herself alive on the scanty stores of provisions they still had in the house for all that time and became sadly malnourished. I have kept her here at the house where my men and I are billeted while I have made inquiries about her family. As her closest living relative, I would like to give you the opportunity to take her yourself, if you will. From what she has communicated to me, I gather there has been bad blood in the past between your family and her mother's family, but I am aware this may be exaggerated.

If you would like to arrange a visit with her, I can make it happen. If you do not think she will fit in with your family or are not interested in providing a home for her, my wife and I are willing to adopt her as our own. I have delayed sending Aveline to my wife until I hear from you what your preference is in this matter, so a prompt reply would be appreciated. I would like to get the girl out of the war zone as soon as possible.

Any information you can provide me regarding Aveline's parents and family would likewise be appreciated.

Sincerely,

Captain A. Graham

PRECONCEIVED IDEAS AND A DOCUMENT

GRAHAM RECEIVED THE answer to his letter late on the fourth dreary day after sending it. The men sat in the great room, taking their time finishing their suppers, or smoking and playing cards. Graham sat at the piano, playing and singing as he usually did in the evenings, but when MacFie waved him over with an envelope, he went and joined him at a card table. MacFie poured them each a whisky, but Graham didn't notice, as his mind was entirely focused on the letter.

> *Captain Graham:*
>
> *Thank you for your care of and interest in Aveline. Yes, she is my niece, and you are correct in your understanding of the situation. My father positively disapproved of my brother's marriage. He disinherited my brother and forbade me to have any contact with him, but I had received occasional news over the years.*
>
> *My father is dead. My wife is hesitant to have the girl come live with us; she is concerned about her upbringing and background, as, honestly, am I. If she is willing to go with you, we are willing to let you have her.*
>
> *As requested, I will tell you what I know of the girl's family. Marie, her mother, was the child of a whore in Amiens or Albert—I cannot recall which—and I don't know her name or family. Nobody decent would have had anything to do with her. My brother met Marie serving drinks at a tavern in Amiens when he went there on business for our father. He found excuses to stay there "for business," and six months went by before my father became suspicious. He investigated Marie's background and forbade any union, but my brother said he would give up everything to have her. She was*

already with child by that time, and my brother used this as an excuse and stubbornly refused to listen to reason.

My father offered Marie a substantial sum of money to give up my brother and relinquish any claim to the family name, but she declined to take it, and they were married in spite of our father. They tried to flatter him by naming their child Armand after him, but it changed nothing. I am sure they lived in grinding poverty, but my brother was too proud ever to come back to ask help. He died of polio shortly before Aveline was born, and I believe Armand also may have had polio.

The circumstances of Marie's death I do not know, but afterward, Armand wrote to my father asking for help, but my father wrote back saying it would be better for Armand and the girl to starve to death and relieve the world of their bastard existence.

Sincerely,

Philippe-Marceau Perrault

Graham crushed the paper in his hand. MacFie glanced over, and Graham tossed it to him. "Read that," he said.

MacFie raised an eyebrow and tossed it back. "I'd as soon listen."

Graham blushed deeply. He always forgot MacFie could barely read English, and this was in French. "Sorry," he murmured, and MacFie shrugged and puffed on his pipe, listening as Graham read it to him, barely containing his anger with Aveline's grandfather.

"Armand was thirteen, and Aveline hardly more than a baby, and he said that to his own blood?" Graham spluttered. "Why should children always have to pay for things that aren't their own fault? Why should they be marked for life for their parents' indiscretions?" He remembered Mlle Leclair. Suppose Marie's mother had been driven to a harlot's life by the entitled actions of a predator like his father, taking his pleasure and disposing of her when she became pregnant or too much a liability, and not by any choice of her own?

"My bairns are branded for life, too, for who their parents are," MacFie said, calmly. "They've done nae wrong, nor my wife and me, but they'll spend their lives under suspicion and prejudice because it's easier for regular folk to lump us all together as a pack of dirty thieves and beggars. People are afraid of the darkness in their own souls, and instead of working to get it out of themselves, they demonize someone else instead. Easier."

"That's not who your people are."

MacFie smiled slightly. "If Scotland was full of your kind and your lady's kind, it would be a better place for Travellers and orphan bairns both. But you cannae deny that we're used to this sort of thing, and you're not."

"Aye, you're right." Graham leaned his arms on the table, his gaze far away. "That uncle will consider her worthless now she's been raped."

"Aye. So take her hame wi' you." MacFie pushed the whisky towards Graham with one finger. "Drink up."

Graham tossed it back and turned to look across the room to the corner where Aveline, deeply involved in a poker game, was slaying her opponents. She sat cross-legged on the floor with her cat in her lap, while Willie Duncan and two others tried and failed to beat her.

"I canna believe you're no cheating," Willie complained loudly as Aveline grinned and raked in her loot of cigarettes.

"Look at her," Graham said to MacFie. "All that life and energy, and these relations of hers don't even want to meet her. They leap to the assumption she's unworthy, has no potential."

"I ken. Their loss, sir."

Graham disappeared into the study for a moment and returned with a few sheets of paper and a pen. He beckoned George over, and MacFie sat quietly while the brothers worked over a document together. After a good bit of animated discussion, Graham was satisfied at last, and he called to Aveline.

She came and sat at the now-crowded table. Graham explained about the letter from her uncle. "My brother has drawn up a document for your uncle to sign, handing you officially into my care. I want to see if you approve." He read it to her, George filling in and explaining the legal words Graham had no idea how to translate.

Aveline did approve. She was not much interested in the technicalities, and as soon as they were finished, she slid off Graham's knee to go barter her cigarettes with the men for more desirable items. Behind her, her capitaine was speaking again.

"I can arrange leave for you two to go to Paris tomorrow and have him sign this..."

LOVE SPEAKS

AVELINE WENT OUT the back door to where she knew Willie would be.

It was drizzling, and he stood leaning against the house, safe from the rain under the eaves, having a smoke on his last remaining cigarette. She stood close beside him, and for a long time, neither of them moved, watching the rain.

Aveline pulled out her notebook from her tunic pocket, scribbled busily, and handed it to Willie. He angled it to catch the faint light from the great room windows.

I can give you back fifteen of the cigarettes I won tonight.

"What happened to the other four?" he asked lightly.

She displayed three barely-used pencils in answer.

"And what is it you want of me? I'm suspicious of your motives, lassie."

I want you to kiss me.

He looked at her, incredulous, and he said, "Avie, did you no hear Captain Graham warn me just last week I wasna to touch you or else? Are you trying to get me into trouble?"

She took the fistful of cigarettes out of her other pocket and pressed them into his hand. He put them right back into her pocket and said, softly, "Avie, you canna buy or bargain for anyone's love. Love is a gift, and if you have to give something to someone to get it, it's no love anymore. If I kissed you, it would no be for me expecting anything in return. And I widna do it unless we both wanted it."

She remembered her capitaine's words. *Only if both people want it.* And she understood in a flash what it meant that the German had done. He had stolen her body and her self-respect, and tears sprung unbidden to her eyes. She was sure all at once she *couldn't* ask Willie to love her, let alone kiss her, when she had nothing left of herself to give him in return. She turned away from him, trying to stifle a sob.

"Avie-lass, what's wrong?" he asked, alarmed at her tears. He lightly touched her shoulder, drew her close into his arms. She buried her face in his coat. "Shh, now, tell Willie your troubles."

Aveline wanted to use her voice. She was tired of having to write everything. She tried to force sound out of her throat, but again she failed. So she drew back, wiped her nose with her sleeve, and took her pencil again. *The German stole everything from me.*

"Who told you such dirt?"

Nobody, except Capitaine says what the German did is only supposed to happen between people who want it, and now I'll never know what it is like because he took everything away from me.

"He didna," Willie objected without hesitation. "He couldna take your mind or your heart. Those are yours always. You can share them if you like, but nobody can *take* them. *Comprends?*" He laid one hand against the side of her upturned face, and she nodded. They were quiet for some moments, and Aveline nestled back into him, and he held her lightly, resting his cheek on her hair, and she whispered easily:

"You are so kind to me."

Willie, startled, took her shoulders and stooped to peer into her eyes.

"Am I imagining it, or did you just speak to me?" he said, excitement in his voice. "Avie!"

Her mouth dropped open. "I didn't even notice," she said, and she grinned and tore away from him and ran inside.

Willie paused on the doorstep, watching with a pang of unexpected exclusion as the girl threw her arms around Captain Graham, bouncing with joy as she whispered in his ear. He spun her around, beaming his rare smile on her.

Willie quietly found his way to his favorite window seat and did his best to be invisible, reaching into his pocket for another cigarette. There weren't any left, but that was his own fault for letting himself get hooked into another of Aveline's poker games of doom. He sighed, eyes riveted on the vibrantly joyful girl, who now whirled around with Sylvie, whose narrowed eyes clearly conveyed her vexation.

He remembered how trustingly she had come into his embrace, and wished she was still there.

PART NINE

1901-1909

Inverness-shire, Scotland

THE THIRTEENTH EARL
AND HIS BROTHER

GEORGE'S TELEGRAM NOTIFYING Graham of his father's death came to him in Gibraltar. Even for a telegram, it lacked any emotion, saying simply, "Father dead. Come home."

Graham burst into tears—not of sorrow, but of sheer relief. He was glad he had taken the telegram someplace private to read, so he did not have to explain his reaction to the other men. He arranged right away to get leave. It wasn't out of any sense of sadness for the loss of his father; it was an excuse to leave the tedium of his life on Gibraltar a while, and he gladly seized the opportunity.

He arrived on a rainy morning at the end of November. George waited at the castle for him. The brothers seized each other in a ferocious-looking embrace.

"Missed you," George said. "It seems strange, knowing my lifetime of intervention between you and the old man is over."

"How did it happen?" Graham asked as George settled into a chair before the fire.

"The doctor believes he had a stroke sometime in the night. Nobody heard him call for help, and he wasn't found until mid-morning. Not that there'd have been much to be done. He was nearly eighty, after all."

Graham did not sit. He paced, his hands clasped behind his back, restlessly twitching. "It's all mine now," he mused.

"Aye, all yours, Lord Inverlochy."

It startled Graham to be addressed by his father's title instead of "Lord Kirkhill", and he turned to George. "Do you mind? Do you really not mind not being the heir?"

"Don't care one whit," George said firmly. "I'm free to do as I like. You aren't. I do not envy that."

"Aye, I get the burden. It's not fair," Graham said, "that he should die so uneventfully after all those years of showering me with every abuse in the book, and the way he cheated on Mother and neglected her. Poor lonely, unfulfilled Mother. He hurt her worse than he hurt me, I think."

George laughed humorlessly. "Folks at his funeral talked about his military service and decorations and public honor. I was glad you weren't there. It was hard enough for me to take, and I'm not the one he beat up all the time. I wanted to tell them all how mean he was to you, how he treated his dogs better than he did you. But I didn't say anything. Pretty sure my silence was enough."

The rain trailed down the glass, distorting Graham's view. "I'd never have signed on for six years, *like he demanded I do,* if I'd known he would die so soon after. It feels like one last cruel joke."

"Rather," agreed George. There was a long silence.

"Do you suppose any of our governesses were dismissed for being with child?" Graham asked out of the blue.

"Wouldn't surprise me," George said. "He only liked virgins, though. I find it hard to believe he'd have been that unlucky with *all* of them."

"How in the world do you know that?"

"It's in his journals."

"He wrote about his encounters?" Graham looked as if he might be sick right there.

"In lurid detail. With dates and commentary about how much they screamed and the—"

"Stop," Graham said, cutting him off with force.

George joined him at the window and laid a hand on his brother's arm. "Are you still put off by sex?"

Graham stood quiet a long time, thinking back to the day in the stableyard when his father had threatened to find a whore to do him over, and when he answered, his eyes were shaded. He said softly, "So far, I've proved the old man wrong."

George did not ask what he meant. Graham knew neither of them would ever forget that day.

"You don't even pleasure yourself?"

Graham glared at him. "I do not."

"If you ask me, you desperately need a girl. You'd loosen up if you had one."

"What do you mean, 'loosen up'?" Graham folded his arms and lifted his chin defiantly.

"You're so tense all the time. Girls can help ease that."

"Music is all I require to calm myself, thank you. And I *didn't* ask you."

George shrugged again. "Have it your way, then," he said. "But I still say you'd do well to chuck your vow of celibacy and find a girl. Father's dead. It's your life now, and you shouldn't let his bad behavior color your entire life blue."

Graham drifted into the world of his own head a while. To be truthful, he had resigned himself to the idea that eventually his father would choose a wife for him, and he'd have no say in the matter. It was not that pretty girls never stirred anything inside him; he just couldn't allow himself to care for a woman while knowing he could never have her. Not to mention he was outright scared of causing hurt of any kind to any woman. No, he couldn't let his guard down for a minute. It was safer to remain unentangled.

George draped his arm over his brother's shoulders. "You do know there are ways to have fun with a girl without having to worry about ruining your reputation?"

Graham jerked back to the present. "I am not worried about my reputation. What about *hers*?"

"I would recommend trying out one whose reputation's already ruined. Or a married woman. They know what to do. Then you use what you learn on a girl you like."

"Shut up, George," Graham interrupted with disgust. "'Drink waters out of thine own cistern—'"

George sighed. His brother's religious fervor might be an understated part of his life, but he still found it annoying. "Stop quoting at me."

"I'll stop quoting if you stop suggesting I seek out cheap sex."

"It's not cheap sex," George insisted.

"It's not the kind I want," Graham said. "Are you going to shut up now, or shall I quote some more?"

"I'll shut up," George said, assuming the air of a martyr.

Fortunately, Bates came in to announce that lunch was ready and put an end to the storm before it had time to become a hurricane.

CHANCE ENCOUNTER

AFTER GEORGE WENT back to Oxford, Graham holed up in his father's study in the castle, throwing his father's vile journals into the fire and creating long lists of things his staff should do in his absence. Mostly this involved removing all his father's personal effects, updating the plumbing, and installing a telephone. He rode around the estate to talk to everyone and find out how things stood, and had long conferences with Bates and other long-time servants (his father had taught him nothing about what ought to be done). But the house was so devoid of non-servant human company that, after only two weeks, he began feeling a little twitchy.

He packed his bags and went to Edinburgh, where he got a room in a hotel for the night and was surprised to run into an old classmate in the dining room. Horace Cunningham, the third son of an English lord and a Scottish baron's daughter, had been at both Eton and the military academy with Graham. Cunningham had come to Edinburgh for Christmas with his family.

"I'm on my way back to Gibraltar," Graham explained. "I don't have to leave for a few days yet, but I thought I'd catch a concert or two in London on my way."

"You and your concerts," his friend laughed. "I have a better idea. Lord and Lady Livingston's Christmas party is tomorrow night. I wasn't able to go last year, but I'm always invited, and you could come with me. It'd be smashing! Mother and Father and my sisters will be there too. They'd love to see you."

"I don't know Lord and Lady Livingston," Graham said. "I can't come to their party!"

"You *should* know them. Wonderful people. They won't mind if you tag along. I often bring friends with me to their parties. My mother is a friend of Lady Livingston." Cunningham paused, grinning. "And they have the finest piano in Linlithgowshire. They might let you play it."

Graham wavered. Cunningham went on. "And they will have

the best musicians you'll ever find at a Christmastide party. Only the best for Lady Livingston and her daughter, both lovers of music only surpassed by, perhaps, *you*."

Fine music in a more intimate setting than a London concert hall was just the thing Graham needed to entice him away from his former plans. "All right," he said at last. "I'll come. When do we leave?"

"I'll meet you here at six tomorrow."

A MELODY,
SWEETLY PLAYED IN TUNE

WHEN GRAHAM AND Horace Cunningham walked into Livingston House the next night, the place dazzled him— airy and light and swarming with well-dressed people—such a change from his own gloomy, quiet castle. A maid took their hats and wraps and directed them to the parlor with the huge Christmas tree. A number of young people played some variant of blind man's bluff on one side of the room while, on the other side, their chaperones and parents sipped wine and gossiped. Graham's and Cunningham's uniforms arrested the attention of many young ladies, who blushed and whispered behind their fans, but Graham noticed one particular girl immediately. She did not play with the other young people, nor bat her eyelashes at anyone from behind her fan. She sat demurely beside several other young ladies, pretty and blonde and sparkling. Not with the sparkle of jewels, although she wore a diamond pendant at her throat, but something from inside herself, her direct and honest eyes, her queenly self-confidence, her rippling laugh. Everyone not involved in the game, girls and boys alike, clustered around her, and Graham's own vision homed in on her like a compass to north; as if, lost in a storm-tossed sea, he had caught a glimpse of the lighthouse which would guide him home.

Cunningham caught him gawping and grinned. He leaned closer and said in undertones, "I take it you've not met the Earl of Livingston's daughter, eh, Graham?"

"I have not," Graham said, his voice hushed. His eyes were fixed on the girl, and she looked him straight in the eye and beamed at him warmly, and he knew he must accept the unspoken invitation. "Introduce me?"

Cunningham gladly obliged him. "Lady Estelle, may I introduce Lieutenant Augustus Graham, Earl of Inverlochy, home from Gibraltar on leave."

"Good evening, Mr. Cunningham," she said pleasantly. *Her voice is low and sweet, and dark blue is her e'e...* Graham was sure he would never speak again, so constricted did his throat become at the sight of her.

"Pleased to meet *you*, Lord Inverlochy," she added demurely, and held out her hand in its white satin glove. He bent to kiss it.

Their eyes met again, and he heard himself say, "May I have the pleasure of dancing with you, Lady Estelle?" He was surprised at his boldness, that he'd managed to speak at all, but she smiled brightly and handed him her dance card. Two blanks remained, for a mazurka and a waltz. Uncharacteristically impulsive and smitten by her beauty, he filled them both in.

"You have chosen wisely, my lady," Cunningham said. "There will be no better dance partner this evening. Or so I'm told by dozens of young ladies. Perhaps you can get him to sing for you as well." He winked meaningfully at Graham, and she lit up, saying she would be happy to accompany Graham if he would sing.

Graham tried to get out of it, shy of his talents being volunteered, but before he could manage an escape, Horace and Lady Estelle had him over at the piano.

"What will it be, Lord Inverlochy?" she asked, her fine face turned up to him as she motioned to the stack of the music before her.

He paged through the music, his heart quivering with a new intensity and purpose he did not wholly understand, a desire to do anything this girl required of him, if it would only give him a few moments near her. He felt as though the wind had been punched straight out of him. He must choose something romantic, but not something that would be considered fresh. At last, he settled on a Burns ballad, patriotic as well as neutrally respectable. He handed it to her. "This," he said, and her smile widened.

"One of my favorites," she said approvingly.

The sight of her pretty hands dancing over the ivories so

enchanted him that he missed his cue the first time, and she laughed at him. But it was not an unkind laugh, and oh, he loved the sound of it. The faintest flicker of a smile touched Graham's own lips. The second time, he paid attention and sang the song properly. He felt keener to impress this young lady than he had ever had reason or motivation to impress anyone else, ever, even his voice teachers, even Peter Davies.

> *O my Luve is like a red, red rose*
> *That's newly sprung in June;*
> *O my Luve is like a melody*
> *That's sweetly played in tune.*
> *So fair art thou, my bonnie lass,*
> *So deep in luve am I;*
> *And I will luve thee still, my dear,*
> *Till a' the seas gang dry.*

> *Till a' the seas gang dry, my dear,*
> *And the rocks melt wi' the sun;*
> *I will love thee still, my dear,*
> *While the sands o' life shall run.*
> *And fare thee weel, my only luve!*
> *And fare thee weel awhile!*
> *And I will come again, my luve,*
> *Though it were ten thousand mile.*

He did not trust himself to make it through the song if he looked at her, so he fixed his gaze on a potted fern across the room instead. But as the song ended, he allowed himself to turn towards her, ostensibly to bow in thanks for accompanying him, and their eyes locked, and he knew there was something fluttering to life in him in response to something warm and inviting in her. The walls carefully built about his heart over the last thirteen years had been smashed into by the battering ram of this girl's winsome smile, leaving hairline cracks, and he hardly noticed it happening.

"You sing beautifully, Lord Inverlochy," she said softly.

"Thank you," he said, transfixed.

"Come, meet my mother," she said, rising from her bench.

He offered her his arm, and she guided him to her parents. "Mother, this is Lieutenant Graham, Earl of Inverlochy. He's a friend of Mr. Cunningham's. He's on his way back to Gibraltar."

Her mother raised her eyebrows slightly. But she gave him her hand and, in her turn, introduced Graham to her husband.

"You sing well, my boy," Lord Livingston said, shaking his hand warmly, putting Graham at his ease right away. "Perhaps you will sing for us again after dinner—a Christmas carol, or something festive like that?"

"I would be happy to," Graham said.

"And after that, there is a lovely new piece from America I'd love you to sing," Lady Estelle put in.

"You mustn't monopolize the young man's time, my dear," her mother rebuked her. "He didn't come tonight expecting to give us a recital."

"It's all right, Lady Livingston," he said graciously with a little bow. "I would be honored to sing both for you."

"I should have asked if you can read music on sight," Estelle said, still blushing from her mother's reprimand.

"Oh," he said, wishing she wouldn't feel badly about it, but not knowing how to reassure her. He didn't want to sound self-important by mentioning his extensive training. "Yes, I can."

At dinner, his eyes kept drifting along the table to the sparkling Lady Estelle, and his ears strained to catch the sound of her voice.

Afterward, Lord Livingston sought him out and ushered him to the piano again.

"What would you like, Lady Livingston?" he asked, sensing that the countess was highly protective of her daughter and needed winning over. "*Peut-être un chant en français?*"

"Perhaps," she said, eyeing him curiously. He was perceptive. He'd caught the remaining trace of her native accent. "But my favorite Christmas hymn is not French, it is German. Do you know '*Es ist ein Ros entsprungen*'?"

"My German isn't perfect, but I have sung it before."

"I'm afraid this key isn't suitable for Lord Inverlochy, Mother," Estelle interrupted, taking the music from her mother's hand and scrutinizing it.

The urge to show off overtook him. "May I?" He gestured toward the bench. She stood aside while he played a few tentative chords, eyes closed, feeling the music under his fingers. Horace Cunningham had been right; this piano was even better than his own, a pure *delight*. Then he accompanied himself singing the requested song.

When he finished, he saw Estelle's eyes regarding him with serious admiration. He rose quickly and said, "I believe there was another song you wished me to sing, Lady Estelle?"

"Yes," she said, softly. She seated herself again, fixing her eyes on him for a moment before turning through the music to find the song she wanted. He stood behind her, reading along as she played her piece once. He longed to rest his hands on her white and lovely shoulders, but he clasped them behind his back tightly instead and sang. It was a sweet, tragic song, and she surprised him by joining him on the chorus, her voice harmonizing with his.

They are roaming in the gloaming
Where the roses were in bloom,
Just a soldier and his sweetheart staunch and true.

But her heart is filled with sorrow,
And her thoughts are of tomorrow,
As she pins a rose upon his coat of blue.
"Do not ask me, love, to linger,
for you know not what you say,
When my duty calls, my sweetheart's voice is vain,
But your heart need not be sighing,
If I'm not among the dying,
I'll be with you when the roses bloom again.

When the roses bloom again beside the river
And the robin redbreast sings his sweet refrain,
As in days of Auld Lang Syne,
I'll be with you, sweetheart mine,
I'll be with you when the roses bloom again.

The guests applauded enthusiastically, and Graham blushed, giving the slightest of bows before sidling shyly into the sidelines. Much as he had thoroughly enjoyed himself, he knew had been in the spotlight for three songs too many at this point, at a party whose hosts hadn't personally invited him.

When it came his turn to dance with Lady Estelle, he treasured each second he got with her, whirling her about the floor, slender and light as a feather in his arms. "That was a lovely song," he said, and she beamed at him prettily. "Thank you for asking me to sing it. I had not heard it before."

"It's one of my new favorites," she confessed, and when he dropped to one knee so she could dance around him, she bent to his ear and, almost too low for him to hear, added, "I'd pin a rose to your coat of blue."

"I would wear it more proudly than a dozen Victoria Crosses," he replied promptly and sucked in his breath in shock that he had spoken such bold and shameless words aloud. But she only smiled.

He found himself wanting to kiss the top of her gleaming golden head, and the unexpected impulse distressed him. He'd just met this girl; how in the *world* could he already be so taken with her? Surely she was only flirting and did not think seriously of him. But oh, how he wished she was sincere.

His parents were dead. *He* was Earl of Inverlochy now, and he made a decision during that dance. George had been right. He *should* take charge of his own life. He would have this girl—if he could, by any miracle, convince her to fall in love with him.

After their second dance, even more delightful than the first, she took one of the roses from the bunch at her waist and pinned it to his coat and winked at him. "Merry Christmas, Lord Inverlochy," she whispered.

He bowed, speechless, and she fluttered her fan and waited for her next dance partner to come fetch her. He did not catch her eyes again, but he noticed her coolness and formality with the young man she danced with after him. He imagined it was still him and not another man holding her, and all the while, his mind went in circles. Was she spoken for already? He had to find out.

Horace Cunningham fetched him not long afterward so they could be on their way back into town for the night. Graham wanted to catch a little sleep before getting on the morning train to London.

ROSES

THEY RODE ALONG in amiable silence for about ten minutes. Graham, absently humming snatches of "When the Roses Bloom Again," gazed out into the blackness of the night through the window of the carriage.

"She's quite a lass, isn't she?" Cunningham said, breaking the silence.

"Who?" Graham asked, distractedly.

"Lady Estelle, of course," said Cunningham, laughing. When Graham didn't answer, he added, "She liked you."

"You think?"

"Yes. Grim as you are, I can't fathom why—but I've never seen her so taken with anyone."

Graham's pulse quickened, and he struggled to find a response. "Aye," he agreed, "she is quite a lass." Then, attempting to sound casual: "Do you know her well?"

"Have for years," Cunningham said. "Our mothers are friends. When we were children, we played together, she and my sisters and I. Lady Estelle is no ordinary girl. Bit of a handful." He laughed. "She turned sixteen a couple of months ago. Rather stubborn and opinionated. Says whatever she wants and exactly what she means. She'd like to be a suffragette. But she's also relentlessly good-natured and kind and always defending anyone who's being unjustly treated."

"Oh?"

"I've been told she says she'll throw herself out the tower window of her home if she doesn't like the man her father chooses for her to marry. I must say, she latched onto *you* with astonishing speed. As I said, I can't say I know why. No offense, old man, but you're hardly a ladykiller."

Graham, well aware of his awkwardness with women, took no offence. A wave of relief washed over him. *She was not taken.* She wasn't even old enough to officially be out yet. It had certainly *seemed* tonight as if she was attracted to him, so perhaps he had a chance.

In his room after Horace left him, Graham carefully unpinned the rose from his coat and cupped it in his hands: pale pink, half blown, and lovely in its perfection as its giver had been. He kissed it.

All the songs he had sung with or for her tonight had been about roses. Even her name had roses in it. She'd had it written out on her dance card: *Lady Estelle Alexandra Bellerose-Moncrieffe.*

What had she seen in him?

He did not understand what had happened. In one evening—in only a few minutes—his entire wall of self-imposed celibacy had crumbled to rubble around him, and he understood what it was to want someone so much, one would give up everything comforting and familiar to have her.

But not in the way his father would do, not as a disposable thing. He wanted Lady Estelle as his wife, and he would be faithful and kind to her and love her the best he knew how. He would cherish her, give her the kind of love his father would call soppy and mock mercilessly—but what had his father ever known about anything, besides self-indulgent lust and exercise of power?

He blew out the lamp and curled up under his blankets. Closing his eyes, he let his mind wander until he had a vision of his gloomy, quiet castle transformed into a place where love drove out the darkness, and the sound of music and lively children relieved the silence. Whether this was only a dream or a reality that could be grasped, he determined to find out.

LADY ESTELLE IN LOVE

IN HER OWN room, around three-thirty in the morning, Estelle took off her dress and flopped onto her bed, opened her dance card and lightly traced her fingers over one name in particular, written over twice in quirky, unorthodox handwriting: Lt. A. E. J. Graham. She kissed it, rolled onto her back, and lay with it clasped over her heart, warm and giddy inside.

He wasn't particularly handsome, but oh, his voice. So rich and full and deep when he sang, with a clarity rare in a baritone, and unapologetically Scottish when he spoke. Even before he'd sung, she was captivated by his diffidence. Not a single other man with whom she had danced tonight had come close to his grace and dignity, and—and also, when his eyes met hers, a warm feeling had stirred inside her that she'd never felt before.

I would wear it more proudly than a dozen Victoria Crosses. She shivered with pleasure at the memory. Somehow she knew he really meant it. He didn't seem capable of saying pretty things just to flirt. He was so *serious*. A little worried-looking. Utterly earnest.

And fare thee weel, my only luve!
And fare thee weel awhile!
And I will come again, my luve,
Though it were ten thousand mile.

It had been a promise. She was sure it had been a promise.

WRITING LETTERS TO A LADY

EVEN BEFORE HE left England, Graham wanted to write Estelle a letter, but he struggled so much over what to say, he was well on his way back to Gibraltar before he even tried. He spent a long time with scraps of paper, agonizing, scratching out and rewriting and crumpling the paper and starting over at least two dozen times. When, at last, he had composed a satisfactory draft, he lined up his ruled paper carefully under his best stationery, nicked from his father's study. It had the family coat of arms and address embossed on it but no name—elegant and impressive, he hoped—and at last, he wrote, forming his letters as carefully and tidily as possible. Having never been one to waste time perfecting his penmanship when he could perfect his voice instead, his handwriting was a legible but odd backhand scrawl, and he felt self-conscious, wondering if she would disapprove. But she had seen his handwriting before on her dance card. It wouldn't be a complete shock.

For goodness' sake, Graham, you are ridiculous, overthinking something so trivial! If she decides you're not worthy of her because of your handwriting, she's not worth your time.

He bit his lip, dipped his pen in the ink, and wrote.

16 January 1902

Dear Lady Estelle,

I am not sure if you remember me from your family's lovely Christmas party on 14 December. I thank you for your gracious acceptance of my unexpected presence in company with Mr. Horace Cunningham. I had a most excellent evening. It has been a long time since I have enjoyed such company as your gathering afforded me. I have only one brother, my younger twin, and he lives in Oxford. I would have had no Christmas at all otherwise. Perhaps you know my father recently died (my mother has been gone for a few years already). My home, Inverlochy Castle, is inhabited only by staff until I come home again. It is a bleak and lonely place at the best of times.

I wanted to ask if I might be permitted to write to you from Gibraltar. It gets rather lonesome here, so far away from all that is familiar, and I miss Scotland tremendously when I am away. Gibraltar has its beauty, but it is not home.

Yours truly
Lt. Graham, Lord Inverlochy

THE MORNING POST AT
LIVINGSTON HOUSE

"LETTER FOR YOU, Estelle," her father said at the breakfast table one Saturday morning. She stuffed the last bit of scone in her mouth, took the letter, and examined the postmark. Her heart leapt.

"Gibraltar?" she said aloud, forgetting her mouthful of scone. The flush creeping over her cheeks belied the surprise indicated by her words. "Who is writing me from Gibraltar?" She hardly dared to believe she was actually receiving the longed-for letter from the man she had fallen in love with. It had been an entire month since the party; she had almost abandoned hope. She slit open the envelope carefully. She didn't have to look at the signature; she had recognized the handwriting at once. Her heart beat a bit faster. "Oh, it's from Lord Inverlochy!" she exclaimed. "I *did* so like him!"

"Estelle," said her mother sternly. "Give the letter to me at once. And *do* swallow your food before you speak. You aren't five."

Estelle held it out of her mother's reach and scanned it quickly. "He's thanking us for the lovely party. Oh, the poor man had no other Christmas! And he is asking if you will permit him to write to me." She handed over the letter.

"You mustn't push yourself on him," her mother said. "I was scandalized at your behavior at the party." She turned to Lord Livingston. "I don't know, my dear. She's only sixteen. Ought we let her write to him?"

"I liked him," her husband replied promptly. "I don't know his family personally, but he appeared a proper fellow, and if Estelle approves of him, that's something we ought to encourage, don't you suppose? Since she's so dead set on choosing her own husband."

"It is our patriotic duty to keep up the morale of our soldiers," Estelle put in, earnest and lofty.

"You never cared a whit about patriotic duty before." Her father winked at her, and she knew she'd won.

"One must start sometime," she said, nobly.

"He says nothing of marriage," her mother said, striking the letter with her hand. "Nothing at all! She's not even out yet. I will not have him toying with my only child's affections!"

In the end, Estelle and her father won the argument, under the condition that correspondence would be broken off immediately if one single thing were revealed to be unsavory about him.

20 February 1902

Dear Lord Inverlochy,

Of course, I remember you. You are not so forget-table as you seem to think yourself. I am glad our party brought cheer to you at Christmas, and I am sorry you did not have a proper celebration with family. Your singing (and playing!) was sensational. Our friends are still saying how they wish they could have you at their parties. I think you missed your true calling!

I would be happy to write to you, and my parents have granted permission. They agreed with me when I said it was our patriotic duty to help our British army's morale, and I am pleased to do my part. I come home from school at the weekends, so you can send letters to my home, and I will get them. I would far sooner have Daddy read them than my headmistress. She is a terror. It is rather a shame not to have something to make the girls jealous over, though. Perhaps you could send just one to St. Leonard's?

Tell me what you do there and what it is like in Gibraltar. I expect it must be exciting and a good deal sunnier than here. I have been to France many times to visit my mother's relatives, and once we went to Italy, but I haven't traveled anywhere else. Sometimes it is terribly dull being a girl, sitting at home doing needle-work and knitting stockings. I wish I could go to South Africa, as a military nurse or, even better, an ambu-lance driver. Mother is reading over my shoulder and says not to be ridiculous, but I don't agree with her. My father has promised to teach me to drive his new automobile this summer. Mother doesn't approve of that either, but I am sure it will be a Tremendously Useful Skill.

I am

Sincerely,

Lady Estelle

P.S. What do the E and J stand for that you wrote on my dance card?

P.P.S. Do you speak French?

4 March 1902

Dear Lady Estelle,

I admit I forgot you would still be going to school. Mr. Cunningham told me you were sixteen, but you seemed older. As requested, I will send this one to St. Leonard's.

I would be much happier here if I had anything significant to do. It is not as if I am going to war; I do nothing heroic or exciting. All routine. I like quiet, and I like routine, but I must admit I like both better on my own terms.

I did miss my calling. I wanted to be a musician, but my father refused to accommodate me on that wish. My mother, a fine flautist, taught me the rudiments of playing from a very young age. I have had vocal training since I entered school at nearly eight years old, and I have played the piano as long. The army was my father's idea. He named me Augustus after the Caesar, with visions of my going out in blazing glory to conquer for king and country, and I have always been a great disappointment to him. I hate my name. So pretentious and unsuited to me. That is why I prefer simply Graham, which (conveniently) is what I'm generally called anyway, at school and in the army. I am good at what I do, do not misunderstand me—one can do well at anything if one tries, I suppose—but I would be happier following my own inclination, which is music.

I do speak French. Likely not as well as you, but I am

fairly fluent. I learned it in school along with Italian, in order to perform foreign music better. I had a series of French governesses, and one lad in my house at Eton was French.

I appreciate the tedium with which you associate knitting. Because I can only play my harmonica for so long before the men launch into throwing things at me, I have taken to combatting my boredom by darning everyone's stockings. I expect I shall someday be awarded a medal for this valiant service.

Driving an automobile would indeed be useful. I expect someday we all will need to know how. I have resisted the urge thus far myself, but I am so fond of my horse, it seems traitorous to exchange him for a noisy machine, and I am the only one needing transport at home at the moment. His name is Altair, a black Arabian. I have had him since I was sixteen and broke him in myself.

When I come home, may I call upon you?

Lieutenant A. (Edmund James) Graham

28 March 1902

Dear Lord Inverlochy,

Your endless list of talents astounds me. Playing the harmonica and darning socks! You do make it sound as if you never have any fun, though. I hope that isn't the case.

I will confess to you that you happened along the very first time Mummy allowed me to stay up for the dancing and have a proper grown-up dress. What luck for me! I blush to imagine what you would think if you saw me as I usually am, in my babyish school clothes and my hair in beribboned plaits.

The girls were all over me about your letter, wondering who my foreign admirer might be. (I didn't open it until I got home, of course. I swore to Mummy I would not be secretive.) But it is glorious, having something to play lady of mystery about. I drop hints occasionally, and it drives them positively mad. Such fun!

It has rained so much, we have not been able to do anything outdoors for the last week. I am becoming unbearably restless. I am expecting some friends this weekend, however, when I go home. That will be a pleasant diversion.

Altair sounds like a fine horse indeed. I don't have one that is particularly mine, but I like to ride my mother's mare. My father doesn't want me riding the more temperamental ones. How dull. My friends tell me I am lucky to be an only child, but I suspect my parents would be less fearfully protective of me if they had a few spares. Mummy says, "Don't be flippant, child." All the same, someday I shall have a houseful of children.

Daddy says he would love to have you visit our home. He liked you very much.

Lady Estelle

Estelle set down her pen, rested her chin in her hands, and closed her eyes, letting her mind drift. She imagined Lord Inverlochy on Altair, fine and straight. "How I should like to ride Altair with him," she thought, and pictured sitting in front of him, the world speeding past in a blur of heather-tinted sunset. Mostly she wanted the firm pressure of his arms around her, holding her tight. Maybe he'd even lean forward and steal a kiss...

"Well, have you finished?" Her mother's voice startled Estelle out of her happy fantasy.

"Yes, Mummy," Estelle sighed, dutifully handing over the letter for a final inspection. "Oh, Mummy?"

"Hmm?"

"May I send him one of the photographs I just had done? I have one left."

Lady Livingston peered over the tops of her spectacles, and Estelle beamed winsomely. "To cheer him up! Wouldn't it be nice?"

Her mother didn't say no.

14 April 1902

My dear Lady Estelle,

Indeed we have ways to amuse ourselves here. But my ideas of pleasure do not coincide with most men's, and most often, I am left to my own devices, which suits me perfectly.

My favorite way to spend an off-duty evening is to climb the rock of Gibraltar and sing from its peak. My only audience there is an appreciative crowd of Barbary apes, but any audience is better than none, aye?

I am quite certain the sight of you in school clothes would make little difference. A person is still the same inside no matter what they are wearing, don't you think?

Thank you for the photograph. I have propped it on my nightstand between my harmonica and sewing kit, like some sort of Soteria, to watch over things. I offer one of myself in return, although I hardly think the likeness worth wasting good paper on.

Yours,
Lt. Graham

She should not gush. She must not. But the photograph, when it fell out of its envelope, made Estelle squeal with delight all the same. Her schoolmate, Diana, who was spending the weekend at Livingston House with Estelle, snatched it up, took one look, and tossed it aside with a sniff. *"That's* what you've gone all soppy over, Stell?"

Estelle cradled it protectively, lying back on her pillow to inspect it more closely. "Don't be unkind," she scolded. "He's not so bad, really. Anyway, you haven't met him."

"If you say so." Diana shrugged and flopped onto her own bed, and Estelle traced her fingertip over the photo.

"Augustus Edmund James," she whispered. "Someday, if I am very lucky, I shall be allowed to call you something besides 'Lord Inverlochy', but Augustus doesn't fit you at all, and Edmund is stuffy. That leaves James... a good solid name. James? Jamie. I shall call you Jamie." She turned to Diana and said, "It seems positively scandalous to have a man in here staring at us in our nightclothes. We shall have to turn him toward the wall when we're dressing."

Diana chucked a pillow at Estelle, and they both giggled.

"As if you'll be leaving him all alone in here all day. Bet you hide him in your maths book so you have something to look forward to."

15 May 1902

Dear Lord Inverlochy,

I am jealous of the Barbary apes. If I could play half as effortlessly as you, I would be the happiest girl alive. I practice for hours each day, but I simply cannot understand how you transposed that song for my mother out of your head like you did at the Christmas party.

This week, several of my friends and I have been busy writing letters to every government person we can think of to ask them to let women have the vote. I say ask; we aren't quite that subtle. We have a sort of women's suffrage club at school. It's not official; the headmistress disapproves and has her eye on me because I am the ringleader, she says. But there are six girls besides me who regularly meet (on the sly, of course) to concoct ways we can be a collective nuisance to the old men who don't want us to have a say. Perhaps by the time we are old enough to vote, things will be different! Do I shock you with my radical views?

We are going to London next weekend since Mummy must go to the flower show. I will write again when we come back and tell you all about it.

Yours,
Lady Estelle

30 June 1902

My dear Lady Estelle,

Mr. Cunningham told me you wanted to be a suffragette. I do not find this shocking or surprising. At any rate, I don't see why women shouldn't vote, especially ones as fearless, intelligent, and articulate as you.

By the time this reaches you, I will be on my way back to Scotland. I hope you and your family had a lovely time in London. Please honor me with your presence for a visit at my home over opening day? Come on the 9th and stay a week if it is convenient.

Lt. Graham

If Graham could have known the uproar of exhilaration his invitation caused in the heart of Lady Estelle, he would have been very pleased and reassured. As it was, the swift acceptance by Lord Livingston on behalf of the family still lifted his spirits and gave him hope.

IF MUSIC BE THE FOOD OF LOVE, PLAY ON

INVERLOCHY CASTLE WAS a well-kept place, albeit a bit frightening in some respects. Gloomy and imposing outside, and inside a curious maze, haphazardly laid out: myriad tiny rooms and alcoves and niches tucked in amongst all the other rooms that served no logical purpose aside from providing fantastic games of hide-and-seek for small children—or, as Graham considered now, ideal places to kiss one's sweetheart, were one inclined to be sneaky (he was not). Many of the rooms were nearly empty, outright spartan, or covered in dust sheets, while other rooms—the few which he regularly used—were well-fitted and even sumptuous.

After a long morning of anxious pacing in his study, Graham looked up to see Bates standing in the door, informing him his guests had arrived. Graham experienced a brief panic as he walked downstairs, taking as long as possible as he talked himself through his anxiety. *Make a good impression, man. Don't spoil your chances by being an absolute idiot.*

By the time he reached the hall, he had calmed himself enough to welcome Estelle and her entourage with—alas for Graham, only figuratively—open arms. Servants appeared out of nowhere to take bags and boxes to bedrooms, and Graham invited his guests to come to the dining room for lunch. He found himself longing inexplicably for his mother, who would have known all the right things to say and kept the conversations flowing. It was not a talent he had inherited, but he did his best, and as if Estelle sensed how ill at ease he was, she filled in the silences easily. If he wanted a compliant wife, she would not be the best choice, but he liked her spirit. He liked the way her mother had to reprimand her frequently for voicing opinions. He liked her opinions. He suspected most men would not relish an outspoken, unabashedly intelligent girl, which no doubt would help his suit.

In the afternoon, they all took a stroll about the grounds,

Graham with his hands behind his back to keep them off the lovely, vibrant young lady at his side. She had a glint of mischief permanently in her eyes. Best of all, she seemed to like him as he was, not expecting him to ever change. He thought privately they could complement one another quite well. He'd half expected her to be in her "babyish school clothes and hair in beribboned plaits," but she looked as grown-up as the last time he'd seen her. He wondered if Lady Livingston had lost any battles about her daughter's wardrobe for this visit.

After dinner that night, they retired to the drawing room with the best piano in it, and Estelle played for him. She had brought her favorite music along, and he shared his with her. She favored Chopin and Beethoven and popular songs, mostly romantic ones and even ragtime; he liked these well enough, but his collection consisted more of a serious, complicated nature: sacred works and operatic pieces. He was especially fond of Handel.

She played, and he sang or accompanied her on his flute for two hours. They ended side by side on the piano bench, playing duets from a book of Scottish ballads and folk songs, while her parents sat listening and sipping sherry and making what conversation they could over the music. He felt alive and happy beyond words, so happy he even smiled a few times. Estelle alone existed in the room for Graham, Estelle and the music that together they were creating. Her closeness and her *joie de vivre* intoxicated him; occasionally their fingers brushed as they played. His eyes kept straying to her lovely face, casting covert glances back at him. A strand of hair had escaped from its comb. He wanted to tuck it behind her ear as an excuse to touch her.

He wanted to say, "I am so in love with you," but he didn't dare. He wanted to say, "I am so hungry for you," but that would have been even less proper. Nor was he bold enough to try to lure her away someplace where they could have even a few minutes alone.

Instead, he sang her *"Voi che sapete,"* sotto voce, no accompaniment. The controlled power in his voice, even when singing softly, was very intimate and made her come out in goosebumps all over.

"I don't know much Italian outside of musical notation," she said softly when he finished. "What's that one about?"

"It's the song of a young man experiencing love for the first time," he answered, his voice a bit husky. "He wants an explanation for why he feels delight and misery and fire and chill, and whether this torment is love."

"*Is* it love?" she whispered.

He looked at his hands and back at her anxiously. "In my experience," he said, his voice hushed, "no song has ever more aptly described love."

A look of sympathetic softness came into her eyes, but before she could reply, her mother stood and said it was time to retire.

UNEXPECTED RENDEZVOUS

AFTER BIDDING HIS guests goodnight, Graham climbed into his bed with a sense of loneliness so acute, it was physically painful. She was here, in his home, right down the hall. So close, but not in his arms, not in his bed. She might as well have been on another planet. He shut his eyes and pictured her lying among her pillows, her golden tresses flowing about her, her long lashes brushing her cheeks. He imagined how soft her skin must be. He lay awake a long time, tossing, unable to turn his mind away from his longing for Estelle. When, after hours had passed, he still had not slept, he rose, put on his dressing-gown, lit a candle, and went into the corridor.

Silence reigned around him. Night in the castle was so thick, one could almost feel it pressing in. He paused in front of the door of Estelle's room, wishing he had right of entry, then purposefully strode away, back to the drawing room. He turned on a lamp to drive away a piece of the night, took his flute in hand and played, seeking an outlet for his pent-up desire. He thought he might exhaust himself enough to sleep, but instead, he only ended in tears. In the middle of a piece, he felt so overwhelmed by the perceived futility of his life that he sank into a chair near the door, dropped the flute to the carpet, buried his face in his hands and wept.

His life had never been his to control; to some extent, it still was not in his control. Until he could wed this wondrous woman, until they could share everything—not merely their bodies, but their minds and their music, without any barriers of societal propriety and shyness in between—he would be empty and incomplete. All his life, there had been an Estelle-shaped hole in his soul, and the idea that he would likely have to wait for ages still to fill it caused him actual pain. He sobbed unabashedly, leaning forward with his hands hanging limp between his knees.

The door creaked. He looked up, startled, his face still flushed and wet with tears. Estelle stood there, her hand over her mouth. He shot to his feet, stammering an incoherent apology, swiftly wiping his face with the backs of his hands. Surely she would be appalled by him. A man who cries is no man, his father had always said.

"I'm so sorry. I didn't mean to disturb you," she said, her eyes wide. "I couldn't sleep—I came down here to find a book to read, and I saw a light—" She hesitated. "Are you all right?" She didn't look appalled at all. Her concern appeared genuine.

"Yes—no—I mean—" he looked at her helplessly, desperate for the comfort she was ready to give him but also aware of the impropriety of the situation. "Lady Estelle, we ought not be here alone."

"I'm leaving presently," she promised, stepping through the door.

Toward him. Oh, God help him, he would surely die.

"But now—I wish—" she paused. "What has happened? May I help?"

He stood with his fists at his sides, and he kept opening his mouth, trying to say anything, anything at all, and he couldn't spit any of it out. Estelle cast him a look of sympathy and came even closer, so she was mere inches away, and whispered, "The song you sang me earlier, that's what you feel, isn't it?"

He nodded mutely. She was too near. His pulse pounded in his head, and his heart leapt to his throat. She stood on her toes and whispered into his ear, her breath soft against his face. "I don't know if this is any comfort, but—I feel it too."

"Estelle!" he gasped. Tears pricked his eyes again. *Idiot.*

"Jamie," she said. "Don't be ashamed. I'm not."

"Estelle," he burst out, "I love you. I've loved you from the first time I met you."

"I have too." Her own eyes shone softly.

They stared at one another. Graham swallowed and blinked, and Estelle dropped her gaze to the floor.

"You'd better go," he said, his voice cracking.

She nodded, but she didn't move right away. As though he were underwater with her, everything swam about his vision in slow motion. "Good night," she said again at last and disappeared.

He sank back into the chair, stunned. After some time, he put away his flute and went back to his room and fell into an unrestful sleep.

UNEXPECTED INTRUDER

WHEN GRAHAM GOT of bed Sunday morning, he reflected on last night's encounter with Estelle. Had he fallen asleep in the drawing room and only dreamed that she came in?

He didn't dare ask her. He felt self-conscious as they all gathered for breakfast, but Estelle acted as though nothing were the matter: collected and dignified as ever. Surely he must have dreamed it all. She smiled at him, and his heart leapt with joy, all preoccupation with the previous night flying out the window. Now, in this moment, she was here, and he was walking on air.

Everything came to an abrupt halt when the door to the dining room swung open, and with a theatrical flourish, George bounded in, showering Graham and his guests with his golden smile. "Hallo, everyone!"

Graham half-rose from his chair. "*George Winston Cameron Graham—*" he said, more sharply than he intended.

"I came for the shoot on Tuesday," George said, breezily, tossing his hat onto the head of a stone angel in the corner. "You didn't tell me you were expecting other guests," he said.

"I wasn't expecting *you*," Graham pointed out. The two brothers locked eyes a minute.

"Well, I'm here now," George said carelessly, getting himself a plate and loading it high from the sideboard, then seating himself across from Estelle and reaching a shameless hand across the table to her. "I don't believe we've met," he said amiably. "I'm George."

She shook hands, momentarily speechless, and Graham sat back down, his face barely concealing his annoyance.

After a moment, he managed to speak. "Lord and Lady Livingston, Lady Estelle, Jeannine; this is my brother, George."

"Pleased to meet you all," George said. "I'm the younger twin. We adore one another."

Estelle narrowed her eyes appraisingly at the man across from her and the one at the head of the table, as if skeptical about George's last statement.

George tucked into the food in front of him. Graham had gone silent, but George ably filled in the conversation, making everyone laugh at the story of his trip from Oxford.

"Excuse me," Graham said, standing abruptly. "I'm going to church. I must get ready." He bowed a little stiffly and disappeared.

George chummed Estelle all the way to church and back and through Sunday dinner too. Graham scowled at him any chance he got. He wanted to drag him outside and knock him flat. He had never felt this uneasy and threatened by his beloved brother. He managed to get through dinner, but after the ladies went upstairs, he took the opportunity to corner George in the hall.

"Could you *stop* being so damnably charming for a change, George?"

George's mouth dropped open. Graham rarely swore. Then, maddeningly, George grinned.

"You're in love with her! And you never told me a thing, you sly old fox! Jealous over a *girl!*"

"I am barely restraining myself from slapping that smug face of yours right now," Graham muttered, his blood up.

George raised his hands in a gesture meant to placate his brother's wrath. "Relax, brother," he said. "I've a girl of my own, remember!"

"A girl of your own. You always have a girl, and it's never the same one twice. What are you up to, twenty?"

"Twenty-seven, actually. Maggie, her name is."

"All I am trying to say is, with your endless fooling about, she's not likely to be the last. If you make Lady Estelle fall in love with you, I—"

"Listen, I'm only being me." George became serious. "*You*

are being absolutely unreasonable. Your jealousy is fogging your common sense."

"You have had all you ever wanted from the minute you were born," Graham said darkly, gripping George's lapel, "and you know perfectly well I have been a cracking sport about it. But I swear, if you take away from me this one thing, I will never, ever speak to you again. So *stay the hell away from my girl.*" He trembled with an odd sense of power. The idea that he had the authority to have someone permanently evicted from his estate was novel and intoxicating.

"Back off. She's coming," George murmured, and they both looked toward the stairs. Lady Estelle and her companion were descending. Graham let go of George and stepped away. He forgot George momentarily.

"We would like to walk," Estelle said.

"May we join you?" George asked, noting Graham had lost his power of speech.

"Please," she said. George offered his arm to her companion and gave Graham a gentle push toward Estelle. Graham remembered his manners and offered her his arm, and the four of them stepped out into the sunshine. George and Jeannine fell into step several yards behind Graham and Estelle. Estelle looked at Graham and smiled. His heart melted, and he forgot his altercation with George.

"Your brother looks nothing like you," she remarked, studying his face and turning to glance back at George. "Your eyes are the same. That's all."

"Aye," Graham said simply. Now she was comparing him to George, *blast it.* He wanted again to slap his brother, and his expression darkened. He stood to his full six feet and picked up their pace.

"Have I offended you in some way, Lord Inverlochy?" she asked after a few moments.

"No," he said, brusquely.

"You've acted peculiarly ever since your brother arrived."

"I didn't bloody *invite* my brother."

Estelle stopped walking. "Sit with me here," she said, motioning to a bench nearby.

He obeyed her. They watched George and Jeannine pass them by, and Estelle spoke.

"What troubles you, Lord Inverlochy?" she asked. "Tell me."

He struggled to find words to express himself, and it took him several minutes to answer. "My brother has been my best and only friend most of my life. George is right, we do adore one another. But"—and here he scowled again—"George has had everything he bloody wants all his life. He has the good looks and the charm and the love of all he meets. My father favored him out of pure spite to me. I'm merely little Caesar, the horse-face boy."

"Nonsense," she protested. "Surely your father didn't call you such things!"

"It's one of the nicer things he called me."

Estelle, deep in thought, did not smile. Graham leaned his elbows on his knees, turning his hat endlessly in anxious hands. He wished he had his flute.

"I'm so sorry. I did not know that's how it was for you," she said, at last, sure it was a lame thing to say.

He did not answer, only stared sulkily into the far distance.

After a few minutes, she laid a hand on his and said softly, "Is there anything I can do?"

He got to his feet and paced in front of her. He didn't dare meet her eyes; he knew he would lose his resolve if he let himself look at her. "You should find someone better, Lady Estelle."

"But last night—" she protested.

He turned his face enough for her to catch sight of the torment in his eyes. "I've been a fool to suppose you could ever care for me. I am not worth it." And he turned and walked away from her back to the castle.

Estelle heard the huge oak door slamming behind him, and tears sprung to her eyes. Had she been thrown over? What was the matter with him?

A few minutes went by, and George and Jeannine came back. "Where's his lordship?" George asked.

Estelle burst into tears and stood as if she would run away too, but Jeannine and George sat on either side and fussed over her. "He's terribly angry," she sobbed out. "I don't know! I must have done something, said something wrong—"

"What did he say?" George asked, patiently.

She sniffled, and he and Jeannine both handed her handkerchiefs at the same moment. "He said he wasn't good enough for me. Last night, he was sweet and kind, and we had *such* a lovely time. Today, he's completely different! What have I done!"

George sighed. "I am certain you've done nothing, Lady Estelle."

"Then why—"

"I'll tell you. Our father was beastly to my poor brother and would go out of his way to make his life miserable. That's why he doesn't trust anyone easily, and he's convinced himself I've come to take you away from him. But I haven't. I've a girl of my own in Oxford, and he knows it. But he's likely going into one of his black moods now, and we might not see him again for a while."

"Is he often like this?" Estelle asked, alarmed at the idea of someday living with an unpredictably moody man.

"No," George said, offering an arm to each lady and sedately walking back toward the castle. "Only if he feels threatened. He'll hole up in his room with his flute until it passes. It's my fault for barging into his party, I suppose, but I had no idea he would care. I always come, invited or not, and he's never minded before. Don't give up on him, Lady Estelle. He's a first-rate man, I promise you, but terribly lonely, terribly naïve, and terribly friendless. He wants love. He's so afraid of hurting people, he doesn't dare let himself connect with them. If you ask me, it's a miracle he had the pluck to ask your family here at all. Come along back to the house, and I'll see if I can fix things for you two."

Back indoors, George left the ladies in the drawing room and disappeared. Estelle drifted over to the piano. She did not open it to play, but rested her chin on her hands, gazing at the portraits on the walls without seeing them, her mind fully occupied with the man she loved and might lose if she did not make a move of her own. She mustn't depend on George or anyone else to be an intermediary, now or ever. If she couldn't work this conflict out with Jamie herself, they had no future together.

Jeannine curled into a cozy chair to read a new and slightly scandalous French novel, and soon dozed off. Estelle's eyes fell from the portraits to her stack of music still sitting on the side of the piano, and an idea came to her mind.

GEORGE THE MEDIATOR

GEORGE, MEANTIME, KNOCKED on his brother's bedroom door. "Let me in," he called out imperiously. He waited a moment. "This minute, or I'm going to get an ax and a sledgehammer and break down the door."

Another moment, and Graham came to the door, opening it slightly. He was pale and obviously had been crying. George pushed past him casually, closed the door behind him, and put his arms around Graham, holding him tightly.

"Listen, I had no idea you had other guests, and I swear, I am not one tiny bit interested in stealing your girl away from you. Would you like me to go back to Oxford? I will, if you want. I'm sorry for knocking up your day."

"I'm not coming to dinner," Graham said, sulkily, "if that's why you came in."

"You left your ladylove in tears. She was sure she'd done something wrong."

"She doesn't deserve me," Graham said miserably.

"Shut up. You're the best in the world, and she's wild about you," George said fervently. "I want you to see you happy. You'd be happy with Lady Estelle. I'm sure of it. Don't throw away such a chance. It won't likely come again." When Graham didn't reply, George said, "Come down anytime you're ready, all right? I have to dress for dinner, and you should too."

After George left, Graham felt more confused, bleak, and useless than ever. He hugged himself. It was a terrible time to have one of these miserable attacks. He couldn't make himself do anything to shake it off; it clung to him like a heavy weight.

Fear. Always fear. All his life.

Fear of his father and his headmaster. Fear of not being in control of his own life. Fear that, were he to marry her, he would make Estelle as miserable as his father had made his mother, that he would cause her to lose her fresh vivacity and fade into a sad shell of herself. Fear that George would steal her. All irrational. All real.

Another knock sounded on his door, and something slipped under. He walked over and picked it up. Sheet music. He opened the door quickly and looked out, but he saw nobody. He closed the door again and looked at the music.

Whatever fate that after years may bring to me
Of grief or care, my life were joy alone
If only I could have your voice to sing to me,
If only I could call your heart my own.
Could I but know that you would be beside me, dear,
If sunshine gladden or if shadows fall,
Oh! then whatever fortune might betide me,
My life would happy be, for love, for love is all.

If only you were mine, dear,
Then all the world were fair;
When my eyes look in thine, dear,
My world, my life are there.
Life's morn is glad and bright, dear,
It's morn of fair sunshine,
And starlit were the night, dear,
If only you were mine.

I would not ask another joy to fall to me;
I would not pray for other boon than this,
Thy true and tender love were all in all to me.
The heaven of my soul is in thy kiss,
The forest voices keep their sweetest songs for thee.

For thee the wild rose blossoms in the glen.

Come back to me, my darling, for I love thee;

Come back to me and we shall never part again.

At the end, in pencil, one line written: *The sentiment of my heart. E.*

He propped the music on his dressing table and played the song through a few times. The words reassured him, and slowly the black Thing lifted away.

He decided to dress and go to dinner after all. He couldn't leave George to preside over dinner for him; it would be inviting disaster. He was *supposed* to be making a good impression on Estelle's family, especially the prickly Lady Livingston, so clearly reluctant to hand her daughter over to anyone less than the best.

CLEARING CLOUDS AWAY

GRAHAM HAD TO swallow his pride to enter the dining room, but he managed it. He was subdued throughout the meal, and when they retired to the drawing room after dinner, Estelle sat at the piano and started to play. He watched, longing to make it up to her, but having a hard time getting up the courage to speak.

She spoke first. "I have trouble with some of Chopin's chords," she said, glancing over to him. "My hands find it difficult to reach them. I don't suppose you have that trouble…"

"Which chord?" he asked, stepping nearer, glad she had broken the silence between them.

"Sit here, and show me how you play this one," she invited, making room for him beside her. She pointed to the troublesome chord, and he played it for her.

"Keep going," she said softly. "I don't really need help with the chord. I need to talk to you, and it's impossible to be alone."

He gave the slightest of nods and continued playing. "I'm listening."

"Your brother explained to me, about your father. I didn't know." She looked at her hands. "I suppose I took it for granted all families were as happy as mine. I truly am sorry about your father."

She turned the page for him, and he murmured, "I am sorry for behaving badly today. It was unfair to you."

"It's all right," she said.

"You *should* know about my father, but I can't say I want to tell you much. He did many things unfit for the ears of a lady." He went silent for so long, gazing at nothing, lost in the music, that Estelle had to prompt him.

"What can you tell me that is fit?"

"He used to beat me. Hit me in the face with his riding crop and left this behind—" Graham touched the almost imperceptible scar. "His mood could change in an instant. You never knew what would set him off. He never beat George, only me. He never criticized George in public, but he did me. Quite often."

"How humiliating," Estelle said, her eyes soft and sad.

"He was decorated for things he did in the Indian Rebellion. They named a ship after him, revered him as a military hero. He was good at that life. The face he showed to the public was different from what we had at home."

He would not tell Estelle *all* he knew about his father. He'd looked at the man's journals after his death. He hadn't believed George, and paged through a few of them before consigning them to the flames. It had been a disturbing, if enlightening, peek into his father's twisted psyche. He suspected that, after having taken his mother's virginity, sex with her no longer appealed to him. The thought of all those innocent girls, violated and cast aside by his monster of a father, utterly sickened him.

He jumped when Estelle touched his arm lightly. "Jamie?" she said as if prompting him again. He'd stopped playing without noticing. "You've been lost in some other world for five minutes, and you look like a thundercloud. What is it?"

"My father was a beast," he said, spitting out the words. It took him a moment to collect himself again. He needed to change the subject, fast.

He looked directly at her and said quietly, "The song you gave me—"

She demurely dropped her gaze.

He lifted her chin to look into her eyes again. "Did you really mean that?"

"I did. I meant every word."

Something flickered deep in his eyes. He dropped his hand and turned back to the piano. "This is my answer, then." He sang softly, as he had sung to her last night.

Oh, promise me that you will take my hand,
The most unworthy in this lonely land,
And let me sit beside you, in your eyes
Seeing the vision of our paradise.
Hearing God's message while the organ rolls
Its mighty music to our very souls,
No love less perfect than a life with thee;
Oh promise me, oh promise me!

Her hand lightly squeezed his knee, and he looked at her sweet loving face and forgot everyone else in the room, except for her. His arm slipped around her waist to keep her from falling off the bench, and he leaned in and kissed her mouth, hungry, longing, amazed. She made a squeak that startled him; he let go abruptly, pulled back, and murmured, "I'm sorry, I'm so sorry, I can't believe I just did that—" He blushed furiously and looked away, clenching his hands at his sides.

"I can," she whispered, her eyes wide and bright. She did not appear one bit put off. She smiled and laid her hand against his hot cheek. Everything about her face and her touch intoxicated him.

He glanced up. George was there. He'd seen them. But he'd stood in such a way as he refreshed his glass from the liquor cabinet that he'd blocked the others from having noticed the kiss. He winked at them and moved away, continuing the animated story he'd been telling Lord and Lady Livingston all this time. Estelle giggled, and Graham, gloriously happy once more, beamed brightly back at her. Perhaps his life would come out all right after all.

A week later, after the Moncrieffes returned home, Inverlochy Castle settled into its usual quiet greyness, and in September, Graham went back to Gibraltar for another six months. He and Estelle wrote to one another as before, but now, each word she sent him held deeper meaning than it had before.

THE GREATEST GAME IN THE WORLD: HIS MOVE

GRAHAM ARRIVED AT Livingston House in the middle of a rainy afternoon in March of 1903. He had hardly been in the hall a minute before Estelle came to meet him, beaming, clasping his hands in hers briefly and dropping them before her mother or Jeannine had time to materialize and scold her for being forward.

"Mr. Cunningham told us you've been promoted," she said. "*You* didn't tell me, Captain Graham!"

He waved it away self-consciously. "If my father were still alive, he would ask me what I have done to 'only' be a captain at this point."

She took his arm with a look of loving sympathy and went with him to the parlor where her mother was.

Lady Livingston seemed to be warming, albeit slowly, to the idea of Graham's presence in her daughter's life. "Come, tell us all about your brother's wedding," she said.

Graham sat a little stiffly on the offered chair. Privately, he was of the opinion that George had precipitated himself into the engagement and marriage out of some sort of need to reassure Graham he wasn't after Estelle. Or else it was simply convenience: George would find a rich wife a valuable asset as he pursued his career, and Maggie, although pretty enough, was a bit dull-as-in-boring for all her money. Rather like himself, in fact, Graham realized. But he said hopefully, "Maggie will be good for George. Maybe now he will settle down."

"A steady, reliable person can work wonders for a flighty partner, I believe." Lady Livingston fixed her steady eyes on her daughter, suddenly very intent on her needlework. "Isn't that right, Estelle?"

Estelle did not answer, and Graham spoke. "Perhaps you mean spirited, not flighty, Lady Livingston?"

"Perhaps," Lady Livingston said, turning her assessing gaze to her prospective son-in-law. He was oblivious to her scrutiny; he only had eyes for Estelle.

Graham stayed with the Moncrieffes nearly a week. On his last night before going back to Gibraltar, he and Estelle sat across from one another, playing a game of chess. A dream burned in his head; he *had* to ask her tonight to marry him. He was running out of time on this visit. Estelle's parents had even withdrawn to give him the chance, but his nerves paralyzed him. Usually a formidable chess player, tonight he was losing, and badly, and he hardly noticed.

As she put out her hand to capture another of his men for the third move in a row, he abruptly snatched her hand and clasped it, scattering pieces. She looked at him, startled, and he burst out, "I, well, I was—" he hesitated, and when he spoke again his words tripped over one another and tangled. "I like how you have always—I mean, I am—I would very much like if you would be—"

The tension of his grip betrayed how anxious he was, and she longed to reassure him. He dropped to his knees before her and finally managed to continue. "Be willing to accompany me for the rest of my life. I mean, will you marry me? It would have to be a long engagement," he plunged on, still clinging to her hands. "I've three years left in the army, and I want to take you home with me properly—"

"Yes," she said. "Yes. I will!" Her face went pink and white with delight and excitement and a sudden shyness, but with no hesitation at all.

"Do you want to, truly? Do you?"

"I do," she said. "From the moment I set eyes on you, I decided I would never marry anyone else."

He bowed his head against her knees and immediately began to cry. "What's the matter?" she asked, stroking his hair lightly.

"Nobody has ever wanted me before. Nobody. George is the only one left who ever loved me. I have worried for the last two years, perhaps you didn't honestly care for me, and I couldn't let myself think about it. I loved you *so much* from the first moment. Do you *really* want me?"

"Oh, darling," she said, squeezing his hands and dropping her voice to a whisper. "Don't you remember our meeting that night at the castle? I told you then I loved you too. And I will spend the rest of my life loving and wanting you." She wiped the tears off his face with her free fingers.

"I didn't dream it? It was real?" he asked, hope springing up in his heart.

"It was real," she promised fervently, and impulsively, he put his arms around her and gave her a squeeze: not the most graceful embrace in the history of lovemaking, but he'd had no experience, and it did come straight from his heart.

"Oh, my darling, yes, I remember," he said. "You called me Jamie. It made me so happy." He rose and offered her his hand, and he did not let go when she had risen.

She smiled kindly. "Are you going to kiss me?" she whispered. In spite of himself and his undignified tears, he broke into one of his rare golden smiles and framed her face with his hands and did, quickly and chastely, but with such warmth.

"You don't smile very often," she said, gently, her fond eyes fixed on him. "When you do, all the light you keep hidden in your soul shows up. It's beautiful."

For that, he kissed her again and gave her another real smile. "I've a ring for you," he said. "But it's at the engraver's, and he's not finished yet. Shall I have it sent to you, or bring it myself the next time I come?"

"Oh, do have it sent, I shall die of impatience if I have to wait," she said. She couldn't stop beaming either. He put his arms around her again, and she rested her cheek against his chest, closing her eyes blissfully.

O PROMISE ME

GRAHAM AND ESTELLE chose the 9th of June, 1906, for their wedding day.

On one side of Livingston House, Estelle was in her room, being dressed by her sniffling mother and having her hair fixed meticulously by Jeannine. She had a severe case of jitters and had only been able to force down a few bites of the breakfast she'd been brought. Jeannine fussed that Estelle would surely faint during the ceremony if she did not eat more, but Estelle *couldn't*. She thought only of her beloved and how much she wanted to be alone with him.

On the other side of Livingston House, Jamie stood in the middle of his room, playing his flute. George's wife, Maggie, had shooed George out of their room to let her ready herself and their two daughters in peace.

George came into the room to find Graham had shaved and combed his hair and not managed to get any further. Anxious beyond words, he stood playing the flute to calm himself. His brain whirled with fretful possibilities: *What if she changes her mind and doesn't come to the wedding? What if she does come to the wedding, and I start crying and can't stop and disgrace myself?*

George fussed over him, trying to dress him while he played, which didn't work so well. "Wouldn't do to be late to your own wedding, old man," he said. "Put down that thing and let me help you."

Graham did not put down the flute. George snatched it away, and he huffed in annoyance, but submitted to letting George buckle his kilt, tie his tie, pin his plaid, and fix his hair in place with more pomade. When George had finished, he spoke again. "What's troubling you, brother?"

Graham's gaze was far, far away. What was troubling him? He'd scarcely slept, tortured with anxiety and fear that something would happen to prevent the marriage from taking place today. He couldn't get the story of Peter Davies and his Clara out of his head. Would he lose Estelle, as Davies had lost his beloved? He felt tormented by the fact that Peter Davies, the only other person with whom he had shared any deep love, was dead. All the people who loved him died, except for indestructible George. His mother had loved him, in her way; he remembered her tortured final moments and shivered. He feared cursing Estelle to the same fate, by trying to be close to her. He could articulate none of this to George, so he said nothing.

"Don't bristle at me, brother, but—" George gave him a Look. "Do you know *anything* about sex?"

Graham didn't hear him. He kept staring, silent, in some other world. George put the flute back in Graham's hands, squeezed his shoulder, and left him alone.

Graham, George, and George's family were at the church in plenty of time, despite all the fussing that he would make them late.

When the organ played the processional for Estelle to come up the aisle, he turned to watch for her, his heart leaping to his throat, his carefully controlled military bearing threatening to give way when she appeared on her father's arm. *She was magnificent.* She carried a cascade of pink and yellow roses, and her eyes gleamed brightly. But even more magnificent to Graham was the fact that she hadn't gone back on agreeing to marry him. When her father handed her to Graham, Graham's own eyes threatened to spill. She gazed at him with such direct warmth and earnestness, he could hardly bear it.

The ceremony concluded without any mishaps. Estelle did not faint, and Graham did not fall apart crying. As they walked down the aisle and out of the church, showered by rose petals and rice, and as they enjoyed their reception in Livingston House's gorgeous rose-perfumed garden afterward, Graham forgot himself and his demons so thoroughly, he even looked happy for the photographer.

He was cheerful all the way to their hotel room, but when the porter left them alone, they stood there, staring at each other from opposite sides of the room for a long time, and Graham became quiet again. The change came swiftly and without warning, like a candle going out in a cold draft. He didn't seem angry, though, only contemplative. Not like that time she'd visited over opening day, when his mood had been black and frightening. This wasn't so bad.

Estelle had changed from her wedding gown to an elegant navy blue traveling suit before they had come. She set aside her hat and gloves and coat and stood with her hands behind her back. He hadn't said a word yet.

"What do we do now?" she asked, giggling nervously. "This feels illicit."

"Aye," he agreed. This was the time ordinary fellows might reach for a smoke to calm their nerves. No, ordinary fellows were happy for the chance to be alone with their new wives. Ordinary fellows didn't need calming. Why couldn't *he* be ordinary? His eyes strayed to his flute case on the table nearby. "Mind if I play a bit?"

"Not at all," she said.

She was a little surprised he did not immediately take her in his arms. Wasn't that what men did, once they were alone with their brides? She *wanted* him to. She had been waiting for this night for rather a long time.

He regarded her with an unreadable expression as he put the pieces of his flute together and blew into it tentatively. Then he turned toward the fireplace and played. The notes poured out like trilling little birds. Estelle recognized it as a piece by Paganini for violin and was astounded at his ability to play something so complex.

When fifteen minutes had gone by, and he had not yet come out of his little private world—if anything, he had buried himself more deeply in it—she decided she must find a way to redirect his attention. She turned down the bed and set about removing her clothes on the other side of the room. Slowly, deliberately, she took off her shoes and stockings and her blouse. As she stepped out of her skirt, she looked up. Graham turned towards her, still playing, and his breath caught, and the music caught too. He lowered the flute from his mouth a fraction of an inch, lips parted.

Estelle stood still, with her head tilted to one side, hands behind her back. She had his attention now. She couldn't help but smile at his reaction. "Have you ever seen a woman in her underthings before?" Her voice sounded loud in the silence the flute left behind.

He shook his head, speechless.

"Well, let's change that. Want to undo me? I hate every minute I spend in this corset."

He did want to. He stepped closer to her. "How does it work?" he whispered.

"The hooks down the front," she said, demonstrating.

He swallowed, longing but frightened to put his hand so close to her bosom. He reminded himself they were married, and he could do anything he wanted with her. He reached forward and undid the hooks as instructed, and she gave a blissful sigh as the miserable undergarment set her free. She tossed it aside carelessly and looked him in the eye.

"Have you decided yet what we do now?"

"Aye, I already knew that, but I—aye, I know what I want to do," he said, his voice gone hoarse. His hand gripped his flute so tightly it hurt.

"What do you want to do?" she asked, stepping closer to him, her eyes shy, but bright.

He bit his lip and turned away from her, speaking into the fireplace, his voice so low she had to strain to hear. "I want to finish undressing you and get into that lovely bed with you."

"Well," she said, "what are you waiting for?"

A long silence. "I am afraid of myself. Afraid I will become a monster like my father and hurt you."

She gently prised his flute out of his fists and set it carefully aside. "Stop stewing over your father, Jamie. You could never be him. I'm sure of it."

"You didn't know him." In his mind, he went back nineteen years and heard again the muffled cries of Mlle Leclair, and the burden of it stabbed in his chest. He backed away from Estelle, sank into the nearest chair, and hid his face in his hands. He had tried so hard to exorcise that hideous image, and yet there it still was, as clear as if it had been only yesterday. It haunted and angered him.

Estelle knelt before him, watching him, unsure what to say. She waited, her hands lightly resting on his knees.

"I've told you my father was a terrible person," he choked out, "but I haven't told you the one vile thing which haunts me more than anything else he ever did."

"Maybe you should tell me now, then."

"I've never told anyone, except George. We were wee lads. Seven and a half years old. Our third governess had been with us six months. My father was often in the nursery when we had a governess, watching. Wolflike."

Estelle made a face.

"It's how he always behaved with them. George and I—we thought he wanted to know how well she did her job. But after two governesses had vanished, we started to imagine there was more to their disappearances than simple dismissal. And one day, I went to the wrong place at the wrong time, and I saw my father, with her—" He looked as if he might be sick. "It's not right to tell you of such evil. You are too pure and innocent, I'm not sure I should—"

"Go on," she said firmly.

He was quiet a long time, staring reflectively and unhappily into a past she could not see, looking tired and anxious. Finally, he rose and paced while she sat in his vacated chair and watched him.

"There is a room in the castle we call the ghost room," he said at last, "that I liked to practice my music in, because nobody ever went to it, and there I saw—what I saw. The door wasn't even closed, that is how remote it was. And I stepped in, and my governess lay on the floor, trapped under my father. He had one hand over her mouth. She clawed at it, trying to scream for help, kicked at him, and he—well, she made a horrible sobbing moan, and she stopped fighting. She went dead quiet all of a sudden, dead still. And my father whooped in demonic glee and said some very bad words, and I turned and ran away before he could notice me. I should have done something to stop him. Surely some way I could have saved her from—from *that*, but—" he leaned his forehead against the cold glass of the window and hugged himself. "And when he found out I'd seen, he gave me the worst beating he ever gave me and told me all sorts of nasty things a boy shouldn't have to know. I swore I would never be like him, that I'd stay a virgin my whole life as penance for his evil, and it was easy enough—girls never liked me. Then I met you, and my resolve melted. I have wanted you from the first, but now I have the right to your body, I feel as if I ought not exercise it. I don't want to be a beast. I think—I think I am a coward."

Estelle came up behind him and rested her head against his back. "It was not your fault, what happened to your governess. Not your fault that your father abused his power." Her arms slipped around his waist. "Sleeping with me will not turn you into a beast. You'd already be one, if you were going to be. You ought not punish yourself for someone else's sins."

He was quiet.

"Your governess didn't want your father. But I want you. Come, darling, at least kiss me. That won't hurt anything, will it?"

He supposed it wouldn't. After a moment, he turned in her arms and framed her upturned face with his hands and bent to touch her lips with his, gently. Part of him still felt as if he'd get smacked by a chaperone for being fresh.

He pulled away to look into her eyes. "May I take your hair down?"

She turned to make it easier for him. He took his time removing the combs and hairpins from his bride's hair, laying them on a nearby table as precisely as if they were surgeon's instruments, and ran his fingers through the golden silkiness cascading to her waist, combing it smooth with his fingers. It was soft and warm, and he buried his face in it for a moment. It smelled like roses. "All our children will be spectacularly beautiful because of you," he said hoarsely. She turned. He was frozen in place again.

She clasped his hands together between hers and smiled at him.

"Are you cold?" he whispered.

"A little." She glanced at the bed with its invitingly turned down covers. "I know someplace warmer..." She snuggled in closer against him, twined her fingers with his, and stood on her toes.

"*Come to bed,*" she breathed urgently against his ear.

So he did.

NO FEAR

IN THE MORNING, Graham woke before the sun rose. He turned carefully, trying not to wake Estelle, and gazed at her, curled up like a contented cat with her hair wild about her face, still sound asleep. Graham blushed at the memories of last night, but also he felt tranquil and safe. *There is no fear in love,* he thought to himself with delight. *Perfect love casteth out fear. I could take on anything or anyone now.* He brushed her cheek with the back of one finger. Her skin was soft and warm as he had always imagined it would be, and she stirred a little. What it would be like to waken with Estelle at his side every morning for the rest of his life!

She stirred again, and this time, she opened one eye. "How are you this morning?" she said, her voice still sleepy.

"You were right. My father's behavior does not define me. I don't have to pay for his sins."

There was a long silence on her part, and she did not open her eyes, but mischief suffused her voice when she spoke again. "Are you always this deep and philosophical the minute you wake up, Jamie darling?"

He looked self-conscious, and she beamed at him reassuringly and gave him her mouth to kiss. After a blissful minute, he whispered, "I thought I could live my life without this, but I'm not sure how I ever imagined it a reasonable idea."

"I used to lie in bed at night wide awake," she confided, "and I would dream up situations where we might find ourselves alone—all by coincidence, of course!—and you would take me in your arms and kiss me and kiss me and not stop. I wanted to know what it would be like. Now I do." She cuddled close to him under their covers, lightly running her fingertips along his body.

"I can undo my father's evil another way," he said as if to himself. "I can be wholeheartedly faithful to you for the rest of my life instead of leaving you for other women."

She turned his face to hers and said, "*Stop. Talking. About. Your. Father.*"

And, for the moment, he did. He stopped talking at all and let himself be swept along by the tide of this woman's unbelievable passion for him.

NOTHING STAYS THE SAME

GRAHAM FOUND IT was not so hard to be affectionate as he had imagined. It came naturally for him when he was with Estelle. For the first few months of their marriage, they lived in astonishingly blissful near-solitude, making love and music together lavishly, taking long rides on his horse so Estelle could explore her new domain. They got off Altair occasionally to chase each other through the woods or kiss in the heather. He had never been so happy, never felt so whole. He blossomed under the sunshine she poured on his life.

Estelle ran the household and nearly everyone in it, and Graham let her. It left him more time for his music and management of the estate. He no longer aspired to make a career of his music; he played now only for his own pleasure, or for church, or for anyone who asked him to perform. Outside of that, he stayed at home as much as possible. He had found a haven of safety and love; he no longer sought nor needed any external approbation.

"Darling," Estelle said one October night while they had tea in their room, as they usually did when they had no guests. "It is time for you to enter a new phase of your music career."

"Oh?" he said, buttering his toast carefully so the butter went all the way to the edges.

"Yes. Time for you to add some lullabies to your repertoire."

"Lullabies?" He looked at her blankly, knife poised above his toast.

She laughed merrily. "Yes, lullabies. To help put the baby to sleep at night."

"Baby?" he croaked. The butter knife fell from his hand and landed on his saucer, cracking it neatly in two. Startlement, anxiety, and terror tangled inside him, and he gripped the edge of the table. "Are you telling me what I think you're telling me?"

"You are going to be a father," she said.

He pushed away from the table and went to the window to

look out into the night, one fist pressed against his lips, so lost in his introspection that he jumped when she came up behind him and laid a hand lightly on his arm.

"Darling?" she asked. The coy glint had left her eyes, and in its place he saw concern and hurt over his reaction. "Aren't you happy?"

He took his time answering. "I should be," he said.

"But you're not?"

"I don't know, I—I don't want anything to change, that's all. These last few months have been nothing but joyous to me, and I want it to go on like this forever."

"Nothing stays the same forever, Jamie. But that doesn't mean it has to get worse in changing. If we want it to keep getting better and better, it can."

"I—I don't know how to be a father, Estelle. I might feel happy if I had any reason to believe I could be better than my own father was to me. But I don't know I can."

"Darling," she said again, putting her arm around him and leaning against his shoulder. "Don't be afraid. We are in this together. We'll help each other the way we always do. You'll make a wonderful father, the same way you are a wonderful husband. I'm sure of it."

Another long silence. "*Am* I a wonderful husband?" He sounded a little surprised and a good deal longing.

She sighed. "Yes," she said firmly, holding him tightly. "You *are.*"

Together they stood by the window until Graham had wrapped his head around the news and was ready to finish his tea.

GOOD CHANGE

A S THE MONTHS went by, Graham got used to the idea of becoming a father. Nothing much changed for him or Estelle right away. She looked the same for several months, and even when she started to show, it happened so gradually it never shocked him as much as he expected it might. They still spent their evenings making love and music, and the sameness of their routine cheered and comforted him. Perhaps whatever changes lay ahead would be likewise minimal.

Estelle was never ill, only more sleepy than usual, and he became used to finding her curled up sleeping in unorthodox places and uncharacteristically scatterbrained.

He met his offspring for the first time early on a June evening. He'd been banished from the bedroom that morning at an hour when even he was not usually awake, and spent an unproductive day pacing in his study, worrying, playing his flute, trying to sneak in to see Estelle, and being shooed back downstairs by Jeannine. Finally, Jeannine promised to come every half hour to give updates, if he would stay where he was supposed to.

An endless number of half hours later, she sailed in, beaming, with the news that he could come now.

Estelle reclined prettily among her pillows with a tiny bundle in her arms when he entered. Everyone else had left, except Jeannine and Estelle's mother, who stood in the background while he sat beside her on the bed. Before he had a chance to refuse, she put the bundle in his arms. He held it awkwardly, speechless. He'd never held a baby before in his life.

"It's a boy," she said softly, unable to fully contain her amusement at his consternation.

He looked at the tiny red-faced creature a long time, surprised by its warmth. "Do they always look like this?" he asked, at last.

"He does look a bit like an old man, aye," she said. "The midwife swears he'll look human in no time."

The baby opened his eyes and fixed them on his father so certainly that Graham gave a little choked laugh. "He's looking at me," he said, and tears sprung unbidden to his eyes. He stroked the infant cheek with the back of a finger. Its skin was so soft, it almost felt like nothing at all.

Estelle adored the baby, whom Graham named Peter, and wanted him near her most of the time. Graham might have been jealous, had she not proved herself more in love with him than ever.

He particularly remembered a day when Peter was about five months old, and Graham had been in his study, staring out the window at the grounds below, with his flute in his hands behind his back. At the sound of the door clicking softly closed, he turned.

Estelle had come in.

"Darling," he said softly, dropping his flute onto the window seat, holding out his arms to her, "I can't concentrate on anything this morning."

"I can't either," she said. He drew her close, gazed fondly into her eyes, framed her face with his hands, warm and contented inside. She stood on her toes and kissed him and worked her hands underneath his kilt, and he sighed in bliss at her touch.

"Foxy today," he murmured, approvingly.

"I am," she agreed, kissing him as though the world was scheduled to end in thirty seconds.

"In here or somewhere else?" he asked obligingly when he could speak again.

"In here," she said. He let her push him gently by the shoulders into his leather chair, and she climbed on his lap. In his turn, his hands wandered up her legs.

"Not wearing anything under your frock?" he said with a light in his eyes which she loved.

"I'm pretending it's a kilt. Hurry up, I'm gasping for you."

NOT SO GOOD CHANGE

THE NEXT YEAR, they had another son. Estelle named him Thomas after her father. And the year after, Vincent was born, and Vincent did change everything. He was a feisty handful whom nothing and no one could comfort. Estelle and Jeannine, now the boys' nanny, along with the nursery maids, tried everything they could dream up, and none of it worked to soothe the savage beast.

Graham had never directly had much to do in the daily maintenance of his sons. He saw them frequently enough, for Estelle liked having them follow her about, but he didn't know them. Vincent was obviously troublesome, but Estelle always had been so plucky and cheerful with the previous two that he did not register at first how much this latest addition was taking out of her.

Even with Jeannine's help, it took both women and a troupe of nursery maids to keep Vincent in any state of contentment. Estelle's nerves were worn thin. She was moody, and the worry that she did not love him anymore nearly broke Graham's heart. He needed her so much, he couldn't bear her sudden unwillingness to let him make love to her, and she exploded at him for the first time since he'd known her.

"Do you think I don't want you?" she said. "I do. I need you as much as you need me. But I cannot handle any more babies. You have your heir and then some, and now I need you to keep out."

It ended with both of them in tears. Initially, he felt rejected and resentful, but as time went on, he respected her for her honesty. He had loved her frankness before they were married; why should he stop now? And it wasn't as though they could never be intimate again. It just had to be when she said it was all right, not whenever the urge came upon them.

PART TEN

October 1916

France

LOOKING LIKE A GIRL

THE NIGHT AFTER reading the letter from her uncle, Aveline woke. Finding it impossible to go back to sleep, she wandered the château. A dim light burned in the study, and she looked in to find her capitaine had fallen asleep at his table over a half-finished letter to his wife. His hat was off, his close-cropped chestnut head lay on his right arm, and his pen had dropped to rest on the table under his open left hand, relaxed and loose in sleep. She silently corked the ink bottle so it wouldn't spill if he jerked awake, and pinched out the almost-exhausted candle.

She went to stand by the window and lifted the curtain, feeling deeply grateful her capitaine had saved her from the awful fate of being sent to her relatives in Paris. The clouds scudding across the sky kept the half-moon's light fitful at best, but a shadowy figure definitely paced the grass outside.

Most likely Willie; she knew his stride. She laid her fingertips to her mouth, contentedly imagining what it would feel like if he ever did kiss her. "William Duncan," she whispered slowly several times, trying the name on her tongue. She liked the sound of it. She found herself wishing she could run outside, despite the cold night air, into Willie's arms.

The next morning, Capitaine Graham spoke on the telephone for such a long time, Aveline became tired of waiting for him. She decided to try on her new clothes. She carried them into Mme Blanchard's room, locking the door behind her, and laid everything out on the Blanchards' bed. She had difficulty with all the fastenings, especially on the boots, but she managed at last. She took a step across the floor and nearly fell. She'd never worn anything with a high heel before.

Well, it would take more than a pair of silly shoes to beat her. She pressed her lips together and practiced walking back and forth until she felt steady enough not to disgrace herself.

She put on the hat, and finally dared to take a peek in Mme Blanchard's mirror. The stranger looking back at her scared her, and she blushed deeply at the idea of being Seen in these clothes. She felt more than uncomfortable; she felt ridiculous. She quickly took them all off, returned them to their boxes, put on her regular things again, and ran outside.

FOUR SECRETS

SHE FOUND WILLIE out back chopping kindling. She leaned against the fence where he had draped his tunic and watched him.

He had his sleeves rolled up; his arms were as lithe and strong as the rest of him. Aveline liked watching him swing the hatchet. He glanced her way with a shy grin. She had grown so used to not talking that it didn't occur to her to strike up a conversation until he had finished filling the old wooden crate and lifted it to carry it inside.

"Couldn't you sleep last night?" she asked him. "Was it you walking out here?"

He smiled crookedly. "Aye, I couldna sleep. But what were *you* doing awake, spying on me?"

She had no answer. She trailed after him as he deposited the crate in the kitchen and then went into the stable. One of the mares had given birth to a most precious wee foal two days before. Aveline liked it because it was the exact rich chestnut color of her capitaine's hair. Willie liked any excuse to take small breaks from his duties.

Aveline stood as close to his side as she could get and leaned over the stable door, and they both watched the little creature peeking at them from behind its mother. "Tell me what you'll do after the war ends," she said.

"I dinna ken yet," he said. "But I'll be somewhere near the sea, I hope. I miss that—I didna want to be a fisherman like a' the other men in my family, but I do love the sea."

"If you like the sea so much, why didn't you join the Navy instead of the Army?"

He blushed. "I shouldna tell. You'll laugh at me."

"You told me your real age," she said, leaning in conspiratorially, eyes glinting. "Tell me another of your secrets."

He hesitated before he whispered into her ear, "Dad used to say I'm no his son, seeing I get seasick in boats. Any boats. I like being by the sea. Just no on it or in it. All the men in my family are fishermen, but I widna be out for a minute before I'd be fair dying. I first went out when I was seven, and it took four months before Dad agreed I was sick and no just pretending to get out of doing the work. So I stayed onshore. I took care of the boat and the nets instead, and all the girls laughed at me." Willie's eyes darkened a little. "He always looked at me like he didna much care for the sight of me anyways. He liked my sisters better. I've three. The oldest one is the age I'm supposed to be. Twenty."

"You never told me you had sisters."

"I ken. Count that as the third secret out of me. I dinna let myself think much on them, because I miss them. Canna write to them. They might make me come home if they found where I was. I dinna want to go home. I'd sooner be shot."

Aveline wondered at his ferocity, but she didn't ask about it.

"I've never seen the ocean," she said. "Can I come with you when the war is over, and you go to your place by the sea?"

He lit a cigarette and took a long drag, sighing out a cloud of smoke. "You belong wi' Captain Graham now. Why would you want to come with me? I'll be a poor wanderer."

She studied his face. "Wandering isn't a bad thing."

"Not something two people can do very easily, I dinna suppose." He changed the subject. "What do *you* want to do after the war?"

"I'm going to be a famous artist," Aveline replied promptly. She leaned her head against his shoulder. He didn't move to put his arm around her, as she'd hoped he might. "I tried on the new clothes from Amiens a while ago."

"Why're you no wearing them now?"

Aveline blushed. "I was afraid of them."

He laughed. "Och noo, clothes never hurt anyone!"

She looked down, and he lifted her chin. "Nae bother, Avie, no matter what you wear, you're bonny. They're only clothes, aye?"

Aveline met his eyes. "I'm not used to them. I never even had shoes except in wintertime before Capitaine Graham found me."

He nodded, dropping his hand and taking another drag on his cigarette.

"Would you kiss me?"

Her words were so unexpected he paused with the cigarette halfway to his mouth. "What?" he asked.

"I said, would you kiss me?"

He laughed. It sounded forced to her. "Captain Graham will have me head. You know that." He sucked furiously at his cigarette. It was almost smoked out.

"He doesn't have to know," she pointed out. "I won't tell."

"You dinna ken what you're asking, Avie."

"Have you kissed many girls?" she asked.

"No so many," he admitted, cautiously. "Two."

"Who were they?"

"Nobody particular," he said, attempting to sound dismissive but blushing too much to be convincing.

She clasped her hands together and beamed. "Can I be third? You must be awfully good at it by now, if—"

"Oh, hisht," Willie said, his eyes darting away from her steady gaze, but his mouth twitched trying not to smile back at her.

She laughed aloud, and impulsively he bent down and chastely pecked her cheek.

"That," he said, lifting a reproving finger, "is the only kiss you're getting out of me. Now, unless you want me reduced to peeling tatties for the rest of the war as punishment for what I've just done—*scoot*." He waved toward the door.

Aveline scooted.

But, reproachful as his tone may have been, he'd *winked* at her as he waved her away. She beamed all the way back to the house.

YOUNG PEOPLE IN LOVE

AFTER THAT DAY, Aveline shadowed Willie any chance she got. She didn't ask him to kiss her again. But they exchanged many glances, and whenever he had opportunity, he would smile warmly at her or find excuses to let his hand brush against hers.

If he was honest with himself, Willie would have been decidedly interested in kissing Aveline—*if* she were somebody besides the captain's daughter. He knew he couldn't risk it, and he would resolve to stay away from her, and the next moment, she would beam adoringly at him, and he felt himself turning into her slave all over again. For the first time since he'd run away from home, he wished he could be the sixteen he really was, instead of the twenty-year-old he had to pretend to be.

One evening, Aveline stole out of the great room to the balcony where Willie stood and sidled up next to him.

"You shouldna always hang about me, Avie," he said, trying to sound stern but failing. "I'm worried about you getting into trouble."

"You want to *really* kiss me, don't you?"

"Of course I—I mean, it's—" He paused, studying the cigarette in his fingers. "I'm supposed to be responsible. Captain Graham trusts me. I darena—"

She hoisted herself to sit at his level on the balcony railing. "I know."

He regarded her, half-smiling. "I do like you fine, you ken."

She took his hand and drew him closer to her so she could slip her arm through his, and leaned her head on his shoulder. For a long time they stood there, saying nothing.

"I'd like to wander with you, Willie Duncan. You'll need someone to help you carry all your photography things, after all."

He laughed. "I *can* carry my own things."

"I could help."

"You're to go to Scotland and get a fine lady's education, Avie. I'm no but a fisherman's son. You'll marry someone fine and fancy and have a much better life than I can ever hope to have."

She sighed, tracing the lines of the plaid kilt with her fingertip. "I haven't even met the rest of this new family I'm supposed to have. What if I don't fit in? I'm just a poor country girl. Nobody. Like you."

She turned her face back up to his, and their eyes met. He bent close, almost close enough to kiss her, then abruptly pulled away. "You'd better go back inside, Avie," he said gruffly, "before anyone notices you've gone."

She smiled shyly, reluctant to leave, but after a moment, she slid off the railing and disappeared inside without another word.

TRENCHES AGAIN

THE MARCH BACK to the trenches on the 8th of October distracted Aveline for a while.

There had been another argument about whether she would be allowed to come; Mr. George had actually *shouted* at her cap-itaine when he heard he intended to bring her along again.

She'd been sitting with Capitaine Graham after supper, and none of them had any idea she was still there hiding behind the curtains in the study, when Mr. George came in, furious.

"Duncan just told me you're taking Aveline with you. She does *not* belong in the trenches, Jamie," Mr. George had said. "Have you lost your damn *mind?* It was one thing for her to sneak there after you first found her, but there is *no reason in hell* for her to come this time."

Capitaine Graham had just blinked at his brother. "She needs me," he said, with a slight shrug.

"She needs to stay alive," George said. "You're just... just... *pathologically delusional*, Jamie!" He turned to MacFie. "MacFie, man, talk some sense into my brother, will you?"

"Who is the superior officer here?" Capitaine Graham asked, voice cold, before MacFie could open his mouth.

George rolled his eyes and sighed. "Aye, sir," he said, with a dramatic bow, and Aveline gasped to see her capitaine seize Mr. George by the arm and growl at him warningly, like a territorial dog.

"You are *under my command*, Lieutenant Graham," he said, inches away from his brother's face. "You do not question my decisions, is that clear? And you decidedly are in no position to pit Private MacFie's opinions against your captain's."

"Jamie, everyone knows he's all that's keeping you sane—"

Her capitaine *slapped* him into silence.

George, shocked, stared agape for an instant, then stood to

his full height, incensed. "SIR," he corrected himself.

"Get out of here, George," Capitaine Graham said, crisply, and George gave him an exaggerated salute and stalked out.

"He's right, my lord," MacFie said, quietly, after George shut the door behind him and Capitaine Graham sank into his chair.

"Oh, shut up, Oliver," he snapped, but his hands trembled and something terrible came into his eyes. He pressed his fists into them, and MacFie came up and laid his own hands on Capitaine Graham's shoulders.

"My lord, you *ken* he's right. Dinnae risk the girl. She'll stay with Mme Blanchard this time, I'm sure of it."

Capitaine Graham lifted haunted eyes to his man. "I am... I *am* losing my mind, am I not, Oliver?"

MacFie sat beside him, one hand still firmly on his shoulder, and held his gaze. "You just hold fast, my lord. You'll make it, I swear, if you just hold fast. What's that you say, 'Hold thou me up, and I shall be safe'? You dinnae *need* me to hang on to, but I'm here to do what I can. A' right?"

Aveline didn't like the bleak, frightening look in her capitaine's eyes as he nodded mutely, and she vowed that absolutely nothing would keep her away from his side now. He needed her.

And that is why, once again, a girl haunted the trenches of Captain Graham's company, while the rain came down in torrents, and mud slowed every move to a crawl.

She had not known the trenches could be worse than they had been last month, but ahead of them lay days and days of doing little else but trying to keep the trench clear of water. Many of the men did not even have the luxury of dugouts this time; they dug shelves into the walls of the trench instead, wrapped themselves in their groundsheets, and prayed they wouldn't freeze. Aveline, particularly, had a difficult time slogging from one place to another in two feet of standing mud, and she was immensely frustrated that she couldn't roam freely as she had before. She didn't complain aloud, though; she hadn't *had* to come. She could have stayed at the Blanchards'. She had nobody but herself to blame for being here.

She mostly stayed put in her capitaine's dugout, alternately bored and frightened, the same as everyone else. Very little fighting happened, and the medic didn't have any extra work for her. Capitaine Graham went to the front line at two o'clock each afternoon and serenaded the Germans across No Man's Land with rousing battle songs. Aveline, desperate for diversion, would follow him as near as she could get without drowning, and listen.

> *Scots wha hae wi' Wallace bled,*
> *Scots wham Bruce has aften led;*
> *Welcome to your gory bed,*
> *Or to victory!*
> *Now's the day, and now's the hour;*
> *See the front o' battle lour;*
> *See approach proud Edward's power—*
> *Chains and slavery!*
>
> *By oppression's woes and pains!*
> *By your sons in servile chains!*
> *We will drain our dearest veins,*
> *But they shall be free!*
> *Lay the proud usurpers low!*
> *Tyrants fall in every foe!*
> *Liberty's in every blow!—*
> *Let us do or die!*

The Germans on the other side either did not recognize Graham's dark humor for what it was, or they didn't care. They applauded with abandon each time.

MUD: 2 NOVEMBER 1916

AS AVELINE SLOGGED her tiresome way back from the toilet before bed, she met Willie coming the other way, lantern in hand. Her face lit up at the sight of him, and he grinned at her.

"Where have you been?" she asked.

"Sleeping. I'm on a patrol tonight," he said. "It'll be hell. Ye ken how the ground is up there."

She made a face. The ground was riddled with shell craters, all of them mud, and now frosty in the mornings too. She didn't envy him that job one bit.

"It's quiet," he said contemplatively. "Canna even hit anything with the guns, what wi' all this rain making it so you canna make out what you're shooting at."

"I don't mind not having the guns going," she admitted. "I had enough of it last time." In the dim light of his lantern, they locked eyes, and she fell silent, sensing the mood change.

"If I dinna come back..." he trailed off.

Alarmed, she snatched his hand and squeezed it in hers. "You must come back!" she whispered, sharply.

He smiled, sadly. "I'm no worried much about being shot, ye ken. I'm worried about drowning in muck out there."

He reached out a hand and stroked her cheek with his thumb. With some difficulty, she moved closer to him, and he whispered, "May I kiss you for luck, Avie?"

She lifted her face, and he lightly touched his lips to hers, then wrapped his arm more tightly around her and kissed her as if starved for her. She felt safe and warm and shaky all at once—not fear, but a pleasant sort of buzzing. His lips brushed her neck, his moustache soft and tickly against her skin, and she moaned in delight.

At the sound, Willie stepped away very slowly. He leaned back against the filthy sandbags, his hand clenched at his sides, inhaling deeply. "Captain Graham will kill me." He looked at the sky with a near desperation in his eyes. "Kiss you for luck, indeed," he muttered. "Swallow you, more like."

"But I liked it." Her voice sounded thin and childlike in the dark.

Willie sniffed. "If I admit I'm only sixteen, he'll send me home. I told you, I'd rather be shot. And I dinna want him angry at you." His words were sharp, but the choked sob in his voice betrayed the real fear lurking beneath the surface, and it cut Aveline to the heart. She held out her arms to him and he came into them. She held him tightly, stroking his hair, willing him to be brave, while he whispered into her ear. "I love you, Avie. I want us both to be two years older so we can get married and find our place by the sea and wander the world together. I dinna want to stay here in this hell anymore. I want to be *me* again. Wi' you. Will you think on me in two years, when you're old enough to marry me? Oh, God, I am a coward. Why did I come here in the first place?"

She didn't answer. His impassioned outburst was more than she knew what to do with. After a moment, she pulled away from him and brushed the tears off his cheeks with her thumbs. "It will be all right, Willie. Don't be scared. Please. I'll be here when you get back."

He nodded, sniffing again loudly and wiping his nose on his sleeve. "Go on ahead," he said. "I'll be along when I pull myself together."

CHÂTEAU BLANCHARD

BACK AT THE Blanchards', Aveline had the luxury of a hot bath and a delousing in Mme Blanchard's kitchen. Since her kilt and tunic were so filthy, the lady wouldn't hear of her putting them back on until they'd been washed. "You can wear your girl's clothes just this once," Mme Blanchard said, firmly.

Aveline submitted with a huff, but went straight to her room after her bath and took them off again, swapping for her night-gown, and holding Sylvie tightly until the house fell quiet. She sneaked to her capitaine's room, where she pilfered his electric torch and spare tunic. Throwing it on over her insubstantial muslin nightgown, she slipped downstairs again and out into the night.

MEMORY

SHE MOVED ACROSS the frosty ground like a ghost with a cat-shaped shadow toward the stable to visit the mare and her foal. She didn't use the torch until she got inside, lest whoever was on watch tonight notice and come after her.

She rested her arms on the stable door, watching the precious sleepy foal. Sylvie jumped up onto the stable railing and rubbed her head on Aveline's arm. Aveline absent-mindedly scratched the cat behind the ears and thought about Willie.

Oh, Willie, lovely Willie. She relived their kiss in the trench and thought about his impassioned proposal that someday they ought to marry. She wondered why it had to be marrying, and why it had to wait two years. She'd be fourteen soon. She had kept house for Armand most of her life and knew she'd make a fine companion for Willie Duncan.

The memory of Armand stabbed her in the heart. She hated the idea of his dead body in the cellar beneath her feet for almost two weeks. The only reason she'd never opened the cellar during his absence was because she wasn't strong enough to do so. What if *she'd* been the one to discover him there? She didn't believe she could have borne that shock.

Life would never be the same without Armand. Never. It still seemed unreal she would never see him again, that this interruption was not temporary. She couldn't decide, now she'd had a chance to experience life away from the cocoon in which she'd grown up, whether she'd want to go back to that existence if she had the opportunity.

Was it disloyal to Armand to feel she'd suffocate if she returned to that? She felt more alive than she ever had been with him. She had a father now, and a mother and new brothers she would soon meet, and she had Willie Duncan, who gave such lovely kisses, who wanted her to be with him forever someday.

These last two months—so much had happened. Like waking from the long and complicated storyline of a dream to find you'd only been asleep for minutes. Like living an entire life in miniature.

For the first time in weeks, she let her mind relive the German's violence. Capitaine Graham said what the German did *could* be beautiful, in other circumstances. What about Willie? Could she like such a thing even with Willie?

Kissing was one matter; the surrender of one's whole self something else entirely. She trembled all over, half from cold, half from nerves, as she gripped the stall door, trying to breathe normally. It had hurt so much. No, she doubted she'd ever want to try *that* again, not even with Willie.

Behind her, soft footsteps sounded. The torch dropped from her hand and landed with a dull thud on the straw spilling out of the stall, as she whipped around toward the open stable door. She gasped and recoiled at the someone silhouetted there. Her mind flashed back to another silhouette in another barn door, and she froze for an instant, before she dashed up the ladder to the hayloft. She dropped face-down into the hay, crumbling in terror, stifling her panicky sobs. It was as if letting herself think about the German had summoned him to her. *Oh, God, he is coming up the ladder. He's seen me. He's coming for me. Please, God, let me die right now if this is going to happen again.*

The hay beside her rustled. She couldn't move, only lay there braced and waiting for the inevitable, but nothing happened.

"Avie? Is that you?"

It was Willie Duncan's voice, and at the familiar sound, her body unclenched itself and went limp. Her sobs escaped her now.

THE FISHERMAN'S SON WHO WASN'T

"WHAT'S THE MATTER, Avie?" He crawled over to sit beside her, peering into her eyes in the light of the waning moon coming in through the loft window.

"I thought you were the German," she said with difficulty through her tears and great gasps for air. "When he came, he stood in the barn door like you were standing, and I thought—I thought—"

"Shh, now," he said and lifted her into his arms to comfort her. "I'll no hurt you, not now, not ever. I swear. I saw a light in the stable, and I wanted to make sure the horses were all right. I didna know it was only you here, or I'd no have come in." His voice soothed her distressed nerves. "We're supposed to keep an eye out for that German, you ken."

"I'm glad you're here," she said. "You won't let anything bad happen to me." But her tortured sobbing continued.

"I should take you back inside," he said. "You're worrying me, Avie-lass."

"No," she said.

"It's cold out here, and you need to sleep."

"No," she said again, fiercely.

"But why?"

"Aren't you ever just *scared?*" she snapped, accusingly.

"Oh. Aye."

He continued holding her, stroking her hair. It took her a long time to calm herself, and when she finally spoke, her voice was stuffy from much crying. "Why did you say you would rather be shot than go home?"

He hesitated, but at last, he answered, "Because my father came there."

"What do you mean, came there? Wasn't he always there?"

"Aye, Dad was always there, but Avie, he's no my *father*." Willie's voice cracked. "My real father came back to our village in 1914, before the war, right before my fourteenth birthday. I look so much like him, everyone in the village pegged my mother as a whore overnight. It was the first I'd ever known my dad hadna been joking all those years. My mum told me she didna think she'd ever see the man again, that he'd swept into her life for a few days while Dad was out wi' the boats and then vanished. Mum was lonely so much. Dad wasna very warm, and the other man brought some spark into her life, I suppose, and she didna think anyone would ever be the wiser. I got angry at her. Left the next night. I couldna bear the way the village folk looked at her and then at me, like it was *my* fault what *she* did. I had to get into a boat to get off the island. Do ye ken how long it takes? Hours and hours. It's nigh three hundred miles to Aberdeen. I didna eat a bite, but I never stopped feeling like death the whole way, and I spent my first night in Aberdeen shivering in a heap in a back alley near the docks. My family doesna know what ever became of me. I took the other man's last name. Dad's name was William Hutchison. The other man, my real father, is Nicholas Duncan. He's got interests in Shetland; that's why he comes there sometimes. But no so often, *because he gets seasick too*." Willie scrubbed unmanly tears out of his eyes and went on. "I worked my way south, doing odd jobs on farms, and then the war started, but I didna enlist until the next year because I knew I'd no pass for eighteen until I got a wee bit bigger."

"Don't you miss them?"

"I miss my sisters. I dinna miss the mother who lived a lie all those years and made my life a shame."

Aveline didn't speak for a long time, Willie's bitter resentment hanging heavily over them. She reached for his hand in the dark and clasped it.

"I'm not sure, but I think maybe my mother was like your mother. My brother wouldn't tell me about her, and the few times I saw townspeople, they always looked at me like I had two heads. And that was *before* the German." She clenched his hand more tightly. "How much do you know about the German?"

"I know what he did to you," he said. "I'd like to kill him."

"So would my capitaine." She sighed deeply. "Why does it hurt?"

"What?"

"What the German did. Capitaine Graham says it can be a beautiful thing, but I don't see how it can ever be for the woman when it hurts like that."

"I dinna think it always hurts. I expect it hurt you because you're little, and it was the first time."

She didn't answer, only extracted herself from his arms and stretched out on the hay. He lay beside her and took her hand, and they watched the stars moving across the square of sky visible through the loft window.

"Have you done that with a girl?" she asked almost inaudibly.

"No yet," he said. He turned toward her and stroked her cheek. "If you're worried I might do that to you, Avie, dinna be. I promise I'll no hurt you."

She rolled onto her side and said, "I might want it someday. But I don't now. Hold me, please, William Duncan. I am so scared."

"You're cold too." He opened his tunic to share his warmth, put his arms around her and kissed her cheek. "Dinna be faered. I'm here. We're a pair, are we no?"

Her tears fell again, more quietly this time. She was tired, and she kept yawning, but she didn't want to surrender to sleep. She wept for her brother and her lost childhood, for Willie's own family troubles, for the tangle of confusion in her heart about her feelings for Willie.

It was warm in the hay and Willie's embrace despite the cold outside, and slowly Aveline's sniffling subsided, her body relaxed, and she drifted off. Willie, comfortable and calm himself and content to enjoy this moment, decided he would let her sleep a little before taking her back to the house.

YOUNG PEOPLE MISSING

IN THE MORNING, Graham's alarm woke him as usual. He washed and shaved and went to Aveline's closet to check in on her, but she wasn't there.

He turned to seek out Mme Blanchard to ask her if she'd seen the girl, but George appeared and intercepted him with a query of his own. "Where's Duncan?" he asked Graham.

"What do you mean, where's Duncan?" They were still not on the best of terms since their argument about whether Aveline should come with them to the trenches, but the perplexed look on George's face unsettled Graham enough to drop the grudge for the moment.

"He's not in our room. He usually has everything laid out for me by now."

Straightway, into Graham's head flashed a vision of Aveline's behavior the past two weeks. She *had* been unusually bright-eyed and squirrelly, even for her, but he hadn't had time to think much about it. He'd told himself she'd just gained more self-confidence after getting her voice back. Now, though, the lingering glances and the unusual softness and the trailing after Willie all came back to him, and his gut became a cold ball of dread. "So help me, I will beat the living daylights out of him," he said ominously. Before George could speak, Graham was down the hall. The front door slammed behind him.

Graham paused a moment, mentally reviewing all the outbuildings on the Blanchards' estate. The only one nobody used for sleeping in was the stable. It would be the most likely place for a tryst. He strode toward it. The door had been left open. *That* was careless.

His torch lay abandoned by the mare's stall, the battery dead. Graham left it and moved silently toward the ladder, mounting it and looking over the edge.

The sun had not yet risen, but he could see well enough: they were there, fast asleep, Aveline tucked into Willie's protective embrace and Sylvie nestling against their heads. For a moment, Graham stared at them, feeling torn to pieces. He noiselessly pulled himself into the loft, stood directly at Willie's head, and switched on the torch he'd snatched up on his way out of the house, shining it directly into the young man's face.

Willie stirred and squinted, blinded by the light. Aveline also stirred beside him, and he gasped, "Oh, God, what have I done?"

"That's what I'd like you to tell me," said Graham, his voice quiet and terrible.

"Oh, *shite.*" Willie leapt to his feet, stricken, and Aveline sat up, blinking in confusion.

Graham took a handful of Willie's shirt in his fist and pulled him close, eyes flashing. "Did I or did I not explicitly warn you," he said, "that if you touched her, there would be hell to pay? Did I, Duncan?"

Willie swallowed, but he met Graham's gaze steadily. "Aye, sir. Ye did."

"And despite the warning, you lured her out here! How long have you been here?"

"Since before midnight, sir," Willie said.

Graham drew back and slapped Willie in the face, hard. "What *were* you thinking?"

"I wasna thinking, sir. I'm sorry, sir. She was pure done in, and I planned to take her back to the house after letting her sleep a little, but I—I'm afraid I drifted off too, sir."

Graham's eyes penetrated right into Willie's soul. Willie bit his lip.

"Ye impudent wee *bastart.*" Graham's face went pale with disbelief and fury. "Did ye—"

Willie didn't reply.

"Answer me, Duncan!" Graham demanded, shaking him.

Willie swallowed again and whispered, "I didna make love to her, sir, if that's what you mean. And I didna 'lure her out here.'"

"But you were here for eight hours alone with her?"

"I swear, sir, I didna harm her," Willie said, but Graham wasn't listening.

"I have never until this moment been sorry flogging isnae allowed in the army anymore," Graham said. "I would have you out there right now, and I'd do it myself, and I might even enjoy it. That's my opinion about this, Duncan. What have you to say for yourself? What were you doing, if not seducing her?"

Willie glanced at Aveline, who clearly struggled to follow the conversation, and his shoulders drooped. But he looked Graham straight in the eye when he answered. "I was comforting her, sir."

"That's all, is it?" Graham asked skeptically.

"I love her, sir. I tried not to. But I couldna help myself."

"You're *twenty years old.*"

"He's not," Aveline burst out. "He's sixteen. Oh—" she clapped a hand over her mouth and looked guiltily at Willie, realizing she had just spilled his secret.

Graham glanced at her and back to Willie, scrutinizing him as though he'd never really seen him before. "Sixteen," he breathed. "You *are*, aren't you?"

Willie nodded miserably. "Your brother kent it right away, sir. I asked him no to tell on me."

Graham hid his face in his hand, trying to control himself as he worked through it in his head. *He oughtn't be here in the first place. He's lied to me, and that damn brother of mine backed him up. George would do something so stupidly irresponsible. Or else I'm the stupid one for not noticing. How could I not have noticed something so obvious? And Aveline... It is easy to get carried away. She is confused. She's terribly young—but I warned her about this. She knew better, at least, in theory. But I wouldn't expect her to be the moral compass for Willie. Willie is handsome and charming and a decent fellow—but even at sixteen, he is* definitely *old enough to know better. He is the responsible party.*

When he spoke at last, his voice was ominously soft. "She's too young to know her own mind, and I trusted you, Duncan."

"I am sorry, sir. It willna happen again."

"It most certainly will *not* happen again. Go to your room. You are not to leave there until I decide what to do with you."

"Aye, sir." Willie obeyed, glad to get away from Captain Graham's terrifyingly quiet voice. He cast one last glance at Aveline, longing and apologetic, and was gone.

Graham turned to Aveline. She shivered, hugging herself, frightened. "What do you have to say for yourself, lassie?"

She looked at him, her eyes brimming with tears. "Please don't be hard on Willie. He didn't do anything to me. I was sad, and he comforted me, like he told you."

"You leave Duncan to me. What has he done to you? Touched you? Kissed you?"

She smiled softly, pleased in spite of herself at the memory of Willie's kiss in the trench. "He hasn't kissed me tonight. Only held me."

"Does that mean he kissed you some other time?" Graham asked.

"He might have."

"Aveline!" His sharpness caught her off guard. "You *must* tell me everything."

"He already told you what happened."

Graham huffed impatiently. "If he didn't lure you out here, why were you both here?"

"He already told you," she said, becoming frustrated. "I couldn't sleep, I came out here, he found me crying, and he comforted me. That's all! Anyway, I love him and someday I shall go wander the world with him." She raised her chin in that all-too-familiar defiance.

"An entirely impractical idea," he said.

"Why?"

"Aveline, you are not quite fourteen. You need to finish growing up first. You are simply too young to make a serious decision like this."

"But I love him."

"You *think* you love him. That is not the same thing. Regardless, he's just put you in a very compromising situation. Even if he is only sixteen, he should have realized that getting you back into the house last night should have been his only priority." He sighed deeply. "Aveline, I realize you've grown up with no restraint or training whatsoever, and I don't suppose you understand the severity of this situation. You will simply *have* to trust me on this."

She looked at her hands. He was picking out the stones of her castle in the air one by one. Didn't he believe she had told the truth about what had happened? "Are you going to punish him badly?"

"I haven't decided yet what I'm going to do to him. But that doesn't concern you. I do know what your consequences will be, however. You will need to stay in my sight at all times, and you will not be permitted to spend any time with Duncan. None at all, supervised or otherwise."

She didn't speak or look at him, and he lifted her chin.

"Lassie, I love you. You might drive me to an early grave, but I do love you. I want you to have the best life I can possibly provide for you, and dashing into a very physical love affair when you're thirteen is not part of my plans. You're coming home with me, remember? I'm going to cable my wife today to tell her when to meet us in Calais so she can get you away from here. Give it a few years. If you and Willie still love each other, well—we'll cross that bridge then. Fair enough?"

Her eyes filled with tears. He *was* being fair, she knew, but she resented the prescribed restraint nonetheless. "Will you let us say goodbye before I leave here?"

"Perhaps I shall, if you and he both stick to my conditions about not talking to each other between now and then." He dropped his hand. "When did he tell you he was sixteen?"

"The first time he ever talked to me, he told me. He didn't mean to, I don't think."

Graham stood staring out the loft window, musing something she only half heard about lies, cluelessness, and George; then he helped her down the ladder, and they walked back to the house.

FEAR

IN HIS ROOM, Willie, deeply afraid, did not lounge or even smoke.

He had blown everything. Even though he had not made love to Aveline, there was no real way of proving it, if proof was needed. He would be shipped off home to Shetland in disgrace—if he wasn't court-martialed and shot first. All his hard work and hopes for the future blasted because he'd had to be such an absolute *idiot*.

In the hayloft last night, he'd simply seen a frightened friend in need of comfort. Knowing what had happened to Aveline made him value her more, somehow. Sharing his secrets with her had been the most freeing thing he'd done since he had discovered the truth about his father. Much as he'd enjoyed the kiss they had shared, he didn't need that as much as he needed her friendship. He suspected she felt the same way.

He got off his bed and paced the little room he shared with George, sick inside. How long would Captain Graham make him wait before meeting his doom? The waiting was the worst. If he could know what to expect, it would be easier to bear.

LOST BOY

MEANWHILE, GRAHAM FOUND George and asked sharply, "If you knew Duncan was underage, why didn't you tell me?"

George answered with maddening calm. "He asked me not to."

"You've been letting him risk his life, knowing he shouldn't even *be* here? You want to have his death on your conscience?"

George met his brother's eyes. "His dad hates him, and he's terrified to go home. I didn't think you'd want him to go back to that. Would you?"

Graham blinked at George, wordless.

"*I* certainly didn't want him to."

"What's the difference?" Graham shot back. "After all the grief you've given me about keeping Aveline here, how is Duncan any different? How can you justify *that*?"

"Aveline has somewhere safe to go," George said. "Duncan reminded me of you, Jamie. I couldn't send him back to an angry father and have *that* on my conscience."

Aveline spent the rest of the day subdued and mopey. She trailed after her capitaine as required, but she wasn't her usual happy self.

She could not erase the memory of Willie's words: *He could have me shot.*

TELEGRAM

WHEN THE TELEGRAM arrived, Estelle panicked. She sat to open it with Jeannine close at hand, in case.

DARLING ESTELLE STOP

MEET ME CALAIS 9TH NOVEMBER ON EARLIEST POSSIBLE SHIP STOP

BRING LEASH FOR AVELINE

OR PERHAPS AN ARMBAND WITH JINGLING BELLS

OR A BALL AND CHAIN STOP

YOUR JAMIE

She burst into relieved laughter to see it was not bad news, and at the recommendation to bring restraining devices. Her pulse quickened at the idea that she would soon meet her husband, even if only for a few hours. She wasn't sure if or how they would manage to ever be alone, but she would kiss him. *Oh*, how she would kiss him.

PART ELEVEN

12 November 1916

Allonville, France

THE TRAVELLER'S SIDE OF THINGS

JAMIE WAS STILL fevered and unconscious the next morning. He opened his eyes at times, but without responding to anything. Still, he was alive, and the doctor promised to arrange for his transfer to a British hospital as soon as possible.

Estelle did not want to leave her husband alone for even a moment, but she had one thing yet to do before she left this place. She wanted to meet Oliver MacFie. Fortunately, George showed up again around eleven o'clock, and she forgot the annoyance she'd felt toward him the previous night in gratitude that he could keep vigil awhile.

MacFie lay in a corner bed at the opposite end of the hospital, swathed in bandages. He saw her and lifted his head from the pillow. "Lady Inverlochy," he said hoarsely, with a faint smile. "I'm sorry I cannae stand—"

She sat beside him and laid her hand lightly on his shoulder. "Nae bother," she said, and he smiled and relaxed at her casual tone. "I wanted to thank you for all you've done for my husband."

"Is he a' right, ma'am?"

"He's still alive, but he's fevered and unconscious. They had to take off his foot last night."

MacFie's hopeful expression fell. "Oh, he'll hate that," he said sadly.

"It can't be helped," she said. "And he'll hate it less than losing his hands. What happened to you?"

"Shot in the chest, ma'am. Lucky shot, didn't hit anything important, but I'll be laid up a while. They'll send me on to England soon."

"Is there any message I could carry home to your people?"

"Could you write a letter for me?" he asked, a light in his eyes. "Captain Graham used to, but of course he cannae just now..."

"I would be delighted to, Mr. MacFie."

"You can address it to the vicar MacDuff in Invergarry. He and his wife keep an eye on my lady and the bairns for me."

After she sealed the letter and tucked it safely in her handbag, MacFie asked, shyly, if she had a moment to talk.

"I have all the time there is until they get Jamie and me out of here," she said with a deep sigh.

MacFie stared thoughtfully at some invisible thing on the far tent wall. His tone, as always, was dry, but his eyes sparked with humor. "I saw Duncan here last night. That boy deserves a medal."

Estelle eyed him. "Whatever for?"

"You know the thing his lordship says about you, terrible as an army wi' banners?"

"Of course I do."

He went on, not so much as cracking a smile. "Duncan came to see me, last night, after you spoke wi' him. He looked like he'd seen a ghost and said 'terrible as an army wi' banners' was an understatement, and how if General Haig sent you after the Huns, the war would be over in minutes."

Estelle didn't say anything, just narrowed her eyes at him, trying to determine if he was serious. "I thought I was rather nice to him, considering."

"Never mind me, Lady Inverlochy. Did the lad tell you much of anything?"

Estelle watched him a moment longer before she answered. "He was distressed. I got the whole story of him and Aveline, after two hours of prompting and trying to get him to stop crying. He wanted me to forgive him since Jamie might not. And he went away without giving much detail about what happened out there by the farmhouse. He didn't seem to want to talk of it."

"Well, I can tell you that better anyway," MacFie said. "I was in the farmhouse, and he wasnae. But he probably didnae tell you it was him saved Captain Graham's life."

"No, he didn't."

"Aye, twice over. First by getting a tourniquet on him and tossing us into a wagon and driving like mad to get us to help. I was conscious, but barely, up 'til then. The ride knocked me out. Then we got here, and he pestered them to let him give some of his own blood to keep his lordship alive. I saw the lad afterward. White as a sheet he was, telling me how his lordship had fallen into a heap in the trench, the water red all around him wi' the blood pouring out. He was always like that, Duncan was, telling you things that scared him. Like a bairn telling its nightmares."

"Did you know anything about this... this supposed indiscretion between Aveline and Willie?"

"Aye, I did." MacFie sighed and shifted on his cot. "You must understand, my lady, that his lordship has been... shall we say... not quite himself for a very long time."

"Yes, I... I had noticed that."

MacFie lowered his voice. "He was doing better, at first, after he found Aveline, and then, sudden-like, he started being verra... pardon me, my lady, but there's nae other word for it. Foolish. Couldnae make him see reason for anything. He's been like that before, a few times, and I'd been able to talk him through it, but the men, they've started to notice." He shrugged his uninjured shoulder. "It's probably best he's oot o' it now, anyhow. He'll soon be himself again, going hame wi' you. But aye, he told me of it, the morning he found 'em in the hayloft."

Estelle sat quietly a moment. "Well, I do thank you for doing what you could, Mr. MacFie, but do tell me, why was Willie so sure it was *his* fault, what happened to Aveline?"

"She had to stay wi' his lordship all the time, remember, because of finding her out in the hayloft wi' Duncan? She *could* hae been safe back at the Blanchards', and none of what happened would hae happened. Because his lordship would never have noticed the farmhouse being amiss, let alone gone in, on his own. We all know that. Wee Aveline, though, she noticed *everything*."

PART TWELVE

6-7 November 1916

France

THE COMPANY OF MISFITS

GRAHAM SAT AWAKE at his table long after the rest of the inmates of Château Blanchard were asleep, a blank paper before him, on which he intended to write to his superior officer about Duncan.

The problem of Willie Duncan chewed at his brain. He'd lectured the boy severely this evening, perhaps too severely. MacFie had advocated weeks ago for the speedy disposal of Aveline to Scotland, and he hadn't listened; tonight MacFie had cautioned him against being hasty in regard to Willie. "After all, my lord, I *did* tell you a month and more ago to get her hame to your wife, even before your brother shouted at you. Why did you wait so long?"

MacFie was right, of course, as always.

What was happening to his own judgement, Graham wondered? A year ago, he'd never have kept the girl here this long. What had George said—"pathologically delusional"? That, too, was true. He made a mental note to apologize to his brother in the morning, both for slapping him and rejecting sound advice. Even if George *had* done basically the same thing with Willie Duncan, he didn't want a quarrel standing between himself and George.

But Willie, not Aveline, was the matter most pressing tonight. In the quiet of his present thoughts, Graham knew charging him with assault would be unfair; obviously he hadn't hurt Aveline, and even more obviously, the two of them were besotted with each other. Now that his initial fury had cooled, Graham wished he could let it go. But he couldn't. He had to follow through with his ultimatum. Either Duncan could choose court-martial like the man he had pretended to be, or he could be sent home to his parents in shame and disgrace.

Graham himself would have to answer for it if he lost hold of his authority over his men. He was sure most, if not all, of them knew that MacFie was the one really running things here, and that combined with letting Duncan off with a slap on the hand was a slippery slope he didn't think he could recover from.

And if it became common knowledge he'd had a girl here this long, actively enabling her presence, well, *he* might be the one being tried instead. MacFie had reminded him of this as well.

He wished he could get Aveline to Estelle now, this minute.

Graham was angry with himself for not having noticed what had been so obvious to George from the start. Of *course*, Duncan was too young to be here. He stood up and began pacing the room, attempting to force his thoughts into some semblance of order.

He remembered the day Willie Duncan had shown up at Aldershot, where Graham had been sent in 1915 to help bring the unruly hordes of volunteers crowding into the ranks into good military discipline. The boy had been almost too enthusiastic, too determined. He never wrote letters home or received any, and he had a childlike innocence about him that showed in sharp contrast to the coarseness of many of the older or more worldly-wise men. At the time, Graham had attributed this to the limits of the sheltered life remote islands to the north of Scotland provided.

Willie went out of his way to prove himself, and Graham liked the boy and began teaching him French in the evenings. They weren't friends as such; Graham had looked on him as a project more than a person.

MacFie had showed up at about the same time as Duncan. Unlike Willie, Oliver MacFie did not want to be in the army at all. He had, like far too many others, been mercilessly pressured into enlisting. "Nobody wants a tinker unless they can get something out of him," MacFie said. "I've a woman and bairns to care for. This isnae my war. But here I am. Tell me what I should do."

Graham liked him right away. Thinking MacFie might be marginally safer as his orderly than he would be otherwise, he quickly snatched him. He never dreamed then that it would be he, and not MacFie, who was going to need the protecting.

INESCAPABLE GEORGE

G RAHAM'S GREATEST SURPRISE, however, had been the morning George turned up in Aldershot in uniform. Graham met him outdoors while on his customary pre-reveille walk.

"What are *you* doing here?" was all Graham could say.

"I'm going to war with you," George answered.

Graham stared at George, speechless for minutes. "But your career," he objected at last.

"There'll still be lawsuits after this is over, aye," George said. "I'll not have you in the thick of things without me there looking after you."

Graham sighed. Over the past few years, the differences between him and George had widened until the two of them hardly spoke. George came to the castle each summer with his wife and four daughters for the Twelfth, but for the last two or three years, that had been nearly the extent of their interaction.

Graham wasn't entirely sure what had caused the rift. He'd sensed unhappiness and strain between George and Maggie, and he did not want to get embroiled in someone else's marital woes, even if the someone was his George. He had chosen to turn a blind eye to his brother's difficulties. He still loved George, of course, but George lived a long train ride away from Inverlochy Castle, and Graham had, subconsciously, left his brother to fend for himself.

"Wake up," George said five minutes later, perceiving that Graham was lost in his own head. Graham started.

George sat on a stone wall nearby and took Graham's hand, making him take a seat beside him. "Listen," George said, "we've hardly spoken for years, and it's as much my fault as anyone's. I guess I was put off by the way you're always so right." He poked at some loose gravel with the toe of his boot. "You used to tell me I needed to settle down and stop fooling with other women.

Water from your own cistern and all that. And I thought you were overzealous, and I could do whatever I wanted and get away with it. I did for a long time, but I've found out I can't really, not forever."

Graham sighed. "What have you done now?"

"Maggie found out I had been dallying with Alice-who-lives-down-the-street."

"And who is this Alice?"

"You've met her," George said. "A few years ago she and her husband came to the castle with us over the twelfth."

Graham couldn't remember, but George continued. "Anyway, she's Maggie's best friend—*former* best friend," he amended. "A mighty pretty widow."

Graham leaned his face into his hands. "George, George, *George...*"

"She couldn't have children, so we didn't bother with any—you know. We have unfortunately learned it was actually her dead husband who couldn't produce children." He looked at the ground, and Graham lifted his eyes heavenward in exasperation. The confession did not surprise him, but it did appall him.

"Mercy on us, George," he said, with undisguised outrage. "How could you do that to Maggie?"

George still kept his eyes fixed on his feet. "I've never really loved Maggie. I was after her money, I guess. I see a pretty woman, and I lose my head. But usually, they've been one-night things, far from home, and nobody's been any the wiser. Well, I mean, Maggie *knows*—she's sharper than she looks, behind those cow eyes of hers—but I kept telling her lies to keep her from completely turning on me. For the girls' sake, you know?"

"Behaving in a way that kept you from having to lie in the first place would have been far better for the girls, George," Graham pointed out. "So you've joined up to escape?"

"I tried to patch it over with Maggie, but she says she's over-looked my traitorous behavior long enough, and she doesn't want anything more to do with me. Of course, she feels betrayed by Alice, too, which I suppose is natural. And now I have Alice's child to consider also—"

"It's not only *her* child," Graham reminded him.

"I know."

Graham had never seen George in this genuinely ashamed and uncertain attitude. Pity rose in his heart in spite of himself, but he knew better than anyone that George could be a master of emotional manipulation whenever it would help him, and he steeled himself against falling for George's wiles.

"If you want me to believe you truly regret any of this, it will take proof," Graham said sternly. "You can't hoodwink me, George. I know you better than Maggie ever did or Alice ever will." He paused. "I expect you know what I *want* to say to you."

"'Be sure your sin will find you out'?"

"Aye. Perhaps also 'Can a man take fire in his bosom, and his clothes not be burned?' But you hate when I quote at you, so I won't."

George looked up at last. "I'm still not sold on your religious convictions, but in this, at least, you were right. I'm sorry I didn't listen to you. I want us to be friends again."

Graham suspected George only felt sorry because he had been caught, but he didn't say so. "What are you planning to do about Alice?" Graham asked.

"I'll support her and the child, naturally," George said. "I won't be able to get out of it, now I've told you, will I?" He meant it humorously, but there was no trace of jesting in his tone nor any light in his eyes. "Frankly, Jamie, barring you, I love her more than I have ever loved anyone else in my life, I really do. She's asked me to pay her passage to America so she can start fresh. She has nowhere to go here to get away from the shame. She's leaving in a month. I found her a place in New York State where there's a good Jewish community she can be part of, and—"

"And Maggie?" Graham interrupted, not terribly interested

in the details about the future prospects of Alice-who-lived-down-the-street.

"She told me she'll burn any letters I try to send the girls and shoot me if I ever come into her sight again. She wants a divorce, but—" he hesitated.

"Wouldn't do your career any good, would it?"

"No, it wouldn't," George admitted. "Maggie's a decent mother, if a shrew as a wife, and I've been a louse. Maybe I should give her what she wants. I don't know anymore."

Graham stood. "Well, for now, you can keep your reputation as an upstanding citizen by running off to fight for your country. Excellent cover for what's actually going on, giving you time to find a way to smooth it all over." He did not attempt to mask his sarcasm.

"Don't be unkind," George pleaded.

"I'm not being unkind. Coddling you is not kindness, and you know it. You prove to me you're really sorry for the mess you've made, and I'll have sympathy and try to help you all I can. But now you're here, I'm your superior officer, and you get nothing better from me than I give anyone else. Fair is fair."

George soon lost his air of subdued misery. It was impossible for him to stay miserable long, especially once he'd left the perceived source of his trouble—Maggie. Graham knew he still wrote regularly to Alice-who-lived-down-the-street, and that he'd even gone to spend a day and a night with her before she sailed for America. But he did not ask George about it. As far as Graham was concerned, George's questionable life choices and their consequences were George's problem. It was hard to regain their former closeness, but they were on speaking terms again, and that was a step in the right direction. George and Willie Duncan, meanwhile, had hit it off right away. They worked well together and had been inseparable ever since they met. George got Graham to fix it so Willie could be his orderly.

Graham had worried George would be a bad influence on the impressionable young Duncan. Now he realized George had only ever tried to protect Willie as best he could, and Graham had to admit he'd done a decent job of it.

In all the time since, not much had changed between Graham and George. They did fight for a common cause, and George truly wasn't as flighty now as he had been at the beginning of the war. Hardship had been good for him. But Graham could not deny that, although all the men respected him, they didn't like him the way they liked George. Sometimes it hurt terribly to not be generally *liked*.

Now he risked losing their respect as well. Here in the wilds of the wider world, Graham was again a misfit, with no real anchor.

Well, one anchor. He took his candle and peeked into Aveline's closet where she lay fast asleep with Sylvie, and smiled sadly. They were both misfits, he and Aveline, and it had taken a cruel war to throw them together. She filled part of him he hadn't known was still empty, but now recognized as a longing for a child like himself. None of his boys were essentially like him. Aveline was. She and he had been fighting a war within their own hearts all their lives, a war against circumstance, abuse, solitude, and fear.

Perhaps now they were together, they could hope for victory. Graham leaned over her, kissed her cheek lightly, and went to bed, but try as he would, he still could not sleep. He knew deep in his heart that Willie Duncan had been fighting that same war too, and his conscience gave him no rest as he wondered again what to do with the boy.

The paper on his desk remained blank.

PERFECTLY ROUTINE SUPPLY RUN

B EFORE IT WAS light the next morning, Graham and Aveline and MacFie were on the road toward the trenches with their wagonload of supplies. Not much was happening in the battle. Two days ago, according to a messenger, the mud had been so bad, the men had to pull each other out of it to go fight. They could make no real progress in such hellish conditions, and all the men hoped the Dread Staff Officers would soon call an end to this for the winter.

Graham was beyond exhausted. It was not his turn to run supplies, but just this morning he'd learned that there was influenza going rampant in the camp since yesterday afternoon. He wondered, considering the shaky state of his mind, if he'd been told already and forgot.

At any rate, now he had to see to this supply run himself, and he was compelled to recruit Willie Duncan to help with the task. Formally deciding what to do with the lad would have to be postponed, at least for one day.

Graham himself did not feel well either, but he didn't have time to succumb to anything at the moment, so he kept going. Besides not having slept well, he'd barely eaten since the hayloft incident. MacFie and Aveline both begged him to rest, but he hadn't time for rest either. He sat on the wagon seat, giving thought to little at all except how he must not close his eyes, lest he fall asleep. The trees of the once-lush wood nearby, blasted to skeletal spires and black against the bleak sky, made him dizzy. He desperately wanted to close his eyes against the sight of them, but he had to keep alert, because he had Aveline with him.

He had not wanted her to come today, but she had reminded him that his own orders had been for her to not be out of his sight, and he'd had to give in. Even without having made such a decree, he knew how she worked. When she had made up her mind about a thing, she clung to it with the tenacity of a tick, and in the end, it was always easier to let her come, instead of wearing himself out arguing with her before he even got out the door in the morning.

To keep himself awake, Graham lectured Aveline on every possible disaster that might happen—there are unexploded shells scattered about, etc., etc.—and reminded her what she shouldn't do (which was, it seemed to her, everything). She let him lecture, mostly not listening. She'd heard it all the day before, and the day before that.

Aveline felt keenly her responsibility for her capitaine's current stress, and although glad Willie had joined their work party today, she knew it was only a temporary respite from whatever fate awaited him afterward. She desperately hoped he would not be shot, as he so staunchly had said he'd rather be than go home. And she wasn't allowed to talk to him. But he was there, and that was enough.

No one spoke much on the ride. Aveline's mind teetered between the absolute desolation she felt that soon—the day after tomorrow!—she would have to leave Willie Duncan behind, and absolute ecstasy that soon—also the day after tomorrow!—she would get to meet her new mother. In the meantime, she felt glad to be back to the comforting familiarity of her tunic and kilt.

When they arrived at the trench, with its icy water and mud deep at the bottom, she stoically pitched in and helped unload in the rain. She looked at her old home as they worked, with bemused detachment, realizing for the first time it *wasn't* home anymore.

She remembered how often she had watched from the window as endless streams of wagons or trucks went to the very trench where she now helped to deliver things, curious about the activity but frightened of being Seen. Now little remained to be frightened *of*; she had experienced it all. She still hated the guns and shells, but she had stopped fearing them. From listening to the men's conversations in the trenches, she'd come to a stoic recognition of the fact that, as long as they didn't come for her, they weren't going to hurt her—and if they did come for her, chances were she wouldn't feel it anyway.

As if by thinking of explosions she had conjured one up, the ground exploded in geysers of mud close by—too close. The three of them dove into the nearest trench, but one of the men collecting the goods said, "It's mined all between the old house and here. I just threw that empty crate, see?"

"I don't see any crate," Aveline said.

"You dinnae see it because there's nothing left of it," MacFie said, grim.

"How long has this area been mined?" Graham asked. "Why have I not been informed?"

"It's new in the last week," the sergeant answered. "We've been keeping sentries here since one of the delivery boys got hit day before yesterday, but nobody has noticed anything. Dinnae ken who's doing it, but they're clever sods."

Graham gripped Aveline by the shoulder. They pressed close side to side and peered over the edge, and when he spoke, his voice was soft. "Get in the wagon, lass, and stay there." She obeyed without question. She kept her head down and her pistol ready in her hand. She knew it was no defense against a mine or any other unexploded thing, but it helped her feel braver anyway.

Her eyes scanned the surroundings. Again she looked toward her old house, and she cocked her head, perplexed. Something was wrong with it. It took her a moment of squinting through the haze of rain to perceive that all the windows had been smashed, and the front door hung open. She shuddered with a sudden chill.

"Capitaine," she said, not taking her eyes off the house, her voice thin and shaky. He acknowledged her with a weary *hmph*, and she pointed to the house. "Capitaine, it wasn't like that last week."

THE FARMHOUSE

H E AND MACFIE followed her pointing finger, and instantly, Graham was on the alert.

"I'm going over there," he said, and before MacFie or Aveline could stop him, he set off running. Behind him, the sergeant shouted to remind him of the mines, and MacFie swore at him for his stupidity, but Graham ignored both of them.

He ran all the way to the house. It looked utterly desecrated. He stood in the door gasping for a moment. It was worse than only broken windows. Everything had been torn apart, furniture broken, drawers tipped onto the floor, mattresses cut open.

The mere sight of the destruction sent that pricking down his spine he'd had the day he found Aveline. As he stood there, Aveline skidded to a stop beside him. He got hold of her hand and would not let go as he strained his ears and eyes for any movement anywhere in the house.

"Keep me covered," he ordered the girl and MacFie, who had been the last to catch up with him, and he walked slowly to Armand's room. The old heavy desk had been rifled through too. Graham searched with his hand for any hidden panel or secret drawer. He struggled for five minutes before Aveline sighed tolerantly, moved his hand away, and reached into the gaping hole where a small drawer had been. She pressed with her finger, and a little compartment opened behind the drawer, and she gestured for him to have a look.

He stared at her. "How did you know about that?"

"I didn't have much to do during the days after Armand went away," she said. "How did you know?"

"Armand's journals," he said. "You knew about the jewels."

He didn't himself know if it was a statement or a question. Her face looked out of focus.

"You need sleep, Capitaine," she urged softly.

"No time," he said. He felt in the little compartment, and his hand came out clasping its contents. Several photographs fluttered to the floor. He opened his palm and saw a pair of diamond earbobs and a strand of gleaming pearls. He turned to Aveline, but before he could speak, she grabbed at his sleeve with her free hand. Her eyes were glued to something in the kitchen, and her entire body went rigid.

"What is it?" he asked, alarmed. She pointed, and he followed her finger to look around the edge of the door. "*C'est lui*," she breathed. "That's him."

He dropped the jewels to the desk with a clatter.

Aveline watched Graham's face as it hardened, and his eyes became steely. He had never looked so dangerous. Alarmed, she laid a restraining hand on his arm.

The man who had materialized in the kitchen was big. Not just tall, also heavy, with a moustache. Unmistakably the same German. He did not appear to be armed. Her capitaine was no match for the man in bulk or height, but there were three of them to one of him. He never took his eyes off the man. "MacFie," he said softly, "your bayonet."

MacFie, in the front door, raised his pistol and aimed, but didn't shoot as he unhooked the leather holder with his bayonet from his belt and tossed it to Graham. "Have a care, my lord," he said softly. "You're going aff again. How about you go on back to the wagon wi' the lass, and I'll tak care o' this…"

Aveline also trained her gun on the German. One glance at her capitaine told her she and MacFie were on their own. Capitaine Graham was not looking at her; he had a strange and eerie smile on his face. Clearly he had vanished into that world in his head which nobody could ever penetrate, and she doubted he'd heard MacFie's warning.

He would be master over this beast. Graham would knock him to the floor, plant one boot hard on his chest, look him straight in his tortured eyes, and say coldly, "You raped my little girl." One bayonet stab. Maybe in the hand or shoulder. Somewhere that wasn't fatal. The man would howl gratifyingly. "And killed her brother." A second stab. "Ye dinnae belong here." Third stab. "Ye've nae right, nae right, to live after what ye did to my Aveline." He would forget all else; his mind would be numb with bloodlust; he would curse and shout and stab with deadly accuracy. "Ye filthy bastart," he would rasp out. All the anger and rage he'd ever had inside him would pour out of him through his bayonet: his anger at his father, and his vicious headmasters and teachers, and his mother's indifference, and out-of-touch Dread Staff Officers, and the pathetic governments that had brought their nations to this war. He would save the miserable whimpering man's face for last with its terrified, unblinking eyes. "And this is for my Aveline. Your life for her honor, Herr Boche!" The crushing, crunching sound of skull and muscle would be satisfyingly horrendous as he would throw every ounce of strength he had into a final plunge. The blade would go straight through the man's face and into the floor under his head...

The loud report of a shot jarred him to consciousness, and he wheeled about. While he'd drifted through his deranged fantasy, the man had leapt past him through the window, mindless of the jagged edges of broken glass, only to be felled by Aveline's ruthless but non-fatal aim to his shoulder. He tried to get back to his feet, but before he could, Aveline had leapt out the window after him.

"Do you remember me?" she screamed at him. "I think you don't. But you'll never forget me now." And, at close range, she aimed at his groin and shot. The man screamed and collapsed. She stood over him, a macabre delight in her eyes. "We are even," she said, her voice low. She holstered her pistol and walked calmly back towards the wagon.

From the window, Graham cringed. She had outdone the wildest ravings of his imagination. But now she walked alone, through a potentially lethal minefield.

He too leapt through the window and finished off the man with MacFie's bayonet. Graham shook all over, adrenaline and shock together surging through his body as he leaned his entire weight on the hilt of the blade. A moment later, he straightened; his rage all spent, the joints of his arms turned to jelly, and he couldn't get the bayonet back out. Chills shuddered through him as he got to his feet, stumbled backward slowly, and turned in a daze toward his own people. Everything went hazy around the edges of his vision, but he clearly saw MacFie bounding toward him, seizing him and dragging him back toward the relative safety of the communication trench, cursing him lavishly for his stupidity. "Och, my lord, you bloody idiot, would you listen to me just this *one last time*? The *mines*, man, mind where ye walk!"

The German hadn't been alone. A bullet whizzed before Graham's eyes and got MacFie; he fell, and a second bullet got Graham in the ankle. He collapsed to his knees, an irresistible target in the open, stunned by the unspeakable pain in his foot.

"NO," he shouted at the sky. "I'M NOT DONE LIVING YET." His defiance disintegrated into sobs, and he bowed toward the ground, clutching the mud.

A voice called. "Capitaine Graham! You must get down, *now!*"

He looked up. It was Aveline.

She had made it back to the wagon. He knelt staring at her, frozen, his hands poised oddly in front of him as though they could not decide where they ought to go. Her face went white as paper, and she vaulted over the edge of the wagon and ran to him, charged at him, pushed him, dragged him, rolled him across the uneven terrain with unimaginable strength, over the edge of the trench. He landed with a splash in the ice-cold standing water in the trench, screaming as a bolt of pain shot through his leg. He could hardly comprehend what happened around him; all was a slow-moving eternity of confusion. Aveline shouted, ran in the direction where MacFie had fallen, apparently intending to help him get to safety. Another shot sounded, and a voice like Willie Duncan's called to her to turn around and get back to the trench. Graham raised his eyes just in time to see Aveline leaping toward him, arms outstretched.

And there was a bright explosion above him, and where Aveline had been, there was no more Aveline, only a million sparkling pieces of her, and then emptiness.

He stared, stunned, and her name tore out of his throat in a roar of denial and horror. He tried to jump to his feet and straightway collapsed in blinding pain.

And warm red darkness swallowed him whole.

CHÂTEAU BLANCHARD

GEORGE JERKED OUT of a doze and leapt to his feet. "Where's Graham?"

"You've been dreaming," one of the other men drawled.

"No," he said insistently, pale and trembling. "Where is my brother?"

The other man looked at him curiously. This was unusual behavior for happy-go-lucky George. "I'm sure he's fine."

"No. No, he's not fine. He's in trouble somewhere." George stood still only a moment before running out the back door.

PART THIRTEEN

November–December 1916

Scotland

OUT OF THE MIST

WHENEVER GRAHAM BECAME at all aware of his existence, he felt heavy and dull and stupid. He couldn't move so much as a finger. He could barely open his eyes. He supposed he still lay in the trench, stuck in the freezing mud. He drifted in and out of sleep even in his dreams, and he had no sense of time. The only thing he *was* sure of was, his foot hurt like the dickens. Infected? Why did nobody come to help him? He felt so cold, and everything was so dark. He dreamed of warm hands stroking his face, or perhaps they were angels' wings. Words of songs brushed about inside his brain in a tantalizing, senseless, frustrating jumble. Any time his mind would get to a place where he thought he might grasp hold of something solid, sleep overcame him—or was it the mud closing in on him?—and he surrendered to oblivion.

He never felt sure of anything at all until he opened his eyes and found he could keep them open, a fact that took a few moments to sink in. He lay in a dim room by himself. All was quiet. He sat up.

Too quickly. His head spun from the sudden change in position. A nurse nearby stood to come to him. He grabbed at her hand and said desperately, "Where am I? What's happened?"

"Aberdeen, sir. Aberdeen Military Hospital."

Aberdeen? Growing sense of dread. How could he have come all the way to Aberdeen from France and never known it? "What day is it? Why am I here?"

"20 November, sir. You've had a fever wasting you away for weeks."

He sat the rest of the way up, gaping stupidly at her, and gingerly poked at his ankle, which still hurt, but his finger went straight to the mattress, and he threw aside the cover.

His foot wasn't there anymore. From just above the ankle down, there was nothing.

Why did it still hurt, if it wasn't even there?

His look of horror caused the nurse to explain quickly, if it counted as an explanation. "Your ankle shattered to bits in France, got infected. You'll be going home soon, now you're awake."

It all came back to him in a suffocating flood, the smoke and explosions and the metallic tang of blood in his mouth and the stench of fear. The pulpy, bloody mess made of that German. But the German was not the only one who died that day. Graham's hand went into a fist, and he stuffed it against his mouth in agony, convulsing with physically painful tremors.

Oliver MacFie had been shot too. MacFie had tried to save his pathetic hide from certain death. So had Aveline. Twice in an hour, Graham had been saved by people who died doing it.

Panic.

He bolted out of the bed, forgetting he couldn't run anywhere, and when he sprawled out on the floor, the nurse had to call for reinforcements to help get him back into his bed. He clung to her feet, sobbing and rambling in French as if he'd lost his mind.

The doctor gave him something to sedate him. A numbing grey haze of melancholy gradually filled his head, and he sat in bed and stared out the window at nothing. His eyes streamed silent tears, his heart was cold, and he would not, could not, respond to the doctor or anyone else who came to check on him.

Graham just sat. Alone. Only his hands moved, with involuntary, unstoppable tremors.

INVISIBLE

ESTELLE CAME AGAIN in the afternoon after having been ordered by the doctor to get a proper sleep. Jamie had been awake for seven hours, they told her when she arrived, but the news of losing his foot had sent him into shock again. Perhaps she could get a response out of him?

She ran to his room, tripping and slipping on her way and barely avoiding tumbling to the floor. She didn't care about dignity at this moment. His fever was gone; he was awake; he would live. *Her beloved would live.*

He sat propped up by pillows, grey-faced and ghostly and as still as death. For a moment, her heart stopped, and she approached slowly and leaned toward him from beside the bed, fearing the worst. She held her hand near his face and felt with relief that he was, in fact, breathing. She sat carefully beside him and said his name, and he slowly, very slowly, moved his eyes toward her, unfocused as if he were unable or unwilling to see anything near him. They looked toward her but not at her, as if he were looking through her. She was invisible.

TORMENT

THE SEVEN HOURS of being awake had felt like seven years to Graham. It was a peculiar sort of hell, to be conscious and yet as unable to respond as if he were not. The doctors assumed he was upset over losing his foot, but they were wrong. The foot was secondary, and for the moment, not in his mind at all. All he knew was the guilt of having caused the death of his two best comrades.

A woman appeared in front of him. "Jamie," she said hoarsely. "Jamie, I've come."

Who called him Jamie? He tried to remember, but it made his head hurt, trying.

She was lovely, so lovely his heart squeezed in his chest painfully at the sight of her. She wasn't a nurse; she was a well-dressed lady in a peacock-blue overcoat. She pulled off her gloves, threw aside her coat and hat, and sat beside him on the bed, pressing a half-blown rose into his perpetually shaking hands, clasping them when she saw he could not possibly hold it alone. Her eyes gleamed with unshed tears. He had to close his own eyes against the pain of her loveliness. The gentle scent of the rose teased at his brain. He knew it; he remembered roses. It was like trying to catch hold of smoke, trying to remember who this person was, and he gave it up, letting himself be in her care.

She spoke to him. He couldn't comprehend her words, but the sound of her voice trickled soothingly through his consciousness like honey from a dipper into tea, and after many, many minutes, from deep in his chest, he responded with a sob. And then another. And he leaned toward her, and she put her arms around him, and for a long time, he wept helplessly and inconsolably onto her shoulder like a child. "Aveline," he kept saying, his voice guttural and harsh and utterly unlike his own. "Aveline is dead, and I am not. Oliver. Aveline is dead. And Oliver. I killed them. I killed them both. I should be shot."

"Shh, Jamie, my love, shh," she whispered desperately. "MacFie isn't dead. I've spoken with him myself. He's all right."

At these words, he leaned his full weight onto her, and she was afraid she might lose her balance. "But Aveline," he rasped. "My little Aveline..."

She had no comfort to give him on this point. She would not press it now, not when he was still in shock. Her tears mixed with his, and she lay beside him and held him closely to her heart until he had cried himself to sleep, and when the nurse came in, she found them both asleep, tear-stained cheeks pressed close against each other.

Estelle woke before he did, and she set to packing his things and arranging for him to come home.

When he woke, he was still dazed. He did not recognize Estelle. He did not speak. A nurse shaved him, and he caught a glimpse of himself in a mirror after she'd finished. In his reflection, he looked like a shadow, like an autumn leaf after the color has gone out of it, beaten and gaunt. He could not think precisely what spooked him about the reflection, but did not want to look at it and turned away. There were two men there in the room as well, and they put him into a wheelchair, and soon he rode on a train, staring out another window at the passing landscape. The golden-haired woman never left his side, and when they got off the train again, a motor car met them. "To take us home," she said.

HANDS

THE PLACE SHE called home looked bleak and uninviting, stony battlements starkly outlined against the white sky and the snow. It all made him certain he'd been plunged into some special, pale, very cold hell, as if he'd been kidnapped by the Snow Queen and lost all his ability to feel. Two men waited at the door and, one on each side of him, helped him through the door and carried him up interminable flights of stairs to a quiet, blue-and-walnut room with a most comfortable looking bed in it. He crawled under the covers into the thick darkness and obscurity they afforded him, and he went to sleep again. He liked it under the covers. He didn't have to look at anyone or anything there. It was like putting himself back into his fever-induced coma.

The golden-haired lady always stayed near him, looking after him, helping him. Helping him eat and drink and shave and bathe and dress and undress. He was so helpless. He may as well have not had his hands anymore, for all the use they were to him now.

He didn't eat much. At first, he couldn't keep anything down except plain soup, and he did not have much appetite. He couldn't sleep, owing to nightmares. He relived the horrific hour over and over and over: wincing at the ever-present sound of the bayonet as it lodged itself into the German the last time, feeling again the splatter of blood on his own face when the blast blew Aveline to bits above his head, and the blinding pain when he'd tried to stand on bones too shattered to support him. He would wake gasping with sobs or screaming in raw terror. He couldn't make himself speak of what he saw in his dreams. The woman would hold him as his whole body convulsed, or bring him tea, speaking soothing words that sounded like poetry, waiting and present for hours while he would stare and stare and weep and mentally curse his useless hands. He couldn't even feed himself. He wanted to talk, but he couldn't make words.

And there were the three boys who came to visit him while

he slumped into his chair as though he had been dropped there from height, unmoving and unresponsive. The biggest one had chestnut hair like his own and blue eyes like the woman, and he would read to him by the hour. The middle one sat calmly at his feet or on the armrest of the chair, saying little, just being there. The littlest one wouldn't come near him, only regarded him suspiciously from behind the woman's skirts.

Their efforts were tireless, yet nothing unlocked his prison of fearful despair.

The woman helped him across the floor from the bed to the bathroom or to his chair. He liked his chair very much. It was safe and comfortable, with a thick, warm shawl he liked to wrap around himself while he sat in it.

One day, sitting in his chair, he noticed his kit bag on the floor in the corner: a familiar sight, something he knew. Had it been there all the time? He slid off his chair to his knees and crawled across the floor toward it and buried his face in its familiar smell of wartime and France and too much damp. It smelled like fear and love and joy and misery all at once. It was bittersweet but oddly comforting to rest his head there. Eventually, he raised himself and reached for the straps. His hands, blast their shaking, unfastened the buckles only after a great deal of trial and failure. He lifted open the flap and there, right on top, lay his harmonica. Shiny and silver, it gleamed like a beacon, like the pole star. He gazed transfixed for some time before he managed to reach out to it. It was cold in his hand, shockingly cold, but he clasped it clumsily, put it to his nose, inhaled the slightly musty, tangy scent of metal and reed, touched it to his lips, and blew.

It felt like coming out of a dream, like having to hop on one foot, uncoordinated and hesitant. But he liked the sound the instrument made, and after a few minutes, it started to make sense, his lips and tongue remembering what his brain could not, notes stringing in their proper order like beads on a string, and the tension slowly melted away from his hands.

O my Luve is like a red, red rose
That's newly sprung in June;
O my Luve is like the melody
That's sweetly played in tune.
So fair art thou, my bonnie lass,
So deep in luve am I;
And I will luve thee still, my dear,
Till a' the seas gang dry.

Till a' the seas gang dry, my dear,
And the rocks melt wi' the sun;
I will love thee still, my dear,
While the sands o' life shall run.
And fare thee weel, my only luve!
And fare thee weel awhile!
And I will come again, my luve,
Though it were ten thousand mile.

As the last note died away, he realized with a sort of primal delight that for the first time in a long time, he had control of his hands. Just like that, they weren't shaking anymore. He gazed at them, holding them in front of his face as if he simply could not believe it, childishly pleased and full of light. His hands no longer shook. *He could play his harmonica.*

He played the same song three times through, not really thinking about what it was or why, fully absorbed in the experience and the strange sensation of success, the notes becoming smoother and less stilted each time, until he became aware of someone singing the words close to him. He looked up, the notes dying away mid-phrase, and he stared at the golden-haired woman with sudden comprehension.

"Estelle," he breathed huskily. "My Estelle." He haltingly raised a hand upward toward her.

She dropped to her knees, and he studied her with an intense scrutiny a less valiant woman would have found unsettling. His harmonica fell to the rug, and he framed her face with his hands a moment. He did not kiss her; he was still too stunned to even contemplate such a thing. His entire body trembled, and she put her arms around him, her beaming eyes full of tears, and he leaned into her, his head buried in her shoulder. "My darling Jamie," she whispered into his hair, holding him tightly, as though she never intended to let go. "You've come home."

PART FOURTEEN

November 1919

Inverness-shire, Scotland

UP THE MOUNTAIN

GRAHAM STOOD ON the mountaintop with his two grey deerhounds, one on either side. He had walked all the way by himself. He could do it. Nobody would guess that beneath his kilt hose, he wore a false foot. Nobody blinked that he limped; it wasn't a secret that he'd been wounded, but not everyone knew *how* he'd been wounded.

It had been overwhelming, coming to. His first shock came when he looked in a mirror and saw that his chestnut hair had gone all silver. He'd seen it before—in the hospital mirror—but he hadn't been able to comprehend it then. Now it was unavoidable.

"I'm only thirty-six," he whispered hoarsely, his expression distressed and horrified. His hands started shaking again, and Estelle took them in hers to still them. "I loved my hair," he said, his eyes spilling tears. He couldn't stop them.

"I loved it too," she said, "and I'm sorry you're upset, but your face is still young, darling. And it makes you look terribly distinguished and elegant."

"I look ancient. I am old and grey and crippled. Why didn't Duncan leave me in the trenches to bleed to death?"

"He cared about you, Jamie-love, and he knew you needed to survive. And he was right to do it. He is a hero for bringing *my* hero home."

Even three years later, Graham still was in a great deal of pain, often debilitating pain. The bullet wound to his ankle and the wrenching of it after, when he had fallen and tried to stand, had done serious nerve damage up his entire leg. Sometimes he would become so dizzy from the pain, he fainted. Sometimes he would momentarily lose feeling in his leg altogether and take a fall. Sometimes he would awake in the night from it tingling and burning. After the long and difficult process of getting him off the morphine after his ordeal, Estelle refused to let him have free access to it, but at times the pain became so unbearable, she would give him a dose or two until the attack eased.

These attacks became less frequent over the years, but when he was overtired or under stress or anxiety, the shaking in his hands would return. He could usually get them under control if he played music. So Graham withdrew into himself much of the time, hiding away in his study, running the estate with characteristic thoroughness and efficiency, frequently interrupting his work for music. He found much refuge in quiet corners with his flute, but he seldom sang for the first year after his return, much as Estelle tried to convince him. Sometimes he managed it, but most often, he would sink to the nearest chair with his chest contracting in agony before he got very far into a song.

"Your love cannot cure me," he would say despairingly to Estelle. "It helps, but it isn't enough."

It was a cold, harsh reality. There was no true cure for the way his mind had come unhinged. But she kept trying anyway, and they would dance together in their room. He could sing to her there, when they were alone. In time, it stopped wrenching at his heart until he was certain he would die. Music had been his first love, and it still lived inside him, patiently waiting for his brain to stop derailing.

As the weeks and months and years went by, the essence of who he was slowly came back into the shell that came home from the war. He immersed himself in the healing power of his music. Once he got past the hurdle of getting himself to sing again, he lived and breathed and bathed himself in music to the point of excess. It was his security outside of Estelle, and he drank deeply of it until he could function again.

The three lads took to following him everywhere he went like a line of ducklings, and he thrived as much on their devotion as on his music. He discovered that they weren't as unlike him as he had previously imagined, and he treasured their company.

Nobody talked of Aveline, not ever. Estelle had strictly

instructed the boys to never mention her to their father unless he brought it up first. And he never did. She was, for them, fading into a dim, elusive memory. But for him, she remained concrete and real. He had all her notebooks and her photographs safe in a lockbox inside his desk, and occasionally he took them out and looked at them. On his worst days, when he could not work up the strength to leave his room, he would sink back into his stunned, comatose state and stare and stare. He would hold the photograph of Aveline and gaze at it, press it to his heart beneath his crossed hands. He would touch the tail of her hair, page through her drawings, longing for a different outcome, weeping until he was so exhausted, he could no longer summon even the tiniest sob.

The cold November wind whipped Graham's kilt and his flyaway hair and ruffled the kinky fur of his deerhounds, attentive and watchful. They were keen to his moods and could sense his episodes coming on before he could. If he was in the company of other people, they would gently tug at his kilt and make eye contact, and he would obey their summons and leave the room to go somewhere alone until it passed. It was like having a canine version of MacFie, he thought ruefully, always looking out for him.

He had decided one thing after these nearly three years of recovery: there was no glory in death on the battlefield. Not like in romance novels or plays. If such things as touching parting speeches ever existed, they had not existed for him at the Somme. Only a sudden, aching, incomprehensible emptiness where human companionship, love, and trust had been.

It was true, Oliver MacFie had survived, and he and his family camped on Graham's estate several times a year. MacFie was as solid and devoted now as he had ever been in France, and Graham treasured him.

Willie Duncan, too, had come through, though not unscathed; he'd been shot in the arm and the war ended before he was well enough to return. Thanks to George's connections,

Willie and his faithful shadow Sylvie had settled in London, apprenticing with a photographer.

But even these things failed to ease Graham's sorrow that there hadn't been time to say anything to Aveline, however. He was only alive as a result of her sacrifice. He wished he could thank her.

Not being able to do that, he resolved he would make the most of his future. He would try to not leave things unsaid. Estelle had given him astonishing amounts of grace, but she still often complained he was in some other world and seldom listened when spoken to. Recently, therefore, Graham had worked hard at curbing his natural dreamy distractedness, his self-absorption and tendency to isolate himself, forcing himself to form habits of attentiveness when people spoke to him. He loved his family fiercely, and he wanted them to know it.

Time. Time would soften all these things, all these memories, ease the pain in his heart.

Estelle would soon have another child. It made him feel still alive, still a man, to create another life with her, and each night, he held her in his arms and treasured her even more.

But this cold afternoon, Graham had come here for Aveline. Three years ago to the day, almost to the minute, she had died, and today he was doing at last what he had promised her he would: taking her to the top of his mountain to see her new home from above. He had her photograph in his breast pocket, and he took it out and held it to the sky, facing out over his demesne. "I wish it were different, sweetheart. But—home, Aveline," he said. "With me and mine, in spirit, always, you are home."

He put the photograph back into his pocket, pulled out his harmonica, and with tears streaming from his eyes, he played her home like a soldier.

I've seen the smiling of Fortune beguiling,
I've tasted her favours, and felt her decay;
Sweet is her blessing,

and kind her caressing,
But soon it is fled,—it is fled far away.
I've seen the forest adorn'd of the foremost,
With flowers of the fairest, both pleasant and gay;
Full sweet was their blooming,
their scent the air perfuming,
But now they are wither'd and a' wede away.

I've seen the morning, with gold the hills adorning,
And red storm roaring, before the parting day;
I've seen Tweed's silver streams,
glittering in the sunny beams,
Turn drumly and dark, as they roll'd on their way.
O fickle Fortune! why this cruel sporting?
Why thus perplex us poor sons of a day?
Thy frowns cannot fear me,
thy smiles cannot cheer me,
Since the flowers of the forest are a' wede away.

The dogs stood at solemn attention, and the notes hung suspended in air, a million sparkling pieces of sound, and then they were gone.

AUTHOR'S NOTE

My characters are fictional, but I credit *A Childhood in Scotland* by the inimitable Christian Miller as one of the primary inspirations for Jamie Graham's upbringing.

The movements and locations of Graham's men in France are loosely based on the Fifteenth (Scottish) Division.

For anyone interested in a practical, day-to-day look at life in the trenches of the Great War, I highly recommend *Eye-Deep in Hell* by John Ellis and *Hot Blood & Cold Steel* by Andy Simpson. These volumes were invaluable to my research.

I also am grateful to John J Graham's Shetland Dictionary, which was very helpful to me in writing Willie Duncan's dialogue. It can be found here: https://www.shetlanddialect.org. uk/john-j-grahams-shetland-dictionary-intro

I also want to thank **Jen Waters**, who read my manuscript aloud to me during its embryonic and terrible early phase, provided merciless honesty and lots of laughs, and saved me the trouble of coming up with a title; my fabulous trio of beta readers: **Samantha Amenn**, **Christopher Gould**, and **Gwen Katz**, who all offered many helpful comments and suggestions on the first edition of this book; and **Karen Heenan**, **Amanda McCrina**, and **Rose de Guzman**, who worked with me on the second edition; **Wendy Cunningham** for naming a minor character (guess which one) so she could get her name onto my thank you list; my husband, for not complaining (much) about my Obsessive Research Book Purchasing and just being the best; **Karen Heenan** and **Meggan Padvorac** for editorial help on the revision for the current edition of this book.

A huge thank you also to those who contributed to my re-release campaign: Amanda, Fayelle, Karen, Robotica83, Leona, Beth, Anna, Lauren, Anitra, Marian, Amanda, Emily, Grace, and Amanda.

Scriptures are taken from the King James Version of the Bible. In order of first appearance:

Psalm 69:1-4; Psalm 69:16-18; Psalm 126; Song of Solomon 6:10; Psalm 46:1-3; Psalm 119:117; Genesis 27:38; Psalm 91:1; Jeremiah 20:9; Psalm 127:2; Proverbs 5:15; 1 John 4:18; Numbers 32:23; Proverbs 6:27.

Songs referenced, in order of first appearance:

"**Care Selve (Come, My Beloved)**," Atalanta by G. F. Handel, 1736 (English translation © 1900 by Boosey & Co); "**Kelvin Grove**" by Thomas Lyle, 1837; "**He Shall Feed His Flock/He Was Despised**," Messiah by G. F. Handel, 1741 (based on Isaiah 40:11 and 50:6); "**Where'er You Walk**," Semele by G. F. Handel, 1744; "**Eriskay Love Lilt**" by Marjorie Kennedy-Fraser, 1909; "**Meet Me, Nannie! Blue-Eyed Nannie**" by William W. Long, 1870; "**A Red, Red Rose**" by Robert Burns, 1794; "**Think On Me**" by Lady John Scott, 1910; "**Annie Laurie**" by Lady John Scott, 1890; "**I'll Be With You When the Roses Bloom Again**," score and lyrics by Cobb & Edwards (© 1901 by F. A. Mills); "**If Only You Were Mine**," The Singing Girl by Harry B. Smith (© 1900 by Witmark & Sons); "**Oh Promise Me**" by Clement Scott, 1889; "**Scots Wha Hae**" by Robert Burns, 1793; "**The Flowers of the Forest**" by Alison Cockburn, 1765.

Eva Seyler was born in Jacksonville, Florida.

She left that humidity pit at the age of three and spent the next twenty-one years in California, Idaho, Kentucky, and Washington before ending up in Oregon, where she now lives on a homestead in the western foothills with her husband and five children, two of whom are human.